# DEATH WARMED OVER

*A GRIM DAYS MYSTERY*

# J. KENT HOLLOWAY

CHARADE
MEDIA

Death Warmed Over (A Grim Days Mystery)
3rd Edition

ISBN: 979-8-9876847-1-9

Copyright © 2023 by J. Kent Holloway
Cover art by J. Kent Holloway and M Wayne Miller
Published by Charade Media, LLC

*To Dr. Bulic...*

*Who taught me so much, listened to my wild ideas, and offered answers to a million and one questions.*

# PROLOGUE

KWAN SU CHINESE BISTRO
JACKSONVILLE, FLORIDA
MONDAY, 7:15 PM

It had been an unusually hectic night at the Kwan Su Chinese Bistro for a Monday evening. For bits of the night, they'd had customers lined up out the door, waiting to be seated for nearly thirty minutes at a time. Despite the wait, however, everyone had been pleasant and patient. Everyone had enjoyed the new karaoke machine the owners had installed. And from the smiles on the customers' faces, everyone had enjoyed the food and the company at their tables. It had been a good night for tips. A good night for the register, as well.

That is, until the woman burst through the doors, screaming at the top of her lungs and sprinting through the restaurant at top speed. She careened down the aisles of tables, casting furtive glances over her shoulders as if she was being chased.

No one else had entered the bistro after her, but still she ran, ducking under tables every so often and peeking out from under their shelter before running to the next table and doing the same thing again.

Bill Ngeung, the manager on duty, eased over to the table she now huddled underneath.

"Ma'am? Are you okay?"

She poked her head out from under the table. Tears streaked her face, making her mascara run in black gashes down her cheeks.

"H-help me," she whispered. Her eyes darted left and right, searching for something unseen.

"I'm trying to, ma'am. Should I call 911?"

Her hand shot out, grabbing him by the wrist. "No! No police. They can't help me. No one can."

Bill Ngeung wasn't about to point out the inconsistency of her asking for help, then denying that anyone could. The woman was unstable. Possibly dangerous. He was going to have to do whatever he could to protect his customers.

"Okay," he said. "Fine. So, what can I do?"

Suddenly, her eyes grew the size of saucers and she screamed, shoving him away. Crouched down as he was, he toppled over backwards and she bolted from under the table and slid under the one directly across the aisle. The occupants of the table scrambled away and gathered in a nearby corner, whispering to each other.

Bill righted himself and followed her.

"Ma'am, I'm sorry. You're upsetting our customers. You need to leave."

"I can't!" she screamed. She was clutching the hem of the table cloth, using it to hide from the outside world. A shaking hand stretched from the shadows of the table and pointed toward the door. "I can't! He'll get me!"

"Who will get you?"

There was a sob on the other side of the cloth.

"Ma'am?"

"Y-you don't see him?" Her finger pointed emphatically at the door.

He turned to look, but no one was there.

"I don't see anyone."

"But he's right there! Right there!" She was beginning to slur her words, making it difficult for him to understand her. Had she been drinking? On drugs?

"What does he look like exactly? Maybe I'm just looking at the wrong place."

"Eyes," she sobbed.

"Eyes?"

"Red, glowing eyes...in a cloud of darkness. A darkness as black as a grave."

*Uh, okay. This woman is just plain freaky.*

"I don't see him. Who is it? Who is chasing you?"

"Death." She said it without the slightest hesitation. Without a trace of irony.

"Huh?"

"Death is here. He's after me. He's been chasing me all night."

Bill's heart slowly crawled its way to his throat. This woman was a real nut. He turned to one of his employees and pantomimed calling 911. The employee nodded her understanding and went to the back to make the call.

"Maybe he's not." Bill hadn't been trained enough in how to deal with psychotic people disrupting his diners. He thought he should mention that to the owners when this was all over. They needed training for this sort of thing. "Maybe you're just confused."

"I'm *not* confused!" she roared, exploding from the table

3

and tipping it over. Heaping portions of kung pao chicken, shrimp, and dumplings toppled to the ground. She lunged at Bill. This time, when he fell backwards, she landed on top of him, pinning him to the floor. "He's after me! I've seen his eyes. Those hideous red eyes. He's coming for me. I'm going to die!"

Customers were beginning to panic now. Many of them were rushing out the door. Probably not paying for their meal as they fled.

"Please," Bill said. He was rightfully panicked at the moment himself. "Let's talk about this."

"But he's after me!" she screamed. "Death is after me!"

She leapt off him, zig-zagging across the restaurant, over-turning numerous tables and chairs. The floor was now carpeted in a slush of food and drinks, trampled underfoot by the crazed woman. Then, as suddenly as she appeared, she ran out the front doors and into the street beyond.

# CHAPTER
# ONE

SUMMER HAVEN BEACH
SUMMER HAVEN, FLORIDA
WEDNESDAY, 12:45 AM

The salty breeze whipped through the man's slicked-back mane of jet black hair as he stood curiously over the body of the dead woman sprawled face down on the beach. His deep-set eyes, nearly as black as his hair, traced the contours of her body against the sand, taking in every crease, every fold of cellulite pocking her naked body. Imagined the feel of her silky black hair through the gaps of his fingers. He sniffed the air, tasting the aroma of death and unexpectedly wincing as he did so.

In all his years, he'd witnessed an incalculable number of such sights. An untold number of tragic souls taken before they'd even begun to live. Each face had been ingrained into his psyche—imprinted into his memory like a carving in stone. But the blood-covered dead woman at his feet now perplexed him. She wasn't supposed to be dead. It wasn't her Time yet. She'd literally been taken too soon.

And the worst thing about it was that he had no idea how it had happened.

He closed his eyes in thought. The silver brilliance of the full moon burned past his eyelids, while the sound of waves crashing against the shore thrummed like a marching band's cadence in which to collect his thoughts.

*It makes no sense*, he thought.

Then again, none of the others had made any sense either.

He released a long-held sigh and let his eyes graze over the murder scene again. The first thing he'd noticed upon finding the body was that the blood was off. It didn't fit somehow, though he couldn't put his finger on it. The woman's back was covered in the congealing crimson. Someone, presumably the killer, had used a finger or some type of stylus to scrawl strange arcane symbols in the blood. But that wasn't what felt wrong about the sight. It was just off somehow. He wasn't sure what it was, but he knew, despite the wicked-looking ceremonial knife plunged deep into her spine, there shouldn't be nearly as much blood as there was. Of course, for now, there was no evidence to support his theory. It was more like a hunch.

*Funny. I've never had a hunch before. Never had any need of them. Feels kind of weird.*

It wasn't just the blood that threw his deductive equilibrium off though. It was everything else too. The position of the body. The drag marks from the road to where she now laid. And of course, the candle sticks placed in a circle around her body. From the looks of them, the candles had only burned a few minutes before being blown out from the rushing wind coming in from the ocean. They wouldn't have burned long enough to conduct any sort of ritual they were left there to convey.

*So, what else is bugging you?*

He knew the answer, of course. It was the fact that the woman shouldn't be dead in the first place. He would have thought it impossible for her to be, in fact. At least, not unless her death had been sanctioned by him. He knew for a fact that it hadn't.

He stepped over to her left and crouched down for a closer look at the dagger. It looked Afro-Caribbean to him. The multi-colored beads—red and white—that wrapped around the handle had a distinct Kongonese flavor to it. Voodoo, maybe. Or Santeria. From the color scheme, he was favoring the latter.

*It's not very smart of the killer to leave the murder weapon. It's handcrafted. You can't buy something like that at your local Walmart sporting goods department. Something like that should be pretty easy to trace.*

His eyes drifted back to the blood. He inhaled and took in another whiff. There was just something strange about it. The smell was wrong. He tilted his head, tracing the spatter across the small of her back.

He began to smile.

*Of course.*

He leaned forward and removed the knife from her flesh. A small dollop of blood bubbled up to the surface of the wound, then settled back into her body as he pulled the dagger up to his eyes.

"You're a wily one, aren't you?" he whispered to the blade. "Or at least, you think you are. You think you're so, so clever."

His smile widened. He was beginning to get a clearer picture of what happened here.

"So, I know what. Now to just figure out the 'who', the 'how', and the 'why'."

He stood, holding one hand under the blade to keep the blood from dripping on the body.

*And with any luck, I'll figure out more than just who the killer is. I'll find out who's behind it all.*

There was a sudden crunch of sand from behind him.

"Stop." The female voice behind him was stern. Confident. "Don't move."

The man went rigid.

"Turn around."

He remained still.

"I said, turn around."

"You also said not to move," the man said. "I'm confused."

The woman behind him sighed. "You understood what I meant."

"Actually, I'm still trying to learn the syntax and subtleties of the English language," he said, holding up his hands, knife still clutched in his right fist, and slowly turned to face the woman who'd so adeptly ambushed him.

She was wearing the navy-blue uniform of a police officer. The shield on her chest, as well as the pins on her lapel, were gold, designating her as someone of power within the police organization for whom she worked. She was pointing a rather large handgun—a .40 caliber Sig Sauer, if he wasn't mistaken.

If he had to guess, he was looking at the chief of the Summer Haven Police Department, Rebecca Cole, known as Becca to everyone who knew her. He'd done some research on her before coming to this sleepy little beach community. She was good. Really good.

The chief's eyes swept from the man to the body on the ground beside him to the knife in his hand. Two other officers could be seen trudging over the dunes, making their way toward them from the parking lot. An aurora of blue and red lit up the night sky in the distance near the beach's public parking lot.

"We received a call about a dead body on the beach," Chief

Cole said. "Never imagined I'd find the killer standing over it when I showed up. That makes things easy for me."

The man rolled his eyes. "Sure," he said. "It does if you're a lazy detective. With a little effort, you'll find I'm the one who called you."

She narrowed her eyes at him just as the other uniforms huffed their way up beside her. The sand near the dunes was high, making walking or running on them difficult for even people in good shape. Given the rotund girth of the two newcomers, it was a miracle they'd even made it to the scene at all.

"I assure you, I'm not lazy," the chief said. "If you're innocent, you've got nothing to worry about. Now, drop the knife."

He obeyed and the dagger dropped blade first into the sand near his foot. He then looked up at her and grinned.

He supposed the woman was attractive. He'd never been a good judge of beauty. His station—the decisions his purpose and position forced him to take—made such trivialities of no interest to him in the past. In fact, such considerations would have been an outright hindrance. Perhaps even a disaster in the universal scope of things.

But he could see the woman was pleasant to look at. She was of average height for a female—around five feet, six inches tall—with a lean, athletic build. Her skin was tanned, but smooth and soft. Her short-cropped light brown hair was tipped at the edges with blonde highlights that helped to accentuate her large brown eyes. Yes, she was definitely an attractive woman...even though those same large brown eyes now glared at him with suspicion as she trained her weapon at his head with steady hands.

He looked down at the corpse, then back at the chief. So far, everything was going according to plan. After the last three unscheduled, unsanctioned deaths, he'd taken it upon himself to investigate. But, he was no fool. He also knew he'd need a little help. Since the death toll was rising disproportionately in this little beach town compared to anywhere else, he'd figured this was the best place to start looking for answers. And Chief Becca Cole was the perfect candidate to assist him.

"Larry," she said to one of the overweight cops panting behind her. "Handcuff him." She nodded in the man's direction.

The officer named Larry reached back on his belt and removed a set of cuffs before walking over to the man. Chief Cole's aim never let up for an instant. The gun barrel never wavered. Didn't betray the slightest tremor of her hand.

*Oh, I'm going to like this one,* the man thought.

Larry stopped in tracks when he came within two feet of the man and sniffed. "Do I smell..." The fat cop shook his head, then looked over at his boss. "I swear, I smell pie or something."

The man's grin widened, but Chief Cole was in no mood. "Larry, just handcuff the man, please."

"Yeah, yes, ma'am." Larry walked around the suspect, slipped one of the handcuff bracelets over the man's left wrist, brought his hands behind his back, and secured the other bracelet over the right with a series of clicks. The fat cop exhaled, wiped a stream of sweat from his brow, and stepped back to appraise his handiwork.

*CLINK.*

The sound of metal hitting the sand drew everyone's flashlight beams behind their suspect to find the handcuffs, still closed, laying casually on the ground.

"I...I...," Larry began to protest, his mouth agape.

"Officer O'Donnell?" Chief Cole looked reprovingly at the bewildered officer.

"I secured 'em, Chief. I know I did."

The man—now a suspect in a homicide investigation—offered Larry an apologetic nod. He brought his hands around and rubbed his wrists before placing them once more behind his back.

Still confused, Officer Larry stooped down, picked up the cuffs, and re-secured them around the man's wrists. Then, he hesitated, pulled on the cuffs' chain to ensure they were indeed secure, and stepped back once more.

The handcuffs fell to the ground again.

"Whatever you're doing, stop it!" Chief Cole told the man.

He chuckled, brought his hands around, and crossed his arms over his chest. "I'm sorry. Merely having a little fun at your officer's expense, Chief. But the shackles are hardly necessary. I'll be happy to accompany you to the police station for questioning. In fact, I'd welcome the opportunity."

She looked at her other officer, then nodded over to her suspect, silently directing the second cop to handcuff him again. "Sorry, pal. Protocol says you need to be cuffed, so cuffed you're going to be."

The man sighed, resigned to allow them the indignity of shackling him like a common hooligan.

Once he was secure, Becca Cole told the officer to take him back to the station to await booking. As they walked past Larry and the chief, the man leaned in.

"Be mindful of the blood, Chief Cole," he whispered conspiratorially. "I believe you'll find that the blood will tell you a great deal about this murder."

With that, he allowed himself to be escorted off the beach and driven to the little police station at the edge of town.

# CHAPTER
# TWO

It had taken about six hours to process the scene. As usual, the St. Johns County Sheriff's Office's Crime Scene Unit, or CSU, had come in to assist, lending their expertise to the investigation. Becca's officers had canvassed the beach houses in the vicinity, waking their occupants up in the dead of night to find out if anyone had seen or heard anything that might help in the investigation. The medical examiner's investigator had arrived near the end of it all and the body was removed from the beach.

Now that she was pulling into the police station parking lot, she sighed. She really didn't have time for this. The town was already in an uproar about a big archaeological discovery some history nerd had found a few miles off the coast. A sunken pirate ship of reported legend. They were in the national spotlight right now with crews from CNN, FOX, and a string of other cable networks coming and going to cover the big story. She hoped a small time murder like this one would creep below their radar. At least until she could solve it.

Of course, so far, they weren't off to the best start. There wasn't much to find at the scene since the body appeared to have been dumped where she was found and they were still looking for the primary murder scene. Thanks to the Florida Highway Patrol and their handy little electronic fingerprint scanners, they knew who their victim was, at least—Andrea Alvarez, who'd migrated to Florida from Bogota, Colombia when she was still in high school. She'd apparently been a local ever since, but Becca had never met her before. Never had any run-ins with law enforcement until two nights ago when she was seen in Jacksonville, the big city in the next county north of Summer Haven, in an altered mental status. She'd apparently caused quite a ruckus in a restaurant there and the Jacksonville Sheriff's Office had picked her up under a Baker Act before transporting her to the hospital for evaluation. She'd already sent an officer to subpoena the medical records. With any luck—and having dealt with them before, she knew it would take a leprechaun's pot full of the stuff—the JSO's incident report should already be on her desk.

She pulled into her parking spot, turned off the ignition, and leaned back in the seat. She couldn't stop thinking about the blood. Like her suspect had told her, there'd been something off about it. Crime Scene had tested it and discovered it wasn't human. Looks like the killer had poured the stuff all over her back himself. The M.E. investigator had told her there didn't appear to be any hemorrhaging in the knife wound— telling her that she had most likely already been dead when the blade was plunged into her.

*So, if that dagger didn't kill her, what did?*

There'd been only a few bruises found on her at the scene, but they appeared to be a few days old. They'd been consistent with many alcoholics she'd seen in the past—but Becca guessed they had more to do with injuries she sustained during her psychotic fit. There'd been no marks on her neck or petechial hemorrhages in her eyes to indicate strangulation or suffocation. The autopsy would reveal more, but at least at the scene, they hadn't even seen a needle mark to indicate a drug overdose or anything like that.

She ran her fingers through her hair, took a deep breath, and got out of her patrol car. A few seconds later, she was in the station and making a beeline for the coffee maker. It had been a long night and, from the looks of things, it was going to be an even longer day.

Despite the early morning hour, the station was already abuzz with activity. They were a small department—only fifteen sworn officers, three reserve officers, and a handful of office personnel. But when things like the murder of Andrea Alvarez happened, her team pulled together and helped where they could. Not only was her office manager, Linda White, already at her desk typing up affidavits and warrants, but a few off-duty officers were also busying themselves with the investigation in various ways.

"I hear we got a crazy one," Sergeant Jeremy Tanner, her second-in-command, said when she walked into the bullpen. "Voodoo ritual or somethin'?"

"Or something," she replied, filling her mug with fresh coffee. "Our suspect?"

"In holding. He's as calm as a cucumber, as far as suspects go."

She nodded. "Eerily calm at the scene too. Downright smug, if you ask me."

"Yeah, well, he's refused to give us his name. Says he'll only speak with you." The sergeant shrugged. "Had no ID on him either."

14

She looked in the direction of the holding cells. "Have you run prints on him yet?"

"Just waiting for the results to come back from AFIS. Then I'll run a background check on him and get back to you."

She smiled at him with a nod. She was thankful she had such a seasoned veteran among all the rookies she'd hired upon accepting the chief's position a year ago.

Suddenly she remembered something the suspect had told her. "Did he have a cell phone on him?"

Tanner nodded. "A burner phone. Untraceable."

"That's fine. Just do me a favor and document the incoming and outgoing calls from it, okay? Oh, and bring him to the interrogation room. I want to talk with him in a few."

Jeremy nodded and went to fetch their mystery man.

"Linda, did we get the police report on Alvarez's little breakdown from a few days ago?" Becca asked her office manager.

"Just came in over the fax." She held up a few sheets of paper. "Haven't had a chance to put it on your desk, but it's a weird read."

The chief took the report and started skimming it. "Care to give me the Cliff's Notes version?"

The auburn-haired Linda looked up from her computer screen. "Well, basically, it says Ms. Alvarez just went nuts. Ranting and raving along Market Street and Main, near the Landing, downtown. She was babbling incoherently. Terrified out of her gourd. Then ran into the Kwan Su Chinese Bistro and started screaming that Death was stalking her."

"I categorically deny that accusation," someone said near the entrance of the police station. "I've never laid eyes on that lady until this morning."

Becca and everyone else in the station looked over at the entrance to see their suspect standing there with a large box of donuts in one hand and a carrier of several coffees in the other. In unison, every cop within the bullpen drew their weapons on the man.

"Whoa, whoa, whoa!" he said with a white-toothed smile. "I just went out to get everyone some breakfast. You guys have had a rough night."

"Chief, he's gone! The door's still secured, but he's not in..." Jeremy ran around the corner from the holding cell area and came to an abrupt halt when he eyed the suspect at the door. "How the...?"

"Apparently our perp and locks don't get along, Jeremy," Becca said, pointing her own weapon at the strange man. "Don't worry about it."

"May I set the donuts and coffee down now?" the suspect asked. "I promise to put my hands up in the air as soon as I do."

Becca rolled her eyes. He was definitely a cool customer. Slippery, too. There was something about him that chilled her every time he was within sight of her. Good looking, yes. Refined with a difficult to identify accent. Perhaps British with a touch of eastern Europe thrown in. He had a dark complexion —maybe a slight olive skin-tone that garnered notions of Italian or Mediterranean in his DNA—and had a well-groomed mane of jet black hair and the darkest set of eyes beneath deep set brows. His pronounced square jaw was clean shaven without the slightest hint of stubble. And, then of course, there was his attire. He was dressed in what she could only assume was a very expensive Italian three-piece suit—all black from jacket to shirt to tie—which gave him the appearance of an overpriced undertaker.

*Or a hit man.*

Becca motioned with the barrel of her weapon to indicate he could lower the breakfast to the front desk. When he'd complied, he was good to his word and raised both well-manicured hands in the air.

"Jeremy, take him to the interrogation room now," she said to her senior officer. "And keep a close eye on him until I get there."

The suspect kept his hands up as the older officer walked over, cuffed him yet again, and escorted him to the interrogation room on the other side of the building. When they were out of sight, Becca blew out a breath and returned her attention to the office manager.

"You were saying?"

Linda stared up at her. "That's it? Don't you want to know how he got out of his cell?"

The chief shrugged. "I'll figure that out in interrogation. Right now, I want to know more about our victim." She flipped through the pages of the police report but was too preoccupied with their Houdini-esque suspect to read them. "So, Andrea Alvarez was having some sort of mental breakdown?"

"Looks that way. Paranoid delusions are what the E.R. doctor said when she was taken to the hospital. She was admitted for overnight observation, but after medicating her, she calmed down and returned to what they call her 'base line'."

"Why didn't they keep her longer than that? She was in obvious distress. Seems like they should have kept her at least a few more days."

Linda shook her head and pointed to the report in Becca's hand. "They couldn't force her to stay. She'd been loud and disruptive, but she'd done no damage to the restaurant property. No one had been hurt. And Ms. Alvarez wasn't suicidal, so they couldn't legally detain her without a court order."

"She thinks Death is stalking her and the doctors didn't think she was suicidal?"

"Hey, I'm just reading what the report says. Hopefully, we'll know more when the medical records department opens up at the hospital and we can get the doctor's notes."

Becca took a sip from her coffee, but instantly spit it back into the mug. It hadn't been that good to begin with, but now it was cold. She eyed the large Dunkin' Donuts coffee cups their suspect brought in but thought better of it.

"Okay, I'm going in to interrogate Mr. Mysterio," she said. "Do me a favor and make sure Jeremy goes to the autopsy. Oh, and have him take Larry while he's at it. The newbie needs to get his first taste sooner or later."

Linda gave her a knowing smile and returned to her work. Becca then made her way toward the interrogation room.

*Okay. Time to talk to our well-dressed escape artist and finally get some answers to this crazy case.*

# THREE

"So, the first thing I'd like to know is why you killed Andrea Alvarez," Becca said as she stepped into the room and closed the door. The man was sitting back in the bolted down metal chair, his feet up on the table, as if he owned the place. He didn't appear to have a care in the world.

She strode across the room, dropped a manila file on the table, and took the chair opposite him before swatting his feet. He pulled them off the table and sat up straight with that same infuriating grin that always seemed to grace his perfectly sculpted face.

"First, you're assuming that I *did* kill her." He leaned forward and placed his hands flat on the table. When he moved them, the handcuffs that were supposed to be around his wrists were left behind. "The assumption, of course, is erroneous. I didn't kill her. If I did, I wouldn't need you, now would I?"

His comment caught her off guard. Of course, almost every suspect she ever brought into interrogation denied having done the crime for which they were accused. That wasn't anything new. It was more in the way he had said it. Like, killing someone was within his nature, but not their current victim. No, that was definitely a new one on her.

"And why should I believe you?"

"Like I said, I'm the one who called the police. The moment I found the body, in fact," he said. "Surely, you've checked the 911 records by now."

"Yeah, let's talk about that." She opened the file in front of her and withdrew a sheet of paper. "The call reporting the body came from an untraceable cell phone. There's no way to know it was you who made the call."

"But it was my phone."

"Which you could have easily stolen. Or found. Or taken off the victim's own body for all we know."

He nodded, acquiescing to her logic.

"We'll get back to that later," she said. "For now, let's start simple. What's your name?"

"Silas Mot."

There was no hesitation when he told her, which was another surprise. She would have bet the man would have played every dirty game in the book to keep her from getting that information. Of course, it could have been a disposable alias, but the speed in which he'd said it made her think he was telling the truth.

"Okay." If he was so easy with his name, maybe he'd be as forthcoming about some other incidentals. "Occupation?"

"Death."

Her eyes snapped up at him.

"Excuse me?"

His grin seemed to shimmer underneath the glaring fluorescent lights.

"I said, Death. The Big Sleep. The Dust Biter, Farm Seller, and the Daisy Pusher. The Grim Reaper. It's what I do." He leaned forward, looking at her from behind his deep-set, predatory eyes. "It's who I am."

*Okay, that's pretty ominous. Of course, the dude is trying to mess with me or he's just plain nuts without the salt.*

"Interesting." She was determined not to show how unnerving his answer had been. "That's quite a job title. Do you get dental with that?"

He shrugged. "Nah, but it has its perks."

*This guy is serious. He's not just being flippant with me.*

"So, you're the Grim Reaper," she said. "And you found Andrea Alvarez on the beach. Already dead."

He nodded.

"And you're saying you had nothing to do with it."

"That's precisely why I'm here, Chief Cole. I most certainly had nothing to do with it. That's what troubles me. It wasn't Ms. Alvarez's Time."

"Her Time? What do you mean by that?"

He leaned back in the chair, placing his hands behind his head to relax. "Just that. Everyone has a ticking clock, Chief Cole. Everyone has a Time in which their number is up. That's when I, or one of my cohorts, show up." He closed his eyes as if remembering a better time in his life. "However, Ms. Alvarez died without my knowledge. I neither know how or who killed her." He opened his eyes again and looked across the table at her. His expression suddenly serious. "And recently, there have been others."

"Others?"

He nodded. "In Summer Haven alone, in the last six months, there have been five unscheduled and unsanctioned deaths. Five deaths that took me completely by surprise. And that's not supposed to be possible."

For the moment, she decided to ignore how insane the man sounded.

"Five deaths? Are you talking about a serial killer?"

"No, no, no," he said, shaking his head. "Nothing so pedestrian as that. It started with Ruth Silvers, an eighty-three-year-old retiree."

"Yeah, I remember her. She slipped in the bathtub, struck her head, and died from a subdural hematoma."

"That wasn't supposed to happen."

She blinked at him, trying to understand what the man was saying. "But accidents happen all the time. Elderly people slip. She was on Coumadin, a blood thinner. Easy to create a bleed in the brain when you're on that stuff." Something similar had happened to her grandmother a few years ago. She knew all too well the risks involved with blood thinners.

"Shouldn't have happened," he repeated, matter of fact. "She wasn't scheduled to depart the mortal plane for another two and a half years. A stroke, I believe."

She shook her head to clear it. "Okay, even if you're right, what does Ruth's death have to do with Ms. Alvarez?"

"Four weeks ago, Adam Patenga. A dump truck operator who happened to lift his truck's bed into a high voltage line while he was still clutching the control levers. Electrocuted to death on the spot."

Becca remembered that case as well, though it had been investigated by the sheriff's office. Where was he going with all these stories?

"Then, two days ago...Elliot Newman. Did you know him?"

She shook her head. "Knew *of* him. Never met him personally. He was the archaeologist who worked for the city of St. Augustine." She looked at her suspect. "What about him?"

"Oh, nothing. He isn't one of the unscheduled deaths actually. It was, indeed, his sanctioned Time. But Elliot was here in Summer Haven, tracking down a lead on an old pirate treasure rumored to have been buried here a few centuries before."

*And there it is.* Becca rolled her eyes. Ever since the story broke about this crazy sunken pirate ship and its missing treasure, every wacko treasure hunter in the area had crawled out from their rocks in hopes of finding it for themselves. *So, is this guy playing some game with me in hopes of finding that crazy treasure?*

"Yeah, he was. Until he was hit by a charter bus on its way to Daytona. I still don't see why he's important. Especially if he's not one of your so-called unscheduled deaths."

Silas Mot looked up at the ceiling as if in thought. "Yes," he said to no one in particular, "It's rather brilliant really. I think we might need Mr. Newman's assistance on this case, now that I think about it."

"Huh?"

"Elliot's knowledge would be invaluable to us in our investigation." He seemed more to be talking out loud than answering Becca's questions.

"Okay, stop." She wasn't entirely sure when her interrogation had taken a left turn into the Twilight Zone, but she needed to put a stop to it now. "First all, I believe I've already caught the killer. No more investigation needed. Second, Elliot Newman is dead. I don't think he'd be much help to us even if there *was* more to investigate."

"No, I really do think Elliot would be most useful indeed," he said, ignoring her argument. "Perfect, in fact."

"Mr. Mot, let's get back to the matter at hand." She slammed her palm down on the table, breaking him from his reverie. He looked up at her, smiled, and gestured for her to continue.

*This is getting us nowhere. Time to switch gears.*

"So, we did what you asked," she told him. "We checked the blood on our victim."

"I'm delighted. What did you discover?"

23

"Don't you know? After all, you're the one who pointed it out to us."

The man shrugged. "I just knew it was off. Wasn't sure how."

"Well, let's talk about those markings written in the blood. Those symbols."

He waved the comment away. "Forget those. They were left as a misdirection. Someone wanted to give us the impression that this was ritualistic in nature. The candles prove that. There's no way those candles could have been used in any kind of magical ceremony. Therefore, the magical glyphs mean nothing."

She blinked at him, trying to find anything that would challenge his assessment. But now that he'd brought it up, he made perfect sense.

"But how did you know the 'blood was off', as you keep putting it?"

"I don't know. It just smelled different to me. And of course, the way it pooled wasn't consistent with her position. I figured it had been placed there after she was already dead."

*Smelled off? Huh?*

"Well, you were right. It wasn't even human blood."

"Oh, then that explains the smell. Humans have such disgusting dietary habits. It affects the odor that comes from their body. Through their pores. And, yes, from their blood. It's quite distinctive." His smile faded for a bit as he looked back at her. "Their diet. I swear. It almost seems like their food choices are what keeps me the busiest in my line of work."

*Humans? Their?* Did this guy really think he was the Grim Reaper? Like literally the personification of Death? She scratched her head while gazing across the table at him. *Seriously, Becca, don't let this guy get to you. He's playing some kind of game.*

"So, if it wasn't human blood, what kind of blood was it?" Becca refused to get sidetracked. She was in control here and she needed to remind her suspect of that.

"How on earth should I know? I'm not a hematologist."

"Look!" She jumped from her chair and came around the table to glare at him. "Could you just give me some straight answers, please?"

His eyes widened at the outburst, then he relaxed again and leaned back in the chair. "Could you please stop wasting my time then?" he answered back. He remained calm, but his demeanor had turned serious. "I've already told you, I'm not your killer. As a matter of fact, I'm trying to find the killer myself. That's why I called you to begin with. I needed your assistance in my investigation."

"'*My*' investigation? What do you mean 'my'..."

There was a soft triple-tap knock at the door and Sergeant Tanner cracked it open without waiting for Becca to respond.

"Chief?" he said, holding up a file. She walked over to him and took it. "There weren't any fingerprint matches to our suspect." He paused, letting his head tilt to one side. "Well, that ain't necessarily true." He handed her a file. It was much thicker than Becca would have expected. "There were nearly ten thousand matches. And AFIS isn't finished processing yet. It's still finding more. This case is getting weirder and weirder by the minute."

She opened the file and flipped through the pages. As she did, she felt her heart thump against her chest and a lump swell in her throat. *Weirder and weirder, indeed.* She glanced back at her suspect, who'd already put his feet back up on the table and crossed his arms with an amused expression on his face.

"Thanks, Jeremy." She closed the door and returned to the table.

"Boy, you should see the look on your face right now," the man said.

She gritted her teeth. His unflappable nonchalance was starting to get to her.

"Well, Mr. Mot, it seems your fingerprints have broken the national fingerprint database." She tried to swallow, but her throat was now almost too dry to do so.

"Really? That's quite intriguing."

"Ten thousand hits on your fingerprints and still counting," she said. "How did you do it?"

"Do what?"

"Whatever it is you did to AFIS. I highly doubt one of your names is Harisho Naguni." She flipped through the stack of fingerprint matches.

"You might be surprised. I've lots of names."

She ignored his comment. "Or Sergei Kersov. Or Brad Pitt!"

He chuckled at this.

"I really loved him in *Meet Joe Black*."

Becca pinched at the bridge of her nose. This guy was starting to give her a real headache.

"This is all a big joke to you, isn't it?"

His face darkened. "On the contrary. I take this affair far more seriously than you can possibly imagine. The scales of balance are teetering on the edge of oblivion and all humanity is doomed unless we can stop it."

Her mouth dropped. She was dealing with a nut job. A certifiable crazy person.

"No, Chief Cole, I'm not insane," Silas Mot said as if reading her mind. There was another knock on the door. He pointed to it. "That'll be a phone call. For you, if I'm not mistaken."

A second later, Linda poked her head into the interrogation room. Her face was ashen, as if someone had just stepped over her own grave. "Sorry to interrupt, Chief, but...but you have a phone call." The office manager glanced over at Silas. "It's about our suspect."

"Can it wait?" Becca asked. "Who is it?"

Linda cleared her throat. "Um, it's the governor. And he says he needs to speak to you immediately about Mr. Mot."

# FOUR

Ten minutes later, Becca Cole opened the door to the interrogation room and looked at Silas Mot.

"You're free to go," she said, gritting her teeth. Her face felt numb as the words oozed from her lips. The governor, however, had made himself very clear: the strange man was not Alvarez's killer. In fact, Silas was supposedly on assignment by the governor himself to investigate hers and the other 'strange' deaths in the area that he'd alluded to during the interrogation. To make things even more bleak, the governor had even insisted that Chief Cole and the Summer Haven Police Department should do whatever they could to accommodate him. In other words, they were to assist him in *his* investigation.

"Excellent!" He jumped up from his chair with a clap of his hands and strolled past Becca into the station's bullpen. "Now, it's time to get started on the real investigation." He spun around on his heels, offered her a slight bow, and looked up at her. "Where exactly should we start?"

"You don't really expect me to work with you on this, do you?"

Silas cocked his head. "Is that not what the governor told you to do?"

"Yeah, but he couldn't have been serious. You're...you're..."

"I'm what?"

"Crazy. Plain and simple...you're insane." Becca moved past him, walking toward her office. She hoped he'd take the hint and just go away. "Which means you're a liability. Any court gets wind of your delusions and they'll throw the case out faster than you could spit."

"But the governor said..."

"I don't care what the governor said. I'm going to figure a way around it. Something." She stepped into her office. Realizing the discussion wasn't over, she waited for him to enter before she closed the door. "Maybe I can find the president's phone number around here somewhere. Someone higher up."

"Oh, I don't know," Silas said. His charming little grin was back. "I'm pretty high up on the food chain myself."

"No, you're insane. No matter what you think, you're *not* Death." She reached into the candy jar on her desk and popped a Lifesaver in her mouth. "Like I said, in—sane."

"Can't I be both?" He laughed. "But here's the way I see it. While we argue about this, your case is growing cold." He nodded over to the blinds covering her office window. "The sun is now up. People are heading to work. Your killer is out there somewhere, mingling among the law-abiding citizens. Perhaps, awaiting their next target to kill."

Becca found herself suddenly exhausted. Back when she'd worked in Jacksonville—in a real metropolitan police department—cases like this would never happen. Sure, there were always lunatics that thought they were Edgar Allen Poe or

Jesus, but they never insinuated themselves into her investigations like Silas was trying to do.

The city was much classier that way.

On top of it all, when she'd worked Jacksonville, she hadn't been nearly as sleep deprived. Back then, she'd only been a cog in the greater machine. Others were there to take up some slack. She was afforded a little rest when she'd been out all night at a murder scene. She had partners to carry some of the burden of her investigation for her. So, she was typically much better equipped to handle mental hurdles like the one that was being thrown at her right now.

But here, in tiny little Summer Haven with its population of maybe six thousand people—not including the snowbirds that popped down here every winter—she was it. Yes, she had her patrol guys, but most of them were so new their shoes hadn't even been broken in yet. And the few veterans she had, like Sergeant Tanner, had never worked any real homicides before. Those kinds of cases had always been handled by the county's sheriff's office. She'd put a stop to that the moment she took over the department after her father, the former chief of police, had passed away.

Now, she found herself wondering if that had been a mistake. It certainly would be nice to pass the buck—and the lunacy she was now having to deal with—onto Sheriff Tolbert and his major crimes unit right about now.

Silas raised his left arm and tapped on his watch. "Tick-tock, Chief. Tick-tock."

She glared at him for a moment before looking up at the wall above the door where her father's old school clock hung. *Eight-forty*. She sighed. The crazy man was right. Time was ticking away and her case was getting cold. She could sleep when she was dead. Heck, Silas Mot could even maybe help with that one day soon. For now, she had a killer to find and she no longer believed it was Silas who'd done Andrea Alvarez in. It was someone else. Someone out there in her quaint little beach town. And she was determined to find out just who it was...whether she employed Mot's assistance or not.

She sighed. "Okay," she said, holding up her index finger. "But you have to answer something for me before we go."

"Ask away." He now stared, as if mesmerized, at the colorful candy jar filled with individually wrapped Lifesavers. "Anything you want to know."

"Who are you? I mean, really?"

He reached a hand into the jar, opened up the plastic wrapper of a green-colored candy, and popped it in his mouth. His lips instantly puckered and his eyes squeezed tight. "Ooooh, that's sour!"

"You got one of my Warheads."

"I like it!" He sucked on the hard candy for a moment before looking back at her. "As to your question, I've already told you."

"Tell me again. Maybe it'll make more sense the second time around."

He puckered up again and shook his head as another burst of sour exploded in his mouth. "Aaaah! That's good stuff."

"Who are you...really, Mr. Mot?"

His face suddenly grew serious, then he shrugged. "I really am who I said I am. I'm Death."

"See? That's where you lost me the last time."

He thumbed his chest. "I'm Death. Black cloak and scythe knocking on people's doors in the dead of night, taking the souls of the dying." He reached into the jar, grabbed a handful of the Warheads, being sure to throw out the more mundane candies like Lifesavers, and stuffed them in his blazer pockets. "The whole bit. It's me. It's what I do."

31

She began to smile, then thought better of it. He wasn't joking.

"But that's not possible. The Grim Reaper...it's a myth. A tale told during the medieval period to scare royal subjects into submission."

"Actually, that's not historically accurate, but close enough. But I can assure you, I'm no myth." He crossed his legs, placing his arm up on the back of his chair to relax. "Look, every religion in the world—from the smallest, unheard of cults to the ancient Egyptians and Mayans, all the way up to modern Christianity, Judaism, and Islam. They all talk about me as if I'm real. Now could all those people be wrong?"

She stared at him. "I...um..."

"Look, you don't have to believe me. I'm good with that. For now, I'm simply Silas Mot," he said, getting up from the office chair and patting his candy-laden pocket with the palm of his hand. "You can just think of me as Silas if it'd make you feel better."

"It doesn't make me feel any better," she said, rising from her own chair. "I thought you were messing with me before. Now I just think you're certifiable." She cocked her head. "What I don't get is how you got the actual governor of Florida to join your little delusion."

"Oh, that's easy. I visited him this morning when I left my jail cell. Had a little chat with him." His grin now could only be described as sinister. "Did him a favor a few years back. Put a little more time on his clock, if you know what I mean. He was very grateful."

Becca shook her head. "No way. I still have no idea how you got out of the cell, but Tallahassee is at least a six-hour drive from here. Another six back. No way you had time to..."

"Hello?" He pointed at his face with both index fingers. "Death! Don't exactly need conventional means of travel here."

"Uh-uh. No. I'm not buying it."

Silas walked over to her office door and opened it. "Doesn't really matter. What matters is that we have a murderer to catch and the trail's not getting any warmer. I hate to pull rank here, Chief, but you've been given your marching orders and it'd be a very bad career move on your part to disobey your state's own governor." He gestured to the open door, ushering her out. "Now wouldn't it."

She bit down on her lip, searching for an argument that would get her out of this fiasco. But there wasn't one. She was trapped. She was being forced to investigate a homicide with a deranged maniac who believed he was the incarnate form of Death and there was nothing she could do about it short of resigning her hard-fought position here as police chief.

She squared off against the man who was about to ruin her life—if not end it altogether—and glared. She'd do this, but she wasn't about to give Silas the satisfaction of showing any more concern for his madness.

"Fine," she said, walking out her office door and making her way to the parking lot. "But I'm driving."

# CHAPTER
# FIVE

SAND CASTLE CONDOMINIUMS
WEDNESDAY, 8:30 AM

They made their way down State Road A1A, heading toward Andrea Alvarez's apartment, in complete silence. Becca was still stewing over her situation, pondering every dwindling proposition she could think of to extricate herself and her agency from the investigation.

*Maybe it's the work of a serial killer*, she fantasized. *The FBI would take jurisdiction if it was a serial killer.*

Silas, for his part, kept his gaze fixed out the passenger window, watching the beach front scenery race by. Periodically, he would whistle or 'ooooh' when something particularly breathtaking would come into view. In many ways, he was almost childlike in his awe of the natural world.

*Heck, we don't even know it is a murder yet*, she continued her whirlwind rationalizations. *Autopsy's not finished yet. We already know the stab wound didn't kill her. Maybe that was just a coinci-*

34

*dence or something and she died from heart failure. Case closed. Mr.*
*Death can be on his merry way.*

After a few minutes, she could take the silence no longer.

"I've got a question," she said.

Silas seemed to snap from whatever mental world he'd escaped to and turned to her. "Shoot."

"What do you think is going on? I mean with Alvarez's death. Do you really think it's a murder or something else?"

He seemed to think about this for a few moments. "Well, it's highly suspicious. And I know that these unsanctioned deaths *must* be done by unnatural causes. Natural deaths—such as heart attacks, cancer, liver failure, those types of things—would all be predetermined and therefore, would be properly sanctioned. So, Ms. Alvarez was definitely killed by something or someone." He paused for a second. "And the Ebo blade stuck in her back would suggest her death was intentional to some degree."

"Ebo blade?"

He nodded. "It's a ceremonial knife. Used in the Santeria religion for animal sacrifices."

"Oh, that's just great."

Becca was aware of the presence of Santeria throughout Florida. Had even heard recent rumblings about local groups around Summer Haven, but she hadn't paid it much heed. She had worried more about the influx of heroin and Fentanyl in her town than any group of hoodoo shenanigans and animal sacrifices.

"Are you thinking Alvarez was some kind of human sacrifice? By these Santeria groups?"

Silas smiled and shook his head. "Nah. Santeria doesn't practice human sacrifice. But with the knife and those glyphs written in the blood on her back, I believe we were supposed to think she was."

Becca returned her attention to the road, letting his words sink in. A few minutes later, she turned into the Sand Castle Condominiums and made her way around the winding parking lot until she came to the building with her victim's unit. She parked her patrol car, reminded herself to breathe, and got out.

She'd parked beside the patrol unit guarding Alvarez's home and, the moment she stepped out of the car, she was met by Officer Tim Sharron. Sharron gave Silas a strange look when he got out of the passenger seat, then glanced over at Becca.

"Long story. Don't ask," she responded to his unspoken question. "How's the scene holding up?"

"It's been quiet," he said. "Haven't seen anyone approaching her place since I got here."

"What about the back entrance?"

He shook his head. "Of course, I can't watch the front and the back at the same time. But I've made random patrols around the property. Haven't seen anyone except other residents leaving, heading for work."

She smiled at the officer. "Good job. Especially with making your patrols random."

Sharron, who'd only worked for the department a year now, beamed at her praise. "Thank you, ma'am."

She patted him on the shoulder. "Stick around, Tim. We're going to look inside. If there's trouble, I'd appreciate the backup."

"Want me to go in with you?" He kept staring at Silas Mot with wary eyes. There was just something about the guy that put everyone on edge.

"Nah, I'll be fine. Just stay sharp and come if I call."

He nodded, then climbed back into his patrol car.

Without acknowledging Silas, she began walking toward building D, and looking for unit number 14—Alvarez's condo.

A few minutes later, she caught sight of it and veered in its direction.

"So, what exactly are we hoping to find here, Chief Cole?" Silas asked, breaking the short reprieve she'd been enjoying from having to speak to the crazy man.

"It's just a good place to start, that's all." She approached the front door and tried the door knob. It was locked. "Right now, we don't know a lot about our victim. We don't know where she died either. The body had obviously been moved onto the beach by the killer. So, her place might give us the clues we need to continue with the investigation."

"And you won't need a warrant to enter her property?"

"It's not hers. She was just renting the place." She retrieved her cell phone from her pocket, searched Google for the property manager's phone number, and dialed it. A short conversation later and she hung up. "Property management is contacting the condo's owner. He lives close by. They said he should be here in five minutes to let us in. If he gives us permission, there's no need for a warrant."

"Ah! Very enlightening."

She pulled her notebook from her pocket and pretended to be reviewing her notes to avoid any more conversation with the strange man. For his part, Silas withdrew another Warhead candy—the crinkling of the wrapper threatening to shatter her last nerve—and plopped it in his mouth for another display of blissful pucker-face.

She flipped through the pages of her notebook with an angry flourish, hoping her new partner would get the hint. But he appeared oblivious to her irritation and began humming a strange tune that sounded like an old Irish ballad she'd heard at a funeral when she was a kid. She rolled her eyes.

*It's only around ten in the morning and I already need a drink. This guy is going to put me in the looney bin.*

37

She was about to ask him to stop his humming when a bright red Mini-Cooper pulled into the parking lot beside her car. A moment later, a portly young woman wearing a pair of leopard print leggings and a black sports bra two-sizes-too-small climbed out from behind the wheel. The woman's hair, short and poufy, was professionally colored as red as her vehicle. Her face—thick with makeup—revealed worry lines creasing her brow when she noticed the police car and then Chief Cole standing near Andrea Alvarez's door. The newcomer rushed toward them, a set of keys in her hands.

"What's going on?" she asked when she was within earshot. "Is Andrea okay?"

Becca stepped forward, blocking the woman from the front door. "Sorry, are you the owner of the condo?"

The redhead shook her head. "No. Just Andrea's best friend." She looked from Becca to Silas. "What's happening? What's wrong?"

The chief recognized the woman from around town, but she'd yet to learn her name. In her line of work, most of the time, that was a good thing. In situations like this, however, it made things a little awkward.

"I'm sorry, ma'am, but I'm not at liberty to talk about it just yet." She withdrew a pen from her shirt pocket. "Can I ask you your name?"

The woman nodded. She was visibly shaking. Her thick mascara now ran in streaks down her cheeks. She was definitely concerned. *I wonder why.*

"S-sure," she said. Her voice trembled. "Ceci. My name is Ceci Palmer. Like I said, I'm Andrea's best friend. Is she okay? She's not dead, is she?"

"Well now, Ms. Palmer" Silas said. He leaned toward her like a famished predator, arms behind his back. His gleaming

38

teeth reminded Becca of those of a hyena. "Why on earth would you ask something like that?"

The woman blinked at him, then turned to Becca. "B-because…" She wiped away a tear and sniffed. "Because of the Death Curse."

Silas seemed to go rigid at the proclamation, though Becca couldn't blame him. In all her years as a police officer, she'd never come across a statement like that.

"Death curse?" she asked.

Ceci Palmer nodded. "Yeah. She's been worried sick about it for weeks. We all have. When I saw your police cars here, I just assumed the curse finally got her."

Becca decided to shelve talk of a curse until they could get inside to look the place over. "And why exactly *were* you coming by here today? If you don't mind me asking."

The rotund redhead shook her head. "I d-don't mind at all. I came to pick her up for the gym. We have spin class today."

Becca glanced over at Silas, who was eyeing the woman with deep suspicion. She then looked down at her watch. The landlord was taking his sweet time getting here to let them in.

"Do you have keys to get in?" the chief asked, gesturing with her thumb to point at the door behind her.

Ceci's tear-streaked face nodded. She held out her set of keys in shaking hands.

Becca took the keys. "Don't go anywhere, Miss. We still have questions. And I'd like to hear more about this death curse you mentioned."

Another nod.

Becca then turned to the front door and riffled through the keys until she found the one that fit the lock. She gave it a quick turn and the door opened with a twist of the knob. She took a single step inside and jerked to a surprised halt. A ghastly visage, hidden within the shadows beyond the door's lintel, stared at her from a pedestal about waist high. A second later, she realized the macabre thing was a statue of some kind —a large oval stone with a face made out of sea shells.

"That's *Echu Eleggua*," Ceci said from just outside the door. "One of the Orisha Warriors of Santeria."

Becca glanced back at the woman. "Excuse me?"

"Santeria, Chief Cole," Silas whispered in her ear. "Our connection to the Ebo knife."

"Andrea practiced Santeria." She pointed at the Mr. Potato-Head-like statue. The thing sat in a bowl filled with small pebbles, assorted hard candies, and a plastic child's whistle. "I'm not really sure of all the ins and outs of her religion, but she told me that the Orisha Warriors were supposed to be placed at the entrance to the house to keep out evil spirits. Eleggua was supposed to be the keeper of the door."

On the right side of the door, resting on another pedestal was a medium-sized iron cauldron with several iron spikes placed within. Next to it was a third pedestal with what looked like an iron tripod connected by a chain at the base.

"The pot, I believe, represents *Ogun*, the master of all metal. Where Eleggua opens and closes doors, Ogun keeps things at bay." Ceci had slid into the condo past Silas and pointed to the tripod. "And that thing...Andrea told me it's supposed to represent a crossbow. It's the sign of *Ochosi*, the hunter. My understanding is that if someone keeps these avatars at their door, it would keep the evil spirits or curses away."

Silas nodded. "I know these guys," Silas said to Becca. "Interesting fellows, each of them. Though they tend to cheat at cards."

The two women blinked at him, then Ceci returned her gaze to the Orisha statues. "There's a piece missing." She pointed to an empty pedestal tipped over on the ground beside the Potato-Head stone. "Osun is supposed to be there. It looks kind of like a silver trophy with a rooster on top. I think it represented Andrea herself...her well-being. Legend said that if your Osun falls over, you're in danger." Ceci paused as if thinking about her last statement, then gasped. "Andrea!"

Before Becca could react, the portly redhead bolted up the stairs of the condo. A moment later, there was a gargled yelp. Becca and Silas ran upstairs and found her in what appeared to be the master bedroom. A nightstand and lamp had been overturned. Strange symbols, similar to those scrawled on Andrea's body, were marked in red on the vanity mirror to their right.

Ceci stared at the bed, which didn't appear to have been slept in recently. She pulled her hand over her mouth to stifle a gargled cry. "Where...where is she? Where's Andrea?"

Becca placed a gentle hand on her shoulder. "Honey, I'm afraid we need to talk."

41

# CHAPTER
# SIX

"The beach?" Ceci asked, blowing her nose into a tissue as she and Becca sat downstairs on Andrea's couch. The landlord had already come and gone, leaving the keys with the police chief. The sheriff's office's CSU was currently upstairs processing evidence in the victim's bedroom. And Silas busied himself in the kitchen, boiling a pot of tea. "What was she doing at the beach? She was supposed to be *here*." She sniffed. "I mean, she only left her house to go to work and that was pretty much it. She was too scared to go anywhere else."

Becca could only shrug in response. "I'm not sure why she was there. Right now, it looks like she was left there by her killer."

"And you said you found a knife in her back?"

"A dagger. Looked ceremonial." She gestured toward the kitchen entrance. "Mr. Mot believes that the knife has something to do with those Osh...Och..."

"Orisha!" Silas shouted from the kitchen.

"What he said." Becca scribbled the strange word down in

42

her notepad. She wouldn't forget it again. "So, what can you tell me about this curse you mentioned earlier?"

"The Death Curse."

"Yes."

Ceci dabbed her eyes with a tissue. A glob of black eyeliner came with it when she pulled it away. "It's a pretty well-known story now. *The Chronicler* ran an article about it. Apparently, Spenser Blakely's on a crusade to clean up all this black magic stuff from Summer Haven." She looked up at the chief. "You didn't read it? It was on the front page of last Sunday's edition."

Silas appeared in the living room, carrying two cups of steaming hot tea resting on saucers. He placed them on the coffee table in front of the ladies and went back to the kitchen to retrieve his own cup.

"You know this might be a crime scene, right?" Becca said to him. "Not the brightest move making tea right now."

"Nonsense." He strode back into the room with that infernal grin plastered on his face and began strolling around the room while sipping from the teacup. He stopped near the sliding glass door and examined the photos of family and friends that hung on the wall. "The kitchen is clean of any and all forensic evidence. I carefully examined it myself. Only thing in there is a wedge of cheese and an empty bottle of wine on the countertops. And I didn't touch either of them." He looked over at Ceci and pointed at the pictures. They all seemed to be focused around that of a young boy—ranging in age from an infant to around four years old. He pulled one of the pictures off the wall and showed it to Ceci.

"Who's this?" he asked.

"Once again...crime scene!" Becca glared at him. "Stop touching stuff."

He rolled his eyes, then placed the photo back on the shelf.

"My apologies, Chief Cole." He pointed at the kid in the picture. "I'm just curious about who he is. He seems pretty important to Ms. Alvarez."

Ceci nodded. "That's Jamie. Andrea's son. He lives with his dad in Hammock Dunes," she said. "Poor boy has a pretty serious form of autism and can be a handful. Because of Andrea's history of mental illness, she figured he was better off with James, his father."

Becca shot Silas a look, warning him not to interrupt the interview again, but he merely waved her off before returning his gaze to Ceci. "Thank you. Now, about this curse...and the man's crusade you mentioned."

Ceci nodded. "Well, there's a pretty high concentration of Hispanics living on the outskirts of town. Andrea herself was from Bogota before she moved here as a teenager." She took a sip of the tea. The cup clattered against the saucer as she set it back down, a clear indication of just how bad her hands were shaking. "Anyway, with this influx of Hispanics, there also came quite a few people who practiced Santeria."

"Santeria," Becca said. "Now, that's like voodoo, right?"

Ceci shook her head. "That's a misconception. Truth is, while they apparently share origins that come over from Africa, Santeria is predominantly practiced by Hispanics. They have a whole other set of rules, gods, and rituals."

"Okay. So, Spenser Blakely ran a piece on all this?" Becca asked.

Ceci nodded.

"Excuse me," Silas said. He'd now moved over to an old travel chest in one corner of the room and was peering inside. "Who's Spenser Blakely exactly?"

"He's the owner, publisher, editor, and chief reporter of our town's newspaper, *The Summer Haven Chronicler*," Becca explained. "But I'll be honest, I rarely ever look at it. It's much faster to find my news on Google."

"Yeah, Spenser was kind of upset when he heard the news about Andrea's curse," Ceci said. "That's when he decided to expose the religion—against Andrea's will—in an article."

"So, Blakely knew Andrea?"

"She worked for him. Did the occasional graphic design job for him."

Becca thumbed through her notes. "But I thought she worked for Tate & Neely, the big advertising agency in the city."

Ceci nodded. "She did. That was her full-time job. She just worked for Spenser on special projects and such."

"I'm more curious about this curse you keep referring to," Silas said, crouching down for a closer look at the chest. He reached inside, moving a few things around before stopping suddenly. His eyes widened for the briefest of seconds, then he turned and looked at Ceci. "Sorry. Tell me about this curse. Specifically."

"Oh, yeah. That." Ceci placed the cup down on the coffee table and rubbed her hands. "Happened a few weeks ago. She and her Santero apparently got into an argument after a ceremony."

"Santero?" Becca asked.

"A priest of Santeria," Silas explained.

"Yeah," Ceci said. "Anyway, a few days later, she received a message from him saying he placed a curse on her and that she would be dead within the month."

"You're saying this Santero initiated a *Brujeria* against her?" Silas looked over at Becca. "It's a ritual of dark magic designed to hurt someone. And it's not taken lightly. It usually takes a pretty big reason for someone to use that kind of magic."

"And Andrea believed this curse was real? That it would actually work?" Becca asked.

"Horribly so. She was terrified. Even had to go see Dr. Fruehan to get her anxiety medication increased just so she could sleep at night."

"Fruehan?"

"Yeah. Emil Fruehan. That's the name of her psychiatrist," Ceci said. "He'd made amazing progress with Andrea before all this happened. He'd all but eliminated her schizophrenic symptoms and her bipolar disorder had become well-maintained. She was like a new woman. Then this Curse business came and all that progress just flushed down the drain."

Becca scribbled down the information. She opened her mouth to ask another question when the sound of heavy boots coming from the stairs interrupted her.

"We're pretty much finished up there," said the head crime scene technician. "Didn't find much. No unexpected fingerprints. All the hairs we found seemed to match hers." The tech held up a plastic bag filled with several pill bottles. "Found these in the medicine cabinet. Psych meds mostly. But they're controlled, so we'll be logging them in as evidence."

"Thank you, Steph." Becca nodded to the kitchen. "Can you do one more thing before you leave?" She looked over at Silas and glared. "There's apparently some wine and cheese in the kitchen. Any way you could take those too? Just in case."

The crime scene tech nodded, then set to work photographing the kitchen. Becca returned her focus on Ceci.

"Ms. Palmer, I understand that Andrea had some kind of nervous breakdown a couple of days ago. Tore through a restaurant, raving about being chased by Death." She glanced over at Silas and gave him a look to warn him from saying anything stupid. "Do you know anything about that?"

"Not much. I was at home watching my boyfriend's kid

when it happened. I didn't hear anything about it until the next day when Andrea called asking me to pick her up from the hospital."

"Hospital?" Silas asked. Becca cringed. She'd intentionally kept that piece of information from him. She was determined to hold as much back from him as she could until she decided whether she could trust him or not. The good news, to her, was that if he truly was the Grim Reaper, he didn't seem to be omniscient.

"Yeah. Instead of arresting her, the cops Baker Acted her," Ceci explained.

"Baker Act?"

"It's where Florida law enforcement can forcibly hospitalize someone who's a threat to themselves or others," Becca told him. "It's limited but can be very effective against suicidal or mentally deranged people."

*Oh, how I'd love to use that against you right now, Mr. Mot.*

"Anyway, the cops, feeling she definitely fit the bill, sent her to University Medical Center," Ceci sniffed. "The hospital held her overnight for observation. That was as long as they could hold her without a court order. After a while, she calmed down and was allowed to go home. That's when she called me. But she wouldn't talk about it with me at all. Said she was just too humiliated about the whole thing. I just drove her home and she went inside and locked everything up."

"Okay, getting back to this Santero who supposedly cursed Ms. Alvarez." Silas, who'd finally taken a seat in a reading chair across from her, leaned forward. "You don't happen to know his name, do you?"

Ceci's eyes widened. "Oh, uh...look, I don't want to cause any trouble for him."

"Why not?" Becca asked. "Looks like he's a good suspect in

your friend's death. Why wouldn't you want to give us his name?"

"Because that dude scares me. He scares a lot of people. Santeria isn't the only thing he's into."

"I promise, Ms. Palmer. He won't know where the information came from. We just need his name."

The girl eyed them suspiciously for several uncomfortable seconds of hand-wringing. "Jacinto Garcia," she finally said.

Becca sat up at the mention of his name. "Garcia? Are you sure?"

Ceci nodded while keeping her gaze steadily at her own feet.

"Who's Jacinto Garcia?" Silas asked. "I mean, besides a death-curse-making evil Santero?"

"He's bad news," was Becca's only reply.

# CHAPTER
# SEVEN

Silas looked over at Becca as she drove her cruiser south along State Road A1A. "So, where are we going now? To see this Jacinto guy?" His voice was garbled because of the Warhead slurping around in his mouth.

She shook her head. "Jacinto Garcia is a member of *Los Cuernos del Diablo*, a local gang with ties to a Colombian drug cartel. He's listed as a person of interest in several unsolved homicides, not to mention a slew of drug charges." She flicked on her blinkers and turned left down a narrow, unmarked road. "Before we go stirring up trouble with him, I need to do some research."

"*Los Cuernos del Diablo*," Silas repeated. "The Devil's Horns?"

She nodded.

"Sounds soft and snuggly."

Becca smiled, then a moment later, she turned into the

49

parking lot of a small single-story brick office with a larger building added to the back constructed of corrugated metal. The sign on the pane-glass window read *The Summer Haven Chronicler* in fancy, Old-English style letters.

She parked the car and the two of them got out and walked into the newspaper's front office. An elderly woman, in a purple and flower-print dress, typed away on an old fashioned electric typewriter behind a long countertop, that acted as a front desk to the office. A chrome bell rested in front of her, but from the spectral fronds of cobwebs covering it, it looked like it hadn't been rung in a while.

"Apparently, our intrepid journalist isn't a fan of modern technology," Silas whispered as they sidled up to the front desk.

"Yes, Mr. Blakely is a bit of a technophobe," the woman said, not looking up from her work. The sound of heavy machinery rumbling in the back of the building made hearing the slight old woman difficult. "If you ask him about it, he'll lament about the fall of real journalism in our country and the assault the Internet has made against traditional media." She finally looked up at him from behind her bifocals. "It gets rather tedious, so don't mention it to him unless you've got a few hours to kill."

"Point taken and appreciated." He cast that ice-melting grin at her, but she appeared just as solid as when they'd entered the door.

"Ms..." Becca glanced at the name plate on the woman's desk. "...Hamilton, I'm Chief Cole."

"Oh, I'm aware of who you are, Chief. We ran a story on your swearing-in ceremony. It was all very exciting." Her eyes darkened. "Though I'm still so sorry about your father's passing, dear. He was such a good man. This town misses him terribly."

"Thank you," Becca said as she opened up her notebook and glanced down absently at it. She always got uncomfortable when her dad was brought up by anyone from town. "Ms. Hamilton, we're here to speak with Mr. Blakely..."

"About Andrea's death...yes, I've been expecting you."

"You have?"

"Of course. Where else would you come? After all, it was Spenser Blakely who broke the story about that horrid curse on that sweet girl. He's been trying to open up the eyes of the Summer Haven community to this weird cult since he first heard about it from Andrea."

"Cult?" Silas asked.

"Santeria. It's like Voodoo, but different. Just as evil though...if not more."

He let out a frustrated groan. "Ms. Hamilton, I can assure you...some of my closest colleagues are involved with Voodoo. One or two dabble here and there in Santeria. These religions —their customs and rituals—may seem bizarre to a Westerner such as yourself, but they're far from evil. In fact, the Kongonese and Yoruba communities from which these religions originated would have found the Romanesque customs of the early colonists who enslaved them most bizarre indeed. It's a matter of perspective, really."

The old woman's mouth went slack as she glared at him behind suspicious eyes.

"Forgive my companion, Ms. Hamilton," Becca interrupted. "He's from out of town."

"Ah! That makes sense," she said, still keeping one eye fixed directly on Silas. "I bet he's from California. Lots of weirdos in California."

"There certainly are." The chief was smiling. "Now, is Mr. Blakely here now?"

"Of course. Of course." She stood, walked over to an aisle

between four cluttered desks, and pointed toward a large green door. "He's back in the print shop. Working on a late edition for this afternoon to break the news of Andrea's death."

"Thank you, Ms. Hamilton," Becca said before taking a step toward the backdoor.

But Silas stopped mid-step and turned to the old woman. "A late edition?"

Ms. Hamilton nodded politely, but Becca could tell she wasn't a big fan of the tall tanned man in the jet-black suit. The old woman was probably a good judge of character.

"That seems kind of expensive. Especially for a small newspaper like the *Chronicler*."

"It is," she answered, going back to her desk and sitting down behind her typewriter. "But Andrea was family. Mr. Blakely feels he owes it to her to get her story out there."

"Of course, it doesn't hurt to sell papers either, I imagine. What with an evil 'cult' being Blakely's chief suspect and all, eh?"

She scowled at him before returning to her typing without another word.

"Come on, Prince Charming," Becca said. "Before you get us thrown out of here because of your utter lack of tact."

At the rate he was going, Silas Mot was going to drive away any and all potential witnesses with his wild, unyielding personality. Not to mention his insane delusions. Fortunately, he'd not mentioned that to anyone but her, but she could only imagine what people would say if they discovered his ridiculous claims.

*No one would talk to me about this, or any other case, if they ever found out. It'd be career suicide.*

Setting her doubts aside, she motioned Silas to follow as she walked to the back of the building and stepped through the door into the larger metal building behind the newspaper's main office. The sound of the printer inside the print shop was near deafening and Becca had to concentrate in order to tune the mechanical grinding out to search for Spenser Blakely.

As far as she could remember, she'd only met the man twice in her life. The first time was when she was fifteen years old and her high school softball team had won the state championship. She, and the rest of her teammates, had had their picture taken by Blakely's late wife, Daphne, while he had interviewed her about her game-winning homerun when their bus had returned home.

The second time she'd met him was during her swearing-in ceremony to become the chief of police. He'd been very polite, offering his condolences over the loss of her father, then proceeded to grill her over how she planned on cleaning up her dad's dirty little police department. Of course, there'd never been any accusations that her father's administration had been corrupt. Nor had any new evidence of corruption come to light after his death. But that wasn't going to stop the struggling newspaper man from trying to sell copies with any scandal he could churn up.

It was one of the reasons Becca had refused to pay any attention to his little gossip rag since returning home last year.

A tap on her shoulder brought her out of her reverie and she turned to see Silas pointing to their left and saying something. With the sound of the printer rumbling off the late edition, she couldn't hear what he said, but the meaning was clear: they should look on the other side of the machinery. With a nod, she walked in that direction, rounded the corner of the massive printer taking up most of the room, and practically bowled poor Spenser Blakely down when they ran into each other.

The journalist was a short, round man, in his early fifties. His thinning gray hair swirled around like down feathers in a light breeze, and he had a thick Burt Reynolds mustache with flecks of gray sprouting here and there like flakes of dandruff that would never fall away.

After a moment of being startled, the man placed a hand over his chest and gave a short drowned-out laugh, before holding up a finger to indicate that she should hold on for a minute. He strode over to the far wall, opened up a metal box mounted there, and flipped a large switch that shut down the running press.

"Ah!" he said, removing the pair of sound-suppressing earphones from his head, and turning back to his guests. "That's better." He walked over to Becca, hand extended. She shook it politely, then introduced the reporter to Silas Mot.

"He's assisting with the investigation involving the death of Andrea Alvarez," she told him up front, hoping to extinguish any curiosity he might develop for the strange man. "An old colleague of mine, who just offered to lend a hand."

"I see." Blakely looked Silas up and down, then turned his attention back to Becca. "So, what can I do for you, Chief Cole? I'm afraid I don't have a lot of time. I need to get this afternoon edition of the paper printed and out to our subscribers as soon as possible. News this important needs to be provided as soon as possible, I think. Not every day Summer Haven sees a murder as grisly as poor Andrea's."

*Newspaper sales*, Becca thought. *It's the only thing the man cares about. He could give two flips about the death of an innocent woman.*

"I'd like to ask you about the article you wrote recently, about Jacinto Garcia and the Santeria practitioners who've recently moved here."

"Just a second," Silas interrupted. "How do you know her death was 'grisly'?"

"Huh?"

"Just then...you said it's not every day your town 'sees a murder as grisly' as Ms. Alvarez's." Silas cocked his head. "Funny. There's been no details of her death released to the public. The autopsy's not even been conducted. So how do you know whether it was grisly or not?"

"Well, I..."

Silas grinned his infuriating grin. "Yes?"

"It's just that...I mean..." Spenser Blakely fidgeted in his spot until Silas laughed.

"I'm just messing with you, Spense." He clapped Blakely on the shoulder. "Of course, every murder in a small town like this would be 'grisly', right?"

"Oh, yes." The newspaper man cleared his throat. "Precisely what I meant. Yes."

Becca's eyes narrowed at her new partner, wishing she had heat vision, before she returned to the question she'd asked earlier. "Anyway, Mr. Blakely, about that article you wrote concerning Andrea's curse and the Santeria group around here..."

Blakely reached up, as if to adjust his tie, then remembered he wasn't wearing one and stuck his hands in his pockets instead. "Ah, well, I wish you had taken the feature more seriously back when I wrote it," he said with a sniff. He was still looking at Silas with derision. "Maybe Andrea would still be alive today if you had."

"I'm sorry, Mr. Blakely. But at the time, I had no reason for concern." She offered him a polite nod of understanding. "Curses aren't really prosecutable, I'm afraid." The reporter opened his mouth to respond, but she cut him off before he could protest. "And last I heard, religion is protected in this country. There's nothing illegal about Santeria and therefore, nothing I could do about it."

"Yes, but..."

"Mr. Blakely, I'll be sure to read your editorial on the subject later. Right now, I just need you to answer my very specific questions." Her face grew stern. "We can either do that amicably right here and let you get back to your work, or we can talk about this at the station. With the latter option, I'm not sure how long it might take. You could be there for hours."

The man's mustache twitched. He glanced from Becca to Silas, then back to the detective and sniffed again.

"Fine," he said. "But in my opinion, the rotten apple hasn't fallen too far from the proverbial tree."

She ignored the comment.

"Could we talk somewhere a little more private, sir?" Silas asked. His face had taken on the sincerest of expressions, like the faux concern of a funeral director consoling a grief-stricken loved one.

He shrugged. "My office, I suppose." He began making his way toward the door and waved for them to follow.

# CHAPTER
# EIGHT

B lakely's office was more lavish than the rest of the building, with its polished hardwood floor and cherry-wood bookshelves, filled with leather-bound tomes, built into the northern wall. A matching desk, neat and tidy—and oddly, no computer—sat facing east with a large picture window looking out at the ocean. The only signs of modern technology in the whole office was a security monitor capturing images of the building's exterior in high resolution infrared.

On the southern wall, hung a collection of wooden masks —they looked African, maybe some Asian, to Becca. A wooden display case sat underneath them and was filled with an assortment of spearheads, knives, colorful beads, and other trinkets of African origins.

The journalist gestured to two chairs on the other side of the desk. "Please, take a seat." He then walked over to the wet bar behind his desk and poured himself a two-fingered glass of brandy. He turned to look at them, his cheeks flushed, as he pulled out an orange pill bottle from his pants' pocket. "Sorry," he said. "I'm a little agitated." He held up the bottle for them to see. "Lorazepam's about the only thing that gets me through the day lately."

He popped one of the pills and drowned it in the amber liquid. He then walked over to his desk and sat down, looking at his two guests with nervous eyes.

"Perfectly understandable." Becca said, although it really wasn't. Drinking brandy and taking anti-anxiety meds before noon was something she would never quite understand. Still, for etiquette's sake, she sat in the proffered seat, then nodded over to the masks and display case. "That's an interesting collection you have there."

"Huh?" He looked in the direction she'd indicated, then beamed. "Oh, yes. It's my pride and joy. Something I started collecting with my late wife—may she rest in peace—twenty years ago on our first trip to the Congo." Blakely paused, as if reminiscing. "We went back every year after. At least, until Daphne got sick, that is."

Becca offered an understanding nod.

"Well, I won't keep you from your work any longer than I have to, Mr. Blakely. But as you know, we're following some leads on Andrea Alvarez's death and I thought you might have some insight."

"I most certainly do. As we were saying, I have no doubt that Jacinto Garcia—known as Omo Sango by his followers—killed her."

"With a death curse." She couldn't believe she'd even uttered the sentence.

"Oh, make no mistake, Chief Cole, the dark magic practiced by followers of the Yoruba people is real. I've become all too familiar with it during my travels." He pointed toward the masks on his wall. "Santeria. Vodun. Palo Mayombe. They all originated in the Congo hundreds of years ago by the Yoruba people. I've seen things on my little excursions that would boggle your mind."

"But you seem to revere this culture," Silas finally spoke up. "You're a collector of their artifacts, after all. Yet, you seem to have great disdain for their belief systems. So much that you would write a scathing article about them in your paper."

"It's all well and good that they practice these dark religions in their own country," Blakely responded. "But when they practice here...in my own backyard...and threaten people I care for, well, I can't abide that at all."

"So, tell me," Becca said, "what do you know of this curse? Why did Andrea get targeted by Garcia?"

The reporter shrugged. "She didn't rightly know. She simply returned home from work one day to find a *bilongo* at her doorstep."

"A bilongo?"

He opened a desk drawer and pulled out a small leather pouch cinched with a drawstring. Opening the bag, he dumped its contents onto his desk. Becca saw what appeared to be a small doll wrapped in seven ribbons of various colors.

"This is a bilongo. It means 'working'," Blakely explained.

"A voodoo doll?"

"Kind of. Not quite. Unlike a voodoo doll, in which a curse can be lifted by destroying the thing, a bilongo is simply a representation of the 'working', not the actual curse itself. It merely acts as a warning." He collected the doll and placed it back into the pouch.

"I'm going to need that as evidence," Becca said, holding out her hand. "When the case is over, you can have it back. Don't worry."

He nodded, then handed the pouch to her. "I was with her at the time she found it." His face turned several shades of red. "We had recently started, ahem, seeing each other. Nothing too serious, mind you. Just dipping my toes back in the dating pool again, one might say. Anyway, I was with her when she found it. The look on her face. My God. It was ghastly. She immediately broke down in a fit of despair. Took forever for her to finally explain to me what it meant."

Becca jotted down some notes on her pad, ignoring the urge to calculate the significant age difference between Spenser Blakely and Andrea. *To each their own, I guess.*

"Funny," Silas said. "We spoke with Ms. Alvarez's friend...a Ms. Ceci Palmer...and she didn't mention that you two were seeing each other."

"Like I said, we had only just begun dating. Though we weren't hiding it, we both felt it was too soon to advertise our relationship yet."

"Did she know why she'd been cursed?" Becca asked, trying to keep the interview on track.

Blakely shook his head. "She was never really sure. Yes, she and Omo Sango had heated words one evening after a ceremony, but that was after he had told her of his intentions to cast the working against her. Before she could protest formally, she was turned away. Excommunicated from their little group, apparently."

"So that's why you began your journalistic crusade against this group?" Silas asked. Becca wasn't sure why he was so focused on Blakely's obvious hostility toward the religion, but she decided to let the question stand.

"I've always distrusted them, Mr. Mot. Always tried to warn people about their nefarious magical practices."

"Yet, you were dating one of their members," he responded. "That seems a touch hypocritical to me." The man in the all black suit leaned forward in his chair, his teeth gleaming back at the newspaper man. "Tell me, Mr. Blakely, how did Andrea feel about your opinion of her religion?"

"I...uh..."

"It's a simple question. She couldn't have been too happy with your little expose on Santeria."

"I don't see how that's important." He started to reach for his non-existent tie again, but remembered his last attempt, and just began fidgeting with his fingernails instead. "She tried to tell me that it's not all bad. Tried to convince me that most of it was good. Peace-loving."

"But you knew better, didn't you?" Silas pointed toward the display case filled with the various trinkets of the reporter's travels. "You'd seen it firsthand."

"Um, excuse me. What does this have to do with anything?" Blakely asked. "I thought you were here to talk about Omo Sango."

"Jacinto Garcia," Silas said.

"They're the same person. It's just the name his followers call him."

Silas leaned back in his chair and glanced at Becca with a wink. "Your witness, Counselor."

*This man is going to get me fired*, she thought, shaking her head. She had no idea what Silas Mot's line of questioning was supposed to have accomplished, other than to frustrate Blakely. *Or worse, sued for slander.*

"Sorry about my colleague, Mr. Blakely," Becca said. "He's a little unorthodox."

"That's putting it mildly," the reporter said.

"Okay. Let's get back to Jacinto Garcia. Of course, I've heard of him. He's the leader of a known gang known as *Los Cuernos del Diablo*."

"I'm very familiar with the group, yes."

"We're aware that they operate out around Gruenwald Commons, but we've never been able to track down their base of operations. Did Andrea ever mention where Garcia hung out? Where he could be found?"

Spenser Blakely nodded, then glared at Silas defiantly. "I'll be happy to tell you as long as you promise to take that horrible man with you."

Silas' self-assured grin stretched even wider.

"You have my word," Becca said, envying her own promise. *I couldn't get rid of him even if I tried.*

The reporter told them what they wanted to know and Becca ushered Silas out of *The Summer Haven Chronicler* before he could offend anyone else that happened to be in the building.

# CHAPTER
# NINE

GRUENWALD COMMONS
WEDNESDAY, 1:05 PM

The Gruenwald Commons warehouse district was about five miles north of Summer Haven, almost equidistant from Saint Augustine further north on A1A. Located near the docks, it was grimy, and cluttered with iron cranes and graffiti-covered brick buildings that should have been torn down decades ago. Technically, Gruenwald Commons was unincorporated. A sort of no-man's land within the county boundaries. But that didn't mean it didn't have its own special governing hierarchy among its denizens.

The area was well known to be run by a corrupt labor union with close ties to organized crime. Despite this common knowledge, however, no law enforcement agencies had ever been able to pin anything more than a parking ticket to the powers that be.

Fortunately, Becca Cole wasn't interested in the upper

brass of this seedy section of her home county. Today, she was after something much more tangible.

"You mind telling me what your little interrogation back at the newspaper was all about?" she asked, keeping her eyes fixed on the road.

"Ah, just as you coppers like saying...playing a hunch, I suppose."

She rolled her eyes. "What kind of hunch?"

Silas shrugged. "Not sure yet. But that little display case inside Blakely's office?"

"Yeah?"

"All those little knick-knacks and doo-dads?"

"Uh-huh."

"I saw a similar collection inside Andrea Alvarez's house."

This caught her attention, though she wasn't quite sure of the correlation. She gave the man a quick glance. "Where?"

"In that travel chest in her living room," he said. He pulled the lever on the side of the passenger seat and tilted it back. "Of course, they weren't knick-knacks and doo-dads in Alvarez's home. They were ceremonial. Not collectables. They were part of her daily life."

"And?"

"Like I said, I'm not quite sure. But something about Blakely's little collection just bothers me." He popped another Warhead in his mouth and grimaced. "Also, Blakely's insistence in calling Garcia by his Santeria name."

"What about it?"

"Well, he kept saying that it was the name his followers called him."

She thought about it for a second, then considered the ritualistic knick-knacks stashed in the man's display case, and a lightbulb lit up in brilliant one-hundred and twenty watts. "Spenser Blakely is secretly involved in Santeria!"

Silas touched a finger to one side of his nose and winked. "Exactly."

"So why the charade? Why go on this crusade against his own religion?"

"That's the hundred-thousand-dollar question. But I bet you dimes to those same dollars that Andrea Alvarez was in on it. There's no way she'd go along with it unless she knew why Blakely was doing it. She certainly wouldn't have been dating the man."

Becca shuddered at the thought. "Dude's old enough to be her dad. And just kind of sleazy. What did she see in him?"

"Dollar signs?"

She shook her head. "No way. *The Chronicler* is only scraping by. I don't know how they haven't gone bankrupt already."

"Then power. Political influence. Whether the paper is successful financially, it's still your community's primary news source. There's a lot of power behind a position like that."

Becca had to admit that it made sense...to some degree. But she'd have to ponder this more later on as she saw her destination coming into view up the road. Checking over both shoulders, she pulled her cruiser into the parking lot of U-Store-It, an abandoned old self-storage facility off Wilkshire Boulevard, and coasted toward the dilapidated brick building that had once been the complex's office.

"So, this is definitely not what I expected from a possible drug kingpin and powerful Santero," Silas said.

"What did you expect? A big mansion and an Olympic swimming pool? These guys are street thugs. Nothing more."

Silas was right about one thing. The place had definitely seen better days. The building's windows were nearly opaque with grime, pollen, and spray paint. A wall of weeds and vines shot up around its exterior, strangling the place in a mesh of vegetation. Gang tags could be easily seen painted here and there along the brick façade.

"Hope you're up on your tetanus shots," Silas whispered while opening his car door to step out.

"Wait!" Becca grabbed him by the arm. "This is going to be dangerous. You need to hang back. Stay with the car."

Silas chuckled. "But I'm Death. Trust me. I'll be fine."

"You might believe that, but I'm not willing to take the chance you're just a nut job with connections to the governor's office."

Gently, he removed her fingers from his forearm and slipped out of the car. "I appreciate your concern, Chief Cole," he said, shifting a piece of candy from one side of his mouth to the other. "But I'm a grown man—in a manner of speaking— and capable of making my own decisions. And if you recall what the governor told you, this is *my* investigation too."

She closed her car door and sidled up to him as he strode toward the front of the office. "Well, are you at least carrying?"

She, of course, knew the answer to that. They had done a thorough search on him when they'd taken him to the station. He'd been unarmed. She shuddered to imagine a man as delusional as Silas Mot carrying a firearm, but it would have at least offered him some protection if things got messy in there. *Los Cuernos del Diablo* were not known for playing nice. Especially with cops. If Blakely was correct and they actually used this old place for their base, they weren't likely to be happy to see them.

"Carrying what?"

"You know what I'm talking about."

He grinned, glancing down at the gun she held in her right hand and shook his head. "No. But I do have this." He held up his hand, index finger pointed up in the air like a finger gun. "Trust me. It's far deadlier than that piece of iron you have."

She sighed before stepping in front of him. "Just stay behind me the whole time we're in there. I'm wearing Kevlar. You're not and these guys in there are serious."

"So am I, Chief." Silas nodded his assent, then gestured toward the door with his free hand while pulling his finger gun up to his chest. "But if it'll make you feel better, then after you."

Her gut reeled with a swarm of butterflies just imagining the million possible ways this could go wrong, but she willed her feet to move forward, walked up to the double glass doors, and pulled on one of the handles. Surprisingly, it wasn't locked. She opened it, kept her firearm ready, and stepped inside. She felt, more than heard, Silas follow her.

The office's foyer was just as deserted as the exterior of the building. An old reception desk, leaning to one side on broken legs, sat directly in front of them. The checkered linoleum floors, almost carpeted in yellowing old papers and windswept leaves, looked like it hadn't seen the business end of a broom in years.

*Six years actually*, she thought. *U-Store-It went out of business six years ago.*

Despite the daylight hour, the room was dim. Moats of dust flitted up from the scant rays of sunlight trickling in from the grime-covered windows.

"Hello? Anybody home?" Silas shouted, causing Becca to jump.

She gave him a silent slap across the arm. "...the heck are you doing?" she hissed. "You trying to announce our presence or something?"

He blinked. "Well, yes. Actually. We can't question this Omo Sango fellow if we can't find him, right? I figured one of his associates might make introductions for us."

Becca pinched the bridge of her nose.

"I'd say his 'associates' would just as soon put a bullet in our heads than take us to their leader. I'd rather find him on our own, thank you very much. It's all about stealth in a situation like this."

"Got it." Silas nodded, then pointed toward a door over to their left with some light shining through a crack near the floor. "Maybe Mr. Garcia is that way."

Becca considered her sanity in allowing this lunatic to continue tagging along on her homicide investigation. He was going to get her killed. Then again, if he truly was Death, wouldn't he be able to tell if they were alone in this office building? Wouldn't he be able to sense the presence of mortals or something? For the briefest of moments, she considered pitching the idea to him, but thought better of it.

*No need to play into this psycho's delusions.*

"Come on," she whispered.

She stepped over to the door, which swung back and forth on hinges, and pushed it open just enough to peek through. Sure enough, the room beyond was lit, but she almost wished it hadn't been. Mentally clearing the room, she stepped into a large chamber with a low ceiling pocked with water stains and sagging pink insulation. An old rusted dolly cart lay without wheels immediately to her right. Beside it, rested a flickering candle. She scanned the room to see dozens more candles lining the walls along the concrete floor and illuminating the room with an eerie warm glow.

But it was what was in the center of the room that gelled her knees to rubber. For a moment, she could only gawk at the grotesque effigy of bones and terror that lumbered more than seven feet tall.

She glanced over at Silas, then back at the statue.

"Oh, this is just great," he whispered. "This is all I need."

She looked back at him, waiting for him to explain what he

meant. The statue, which was straight out of childhood night-mares, was that of an azure robed skeletal figure holding a scythe in one hand and a globe of the earth in the other. A crown rested upon its skull and several bead necklaces of multiple colors hung loose around its neck. Trinkets of all kinds—coins, liquor, bullets, and other shiny things—rested at the statue's feet as offerings.

"No, no, no, no, no." Silas was obviously nervous about something. "Not now. Not here."

"Care to explain yourself, Mr. Grim Reaper?" she asked. She wasn't sure how her new 'partner' was going to deal with seeing a likeness of the mythological being he identified himself with, but she was rather curious to see how it played out.

He placed a palm on his face and shook his head. "Of all the dingy little drug hangouts in all the world, she's gotta be in this one."

*She?*

"What are you talking about?"

"He's talking about me, dear," came a silky feminine voice from the shadows on the other side of the chamber. There was a thick Hispanic accent to it, though Becca couldn't quite place the region.

As if materializing from thin air, a striking woman wearing a white, form-fitting sun dress stepped out of the shadows toward them. The woman had a dark, caramel complexion—probably Latin or Native American—with long, flowing black hair that cascaded over her bare shoulders to the small of her back. Her skin was flawless, unmarred by the typical tattoos and piercings Becca expected to see on anyone associated with the gang known to haunt the Gruenwald Commons storage complex. And her bright, emerald eyes seemed to be fixed solely on her companion with laser-like intensity.

"Esperanza," Silas said with a nod of recognition. "I'm assuming, anyway..." He paused, looking her up and down. "It's always so hard to keep up with what you might look like at any given moment. So many makeovers."

She smiled at this. "Can't say the same about you. Until now, that is. Like the new look," Esperanza replied, gesturing lavishly at his body. "Finally decided to go slumming with the mortals like the rest of us, I take it? Or maybe you had no choice, eh?"

Becca looked over at Silas. She decided it best to ignore the 'mortals' comment. "You know this woman?"

He shrugged. "*Woman* is a bit generous a term, I'd say."

"Oh, he's just being overly dramatic," Esperanza said. "That's what men do, after all, whenever they bump into their wives when they're with another woman."

"Ex-wife," Silas barked. "Most definitely *ex*."

Esperanza laughed at this. To Becca, the sound was something akin to bones rattling in a wooden box.

"This is your wife?" she asked.

"Ex. She's my *ex*-wife," he said. "Don't let her get into your head. You'll never get that mess untangled if you do. Trust me."

"And she's here. Right now. Where our suspect is supposed to be?" Becca felt a growl of irritation rumbling up from her gut, but she suppressed it. Either this guy was more involved in Andrea Alvarez's murder than he claimed or he was trying to sabotage her investigation.

"I know what you're thinking," he said.

"I don't think you do."

"It's not like that. Before you start accusing me of tipping her off to this Garcia bloke, think again. I haven't seen or spoken to Essie in nearly seventy-five years. In Berlin."

"Seventy-fi..." She stopped and looked at the beautiful Latina woman standing just three feet away from them. Surely, she would correct him. Surely, this woman, who obviously knew Silas, would shed some light on his delusion.

"Oh, you've always had such a horrible memory, Ankou," Esperanza said, clucking her tongue at him like a disapproving school teacher. "It wasn't Berlin. It was in Belize. And it was forty-eight years ago." Her eyes narrowed. "You took one of *mine* at the time, if you remember."

*You've got to be kidding me*, Becca thought. *She's as crazy as Silas!* Neither of the two could have been older than their mid-thirties. No way they could have been in Belize forty-eight years ago. *Unless...No, Becca. Don't you even start down that road.*

"Now wait just a minute," Silas said, stepping toward the woman and pointing his non-gun-finger at her. "Sergio Nasgucci was *not* one of yours. There is no *yours* or *mine*. Once someone's ticket is up, that's it. Neither of us have any control of that...no matter what you've convinced your devotees to believe."

"Devotees?" Becca was losing control of the situation in a bad way.

"Yeah," Silas said, pointing to the hideous skeleton statue in the center of the room. "That's not me. That's her."

"Her?"

"Yes. Allow me to introduce the two of you," he said. "Chief Becca Cole, meet her *Glorious Highness* of the Narco drug cartels themselves, *Nuestra Señora de la Santa Muerte*. Or, simply Santa Muerte, if you like. The cartels revere her. Worship her even. They believe she'll keep them from harm at the hands of police officers such as yourself." He looked at the woman and gestured to Becca. "Honey Bumpkin, meet Becca Cole. She's a cop. A good one, by all accounts. And together, we're investigating the death of a woman found on the beach in Summer Haven. An unscheduled death, I might add. And one of your devotees has been named as a suspect. We're here to talk to him."

He squared off against her, his eyes flashing in a silent challenge against the woman. For her part, Esperanza didn't back down.

"So, an unscheduled death, eh?" She grinned at him. Her smile was cruel, nothing like Silas's usual cheeriness at all. "So, it's true. I'd *heard* you were losing your edge."

"Are you going to introduce us to your stooge or what?"

*Yep. I'm definitely losing control.*

Fortunately, it seemed that Silas Mot—or as Lady Death called him, Ankou—had recovered from the surprise appearance of his ex and was back on track. And from the sound of things, it all went back to what he'd told her in her office. People were dying and he had no idea why. Esperanza seemed pleased with the turn of events, which put her up a notch or two on Becca's own suspect list.

"Why should I?" Esperanza asked. "He worships me. Far more than you ever did, *mi esposa*. Why shouldn't I just have the both of you killed now where you stand?"

Several guns cocked from the shadowy corners of the room. In response, Becca swept her own gun around, searching for targets. A large man holding a pump shotgun stood just inside the doorway from which they'd entered the chamber. Two more appeared from another door at the back. Both appeared to be holding H&K MP5 submachine guns.

"Oh, come on, Essie," Silas said. "You know they can't hurt me."

The woman shrugged. "Can't they? I'm not so sure."

Silas edged closer to her. "Don't try me, Esperanza. You won't win."

The Latina woman shrugged. "Even if they can't harm you,

they can definitely hurt your new girlfriend here." She nodded at Becca.

"First of all, I'm not his girlfriend," Becca said. She wasn't certain who to point her gun at first, so she opted for Esperanza's head instead. If these gangbangers really did worship the woman as some type of death goddess, maybe they'd think twice about attacking if she could get hurt. "If they kill us, the Florida Department of Law Enforcement and every agency in northeast Florida will be down on your gang faster than you can blink."

Silas glanced around, his eyes tracking each of the newcomers like a predator about to pounce.

"Esperanza, call them off," he said. "No one here has to die tonight."

"How would you know? Aren't you losing a grip on your kingdom, Ankou?"

"Not by a long shot." He spun around, whipped out his ridiculous finger gun, and pointed it at the shotgun-wielding thug near the entrance to the foyer. "Bang," he whispered, bringing his thumb down.

The man dropped and fell into convulsions before gasping for one last breath and going still. His gun clattered to the floor. A split second later, the two goons with the MP5s gargled gasping breaths and fell to the floor along with their companion.

Esperanza screamed.

"No!" She ran over to the shotgun-wielding man, crouched down, and scooped up his head into her lap. "They're mine, Ankou! They're all mine." She stroked the man's shaved head with delicate fingers. "Bring them back." She looked up at Silas. Tears ran down her cheeks. "Please."

Becca couldn't believe what she was seeing. Silas had simply pointed at the man and he collapsed. The others too.

They had died right in front of her. The way it all went down was just as she imagined a Grim Reaper would be able to do.

*No. Get your head out of that rabbit hole. It's obviously a trick.*

But in her gut, the seasoned police officer knew it wasn't. The inability of Larry, one of her rookies, to properly handcuff the man. His disappearance from his secured holding cell. And now this. It was true. Silas Mot really was Death.

"Why should I?" Silas's good-natured attitude was completely absent now and had been replaced by cold, but calculated fury. "They'd simply try to kill Chief Cole again and I can't have that."

"No! I swear it. Bring them back and I'll offer both of you safe passage while you're here."

"That's what I wanted to hear," Silas said. "And you will also take us to Garcia without any more games?"

The woman nodded.

His face still deathly solemn, he walked over to the shotgun man, bent down, and touched his forehead. The man jolted upright at his touch, gasping and coughing for breath. The others were revived as well, though they still lay motionless on the floor as if in shock from their experience.

"As I told you, Essie...there was no need for anyone to die this afternoon. Returning their lives was of no consequence to my station." Silas stood and reached out a hand to her. When she took it, he helped her to her feet. The gunman laid his head back down on the concrete floor and continued to heave for breath. "Still, they won't be exactly mobile for several hours more, I'd say."

Then, Silas turned to look at Becca.

"You're...you're..." She couldn't quite form the words.

His bright smile returned. "I told you," he said before popping another piece of candy into his mouth. "Now, how about we have that meeting with the Santero, Jacinto Garcia."

## CHAPTER
# ELEVEN

They were led through a dark hallway that descended underneath the *U-Store-It* complex. Becca's mind whirled at the revelation that she was currently walking side by side with the mythological incarnation of Death and was being led by the patron saint of drug cartels throughout all of Central and South America.

When she'd been awakened earlier that morning by the shrill ring of her iPhone that informed her of Andrea Alvarez's murder, she'd had no idea how upside down her world was about to be turned.

"If you're going to stare, at least talk to me," Silas said, keeping his own eyes fixed ahead at his ex-wife. "It's unsettling."

Becca blinked, then shifted her gaze down the hall they were now walking. The sound of their shoes clip-clopping down the cement enclosure was nearly deafening. It had been also eerily hypnotic and she hadn't even been aware she'd been staring at the man next to her.

"Sorry." She tried to swallow, but her throat was far too dry. "I'm kind of freaking out a little right now."

"Don't. I'm still the same annoying man you believed to be nuts just a few minutes ago." She noticed he was keeping his voice low, despite the maddening acoustics of the hallway. "We're about to meet a major player within *Los Cuernos del Diablo*. Now would not be a good time to show fear."

They turned a corner, then descended a few more steps to go deeper underground.

"I've got a question for you, Essie," Silas said, turning his attention to his ex. "Didn't consider the possibility until I realized you were in town. Did you have anything to do with Elliot Newman's death?"

"Who?" she replied, not turning to look back at him.

"So, I'll take that as a 'yes'."

Becca looked over at him. "Elliot Newman? The archaeologist that was hit by a bus a few nights ago? What does he have to do with Andrea Alvarez's death?"

Silas shrugged. "Nothing at all. Just working all the angles is all."

"Well, don't press your luck, *mi esposa*," Esperanza added. "Remember what you said. There's no *your* or *mine*. When their Time is up, it's a free-for-all."

Becca's mind reeled. Silas had mentioned Elliot Newman in her office when they were discussing his interest in the case. Something to do with people dying unscheduled and unsanctioned deaths. Andrea was one of them, but Silas had admitted that the St. Augustine archaeologist wasn't. The only thing she knew about him was that he had been here to investigate an old sunken pirate ship off the Summer Haven coast but was struck by a tour bus before he even had a chance to take his team to look at it.

*Okay. One weird death at a time, Becca. You're having a hard enough time dealing with things as they are.*

A moment later, they came up to a set of large double doors at the end of the hall. Two well-tattooed gangbangers stood on each side of the doors, MP5s in hand.

Esperanza moved to within five feet of the door and turned. "He's inside there. His sanctum where he practices his faith and prays," she said. Her eyes seemed to burn with anger. Perhaps humiliation. Becca couldn't get a good enough read on her. "But there are things you need to know before you approach him."

"Such as?" Becca asked. She refused to let Esperanza see how terrified she was of the woman's very existence.

"First, he doesn't answer to the name Jacinto Garcia. If you call him that, he'll take offense."

"We've heard," Silas responded. "Goes by Omo Sango now."

"Don't utter that name with such contempt, *mi esposa*. It is a sacred name. He didn't choose it. It was bestowed on him by his Orisha namesake. His patron spirit within Santeria." She leaned in toward them as if what she was about to tell them was a closely guarded secret. "Sango."

Silas gasped. "You mean Sango gave him the name personally? He's not just a Santero? He's a..."

"Yes."

"A what?" Becca asked. "What else is he?"

Silas looked over at her. "A Babalowa. I'd just assumed he'd taken the name himself to make his followers fear him even more. Sango is the most feared Orisha of Santeria. Made sense that a drug thug would want a name like that. But the title 'Omo' means 'child of'. Garcia's new name is essentially 'Son of Sango'. The fact that it was bestowed on him by the Orisha is very significant. The nomenclature is reserved specifically for Babalowas of the religion."

"And what exactly is a Babalowa?"

"If a Santero was like a Catholic priest, then a Babalowa would be a sort of..."

"Bishop?"

He shook his head. "A Cardinal. And considering he's believed to be a child of Sango—the veritable King of Santeria —it's like he's royalty as well. The mortal equivalent of an Orisha himself." He turned back to Esperanza. "He's the only one who can read *diloggun* tools for divination and also can confer initiation to other Santeros. Which means he's pretty powerful."

His ex-wife nodded.

"Powerful enough to possess it, you think?"

Becca cocked her head. "Possess what?" She didn't like being kept in the dark—especially in her own investigation— and the secrecy was starting to wear down the last of her patience. "Mot, tell me what you're talking about. I need to know before I go in there and start questioning this guy."

Silas gestured for her to hold on a moment but continued to stare down Esperanza. "Well, is he? Does he have it?"

"Yes, he's powerful enough to wield it, I believe. As to whether he has it, I am not sure."

"And this is why you've come here? To get your hands on it before I can find it?"

She let out an irritated laugh. "My reasons for being here are none of your concern. These men have prayed to me and I have come...just as I've always come and always will."

Silas let out an irritated sigh, then looked at Becca. "I promise, I'll explain all this later. For now, I think it's time for our audience with the Babalowa."

79

"I don't like feeling confused," the cop replied. "It's not in my nature."

"Trust me, Chief Cole. The scenario playing before you would confuse even the most brilliant of minds. But hopefully, after speaking with Garcia—" He paused and glanced at his ex. "Pardon, Omo Sango—everything should be made clear. For all of us."

Silas gestured toward the door and Esperanza nodded to the guards. As one, they pushed both doors open and the three of them strode into a large subterranean warehouse. A set of Orisha Warriors, similar to those they discovered in Andrea Alvarez's house, greeted them at the entrance. Beyond, the room's walls were made of cinder block and patches of rusted corrugated metal. Iron rafters draped the ceiling, giving the structure a hollowed-out cadaverous appearance. Several metal fire barrels were placed around the room, emitting red-orange illumination that seemed to cast dancing shadows in the darkened corners.

A handful of people huddled around the barrels, each packing some type of firearm and seeming to act as sentries against any uninvited intruders. Each was inked with a series of crude, prison-house tattoos that covered most of their bodies. Some had gang tags tattooed on their cheeks, brows, and necks.

In the center of the room, cloaked in a bright red and white checkered robe, sat a large black man, cross-legged on the floor and surrounded by lit ritual candles. He was sitting in front of an obsidian statue of a man clothed in red and white and wielding an axe. Two columns of smoke rose from incense sticks on each side of the statue.

As they approached, the black man looked up to greet them. He wasn't smiling.

"These people are here to see you, Omo Sango," Esperanza

said. The tone of her voice was anything but submissive. In this place, though Jacinto Garcia may think different, she was the one in charge. "I've given them safe passage. They are here under my protection."

*Interesting that she didn't tell him who Silas really is*, Becca thought while stepping toward the candle circle in which the man sat.

"Jacin..." She stopped herself. It wouldn't be wise to antagonize her suspect any more than she needed to. "Sorry. Omo Sango." She nodded silent apology for emphasis. "I've got a few questions for you regarding..."

"Andrea Alvarez." His response wasn't a question. Despite living in America for nearly twenty years, he still had a thick Cuban accent.

"Exactly."

"I didn't kill her."

"I didn't ask."

"You were going to. I was just saving you the trouble."

Becca shrugged. "So, what about the curse? We have a witness who says you placed some kind of death curse on her."

The Babalowa remained seated, his legs crossed. Absently, he fondled a necklace around his neck comprised of sea shells, bones, and palm nuts. Then, he laughed. It was the deep, throaty laugh of a giant. "You don't really believe in curses, do you, *chica*? You think a jury would believe in such a thing?"

"That's not an answer to my question. Did you place a death curse on Ms. Alvarez?"

Omo Sango clambered to his feet. Becca's head craned up to keep her eyes fixed on his nearly seven-foot frame. He wasn't just tall. He was as big around the middle and packed with solid ropes of muscle underneath the flab.

The big man stepped closer and looked down at her with a

sneer. "What's it to you, if I did? Can't prove I had anythin' to do with her death, even if I did."

"You might want to reconsider answering Chief Cole's questions." Silas stepped up to the giant and glared at him with dangerous, black eyes.

There was a sudden hush in the room. The gangbangers, who'd been ignoring the exchange for the most part, all turned to the confrontation and shifted their weapons in their hands.

"Pretty man in a suit. What you think you gonna do to me if I don't?"

Silas's white grin stretched across his face. His eyes narrowed into slits. He leaned forward and beckoned the big man to bend down closer to him. Smirking, the Babalowa complied.

"You see that pretty lady behind us?" Silas thumbed over his shoulder at Esperanza. "I assume you know who she *really* is?"

Omo Sango nodded. "Our holy lady of Death," he replied. "Our protector."

"Right," Silas said. "Do you fear her?"

The big man glanced over at the woman and gave a slight bow. "Yes."

"Okay," Silas said. At this point, his voice was only a whisper. "Now, look into my eyes, Mr. Big Bad Babalowa. Want to guess who I am?"

Omo Sango stood there for several seconds before his sneer dissolved into a frown. His eyes widened. He took a single step back while his jaw went slack.

"Yeah. I'm her old man," Silas continued. "Now where does that put you in the food chain of this room, I wonder?" Omo Sango took another step back. "Now show some respect and answer the lady's questions."

# TWELVE

"I didn't kill the woman," Omo Sango said. His eyes had never moved from Silas even though Becca had been asking him the questions. He'd lost the hard edge of a drug-pushing gangster and now trembled in what could only be described as a 'throne' near the ritual circle in which they'd first encountered him. "I didn't even put a curse on her. I swear it. On my ancestors."

The subterranean warehouse had been cleared of the gang-bangers. The candles in the ritual circle had been extinguished. The only people now occupying the room were Chief Cole, Silas, Esperanza, and the Babalowa.

"And why should I believe you?" Becca asked. "The whole town knows about this curse of yours."

"I'm tellin' ya...I didn't curse her. She was one of my initiates. Why would I do somethin' like that to one of my own?"

Becca glanced at Silas, who only shrugged in response.

"Everyone seems to think you did. Her friends. *The Summer Haven Chronicler...*"

"Blakely and that lousy paper." Garcia spat on the floor. "Not exactly a trustworthy source there."

"And if you did put a curse on her, wouldn't it have looked bad for you if it didn't work? I mean, what kind of power does a Babalowa have if his curses don't actually do what they're supposed to do?"

He glanced over at her, then quickly returned his gaze back to Death. "It would, but like I said, I didn't do a bilongo on her. I didn't perform no curse."

"But the paper..."

"That paper is full of it, chica. Blakely's got it in for me. Has for a long time. He'll do or say whatever he can to spread those lies to anyone who'll listen."

Becca crossed her arms over her chest and smirked. "Spenser Blakely is one of the most respected men in Summer Haven. Why on earth would he have a vendetta against you personally?"

The gangster sniffed. "That's somethin' you should ask him."

"She's asking you," Silas said, leering at the big man.

Garcia tensed. A vein began to bulge from his neck. Then he shook his head. "No matter what's between us, I can't tell you. Ain't my place and the Orisha wouldn't be pleased if I did. *Lo siento, Senior* Muerte, but I can't. Not even for you."

Becca nodded. "Okay. Then tell me...how is it everyone came to think you did place this hex on Alvarez?"

Garcia shrugged. "Don't know. A few weeks back, I *did* have a lady try to pay me to lay the bilongo on her. Offered up two grand to do it. But I refused. Like I said, Andrea was one of mine and she'd not angered the Orisha. I had no reason to curse her."

Silas and Becca looked at each other.

"And who was that?" They both asked at the same time.

The Babalowa shrugged. "Don't know. Nice lookin' white lady. Nice clothes. Expensive car. She just came to me and said she would pay me two grand to do the working."

"Wait a minute," Silas said. "You're telling us that a well-off white lady in a nice car just drives up in your neighborhood —*this* neighborhood—finds you somehow, and asks you to place a curse on someone?"

"Yeah, that seems unlikely," Becca agreed. "Even cops steer clear of Gruenwald Commons unless they can help it."

Jacinto Garcia continued toying with the bones hanging from his necklace and shook his head. "Nah. That ain't how it happened." His eyes darted around the room, then to Esperanza, who gave him a nod of encouragement. He then returned his gaze back to Cole and Mot. "I met her at school."

"Excuse me?" Silas' eyes widened.

"Yeah, yeah. I know. Big bad drug dealer takin' night classes at the state college. Go ahead and laugh it up."

"You're taking night classes?" Becca asked.

He nodded. "I don't want to be doin' this my whole life. If I do, I ain't going to be around long enough to enjoy it. I want out. Military wouldn't take me 'cause of my record. School just seemed like my best bet."

"And is this woman a student? A teacher?"

"I told ya. I don't know. I seen her around campus a few times, but we ain't ever had no classes together or anything." He pulled out a pack of cigarettes and lit one. "One day, I'm walking to class and she comes up to me in the quad. Says she heard I was a Babalowa and that one of my initiates was Andrea. Said she'd pay me two grand to lay the working on her."

"And you refused?" Becca asked.

"That's what I said, isn't it? Ain't no way I was going to use the power of the Orisha—especially Sango's power—to do something like that. It'd turn around on me so fast, I'd be dead within a week."

Garcia took a long pull on his cigarette. Becca noticed his hands were shaking. Not exactly behavior she'd expect from a cold-blooded gangbanger.

"How did this woman respond when you refused her request?"

"Didn't seem to have much of a reaction at all, to be honest." He exhaled a plume of smoke. "She just smiled and walked away. Cool as an iceberg, if you ask me."

"Like she had other options in mind," Silas added.

"Exactly."

"Did you ever see this woman again?" Becca asked.

Garcia shook his head. "Nope. But a few days later, Andrea came to one of our ceremonies freaked out. Got in my face in front of all the others and started accusing me of cursing her and that that creep reporter she'd been dating was going to find a way to stop it."

"Wait," Silas said. "You knew about their relationship?"

"Sure. Everyone did. She didn't exactly keep it a secret. A matter of fact, several people warned her about that guy. He was an initiate of mine a few years back. But somethin' was wrong with him. That dude was dark, man. I mean, yeah we're drug dealers and gangbangers, but he even gave my *hermanos* the creeps." The big man tossed the cigarette butt on the ground and stamped it out with a sandaled foot. "Andrea and Spenser met around the time his wife got sick. A few months later, Daphne Blakely was dead and Spenser was already tryin' to get in Andrea's pants. Took a few years, but he finally wore her down and they started hookin' up."

Becca and Silas gave each other sideways glances. "You

could be right about him," she said to Silas. She turned back to Omo Sango. "You're saying that Spenser was into Santeria?"

"Yeah. An initiate working toward becoming Santero. Until I gave him the boot. Like I said, I won't go into why, but let's just say he was experimenting with some really weird stuff— death rituals and such—after his wife got sick. We already had a hard-enough time getting acceptance from the locals. We didn't need someone like him being part of us."

"Could Blakely have continued practicing without you?"

The big man nodded. "I ain't Yoda and this ain't like Jedi school. It's sort of an individual thing. He couldn't have received an Orisha without a Babalowa conveying it to him, which means he couldn't ever become Santero. But he could certainly continue growing in the religion as much as he wanted."

"And his wife?" Silas asked. "You said he started these strange death rituals around the time Mrs. Blakely got sick. Any chance he used one of those curses on her? Maybe he had his sights set on Andrea long before his wife died."

Omo Sango shrugged. "Possible, but I doubt it. Need at least a Santero for a working strong enough for that. Woman got eaten up with cancer from what I hear. That'd take a lot of juju for something like that."

"Getting back to this woman at your school," Becca said after clearing her throat. "Think you could describe her to a sketch artist?"

He looked over at Silas again and gave a fearful little nod. "Sure."

"Okay. Come to the station tomorrow morning, first thing. If you do, I won't send the sheriff's deputies and highway patrol out to come pick you up." She paused, then shook her head. "No. Scratch that. Come to the station tomorrow morning and I won't send *him*."

She pointed at Silas.

Another nod.

Without another word, Becca turned and beckoned for Silas to follow. The two strode out of the gangster den as the Babalowa and the living embodiment of Santa Muerte looked on.

# CHAPTER
# THIRTEEN

SUMMER HAVEN POLICE DEPARTMENT
WEDNESDAY, 3:48 PM

"Wait, I don't understand," Silas said, craning his neck as she drove past the newspaper office on her way to the police station. "Why aren't we going there and arresting Blakely? He's got to be our guy."

She pulled up to a red light and stopped the car. It was after three in the afternoon and traffic was unusually light for that time of day. No doubt, many of the residents of Summer Haven had heard of the strange death on the beach and rumors were probably already spreading like wildfire. To most of the people who called the town home, it was an invitation to stay indoors until the killer was caught.

"A," she said. "We don't even know how Andrea died yet. I haven't heard anything about the autopsy. We don't even know it's a homicide. I can't accuse the town's newspaper owner of being a killer if we're not even sure there's been a murder."

"Really? Found on the beach with a knife in her back and you don't think it's a homicide?"

"You're the one who told me the knife isn't what killed her," she said, pulling forward the moment the light turned green again. "B. I got two and a half hours sleep last night. I'm exhausted. What we did today...all of it...was just preliminary. We were just looking into Alvarez's life. We'll get down to the nitty gritty of it tomorrow. Hopefully, the M.E. will have something for us by then."

"In the meantime, a bloodthirsty killer is walking around just waiting to strike again."

"Unlikely. If Alvarez was murdered, I think it was by someone she knows. She was killed for a reason. Not out of some random lust for killing." Becca pulled into the parking lot of the police station and drove up into her designated spot. She put the vehicle in park but didn't turn off the ignition just yet. "And C. I'm still freaking out a little about...well, you know..." She wiggled her finger at him.

"Oh, about that," Silas said. "Yeah, you can't tell anyone what you saw me do today. No one can know I'm really Death."

"What? But you blabbed about it all over the station this morning. Everyone heard you."

"Yeah, but everyone thought I was a crackpot too. No one believed me. In hindsight, it was a foolish move, but I was rather giddy with being alive...so to speak. I've never walked among mortals before...at least, not the way Esperanza has. No one had ever seen me...I mean, actually looked at me with physical eyes. The temptation to show off a little was a little too much. But the fact is, someone in this town is a threat to not just Summer Haven, but the world at large. If they find out I'm onto them, it could be a problem."

"Okay," Becca said, shifting in her car seat to look him straight in the face. "That brings us to my next question. You told me I'd get my answers after we spoke with Jacinto Garcia. What's going on? I know you're here because of these unscheduled deaths you keep talking about. But what were you and Esperanza talking about in regards to whether Garcia 'had it'? Had what?"

Silas' eyes drifted down to his hands in his lap, as if concentrating on what to say next. "It's complicated."

"Try me."

He let out a breath, resigned. "Okay. Fine. But it may seem unbelievable to you."

"More unbelievable than the fact that you're the living manifestation of Death and that you have an ex-wife named Esperanza."

He smiled at this. "Touché. But I was only giving you fair warning."

"I'm a big girl."

"There is an object, Chief Cole. An object of intense power. No one knows where it came from or when it came into being. Only mortals can use it. Immortals, such as myself and Esperanza, can't even touch it—even while in material form such as I am right now." He looked out his window, out toward the beach, and paused. "It's called the Hand of Cain and it gives whoever wields it the power over life and death."

"What do you mean 'over life and death'?"

"Just as it sounds. Whoever wields it, in essence, becomes... well, me. The Grim Reaper. The being in charge of who lives and who dies."

"And you think someone in Summer Haven has this...this thing?"

"I do. The largest concentration of unscheduled deaths has occurred in this area."

"When you say 'unscheduled'..."

"As I told you this morning, it means that it wasn't their Time. The most troubling thing to me at the moment is that these deaths have been random. Hodge-podge. I believe whoever has the Hand of Cain is still learning how to use it. He or she has no real control over it and people are meeting their untimely end far too soon."

Becca's thoughts drifted to the death of her father. He'd been only fifty-seven when he died. Granted, he'd had some medical issues, but she didn't think they'd been severe enough to lead to his death.

"My dad." She couldn't get the question out.

Silas shook his head. "I'm sorry. No. It was definitely Hank Cole's Time. He wasn't a victim of the Hand."

A single tear ran down her cheek. She wiped it away with a brush of her hand and looked back over at him. "Well, if Andrea Alvarez was murdered, wouldn't it have been her Time no matter what?"

"I honestly don't know. The longer a mortal has possession of the Hand, the less I can see the fate of human beings. And in human form, my power is even more severely limited. Like you, I now see only the things in front of me with physical eyes. My understanding of the spiritual world enables me to perceive more than you might, but my access to knowledge is limited by the same restrictions as you."

"So that's why you are personally investigating Alvarez's death? Because you honestly don't know how she died."

He nodded. "Precisely. Granted, because of my office, I have a little more insight into life and death than you do, but I'm not even omniscient in my spiritual form, much less this physical body. The cold reality is that the longer the one who controls the Hand remains in possession of it, the more control he'll develop. He will slowly begin to usurp my place. He will, in essence, become Death himself."

"Or herself."

"Exactly."

"What will all this do to the status quo?" she asked. "I mean, is this like that old movie, *Death Takes a Holiday*...where people discover they can no longer die?"

He smiled with a shake of his head. "No. It doesn't work that way. The natural order of things is pretty much fixed, no matter what happens to me. I didn't personally see to the death of every human in history. For the most part, things just happen naturally. In their own Time. However, there are some deaths I'm called to oversee in person. I can't really explain the process, but trust me. It's never random. And never without reason." He glanced down at his watch. "Until now, that is."

"Sounds to me like we need to find this Hand of Cain fast then."

"Which is precisely why I'm here. Why I injected myself into this investigation. And why I think Elliot Newman would be so invaluable to us." Silas popped in another piece of candy, but this time, didn't make a face. "His knowledge of ancient artifacts would be an invaluable resource for us in tracking the Hand of Cain down."

"Yeah, but he's...he's dead, so how..."

There was a sudden tapping on the driver's side window, startling Becca. She spun around to see the sweaty, red face of an overweight man in a rumpled suit. He wiped at his brow with a yellow handkerchief.

"Chief Cole, I need to speak with you please."

"Just a moment, Mayor Hardwick." She glanced over at Silas. "It's the mayor. Probably wants to know where we stand on the Alvarez investigation and it would probably be best if he doesn't focus too much on you. Go inside and see if Linda has any new information for us. I'll be inside shortly."

"Sure thing, boss."

The two of them slipped out of her patrol car. Silas sauntered back into the police station, leaving Becca at the mercy of the town's sudorific mayor.

"People are getting spooked about this murder, Chief Cole," Mayor Ray Hardwick told her the moment she got out of the car. "My phone's been ringing off the hook all day. Tell me you have good news."

"Sir, I'm not..."

"It's an election year, Chief Cole. An election year! We can't have murders happening around here. That kind of thing happens in Jacksonville. Not Summer Haven. So, what's being done about it?"

"Well, I've been..."

"I'm serious. You've got to handle this fast. People have got to feel safe here. They can't feel safe as long as a murderer is walking the same streets as them."

"I understand that, but..."

"You don't understand. I was running unopposed this November." He reached into his coat pocket and withdrew a folded newspaper. He unfurled it and held it up for Becca to see. "Now I'm not."

Becca took hold of the mayor's wrists to hold the paper steady. It was the late edition of *The Summer Haven Chronicler*. The headline on the front page read:

'Ghastly Murder Points to Santeria. Spenser Blakely Announces bid for Mayoral candidacy to Clean Up Summer Haven.'

"Whoa." It was the only word that came to mind. Blakely hadn't mentioned his plans for running against Mayor Hardwick when they interviewed him earlier. Hadn't even hinted at it. And something like that should definitely have come up if the reporter had nothing to hide. *Maybe Silas is right. Maybe Blakely did kill her.* It would certainly get him points from the locals if her death could be pinned on Garcia.

"This has to be wrapped up quick, Chief." The mayor was still rambling. The crisp collar of his dress shirt was now saturated in sweat. "The people have to feel safe. They have to see I'm doing a good job..."

Becca grabbed him by the shoulders and gave them a gentle squeeze. "Ray, calm down. Calm down. This isn't good for your blood pressure." The overweight man took a series of deep breaths as he collected his thoughts. "Listen. I've got some good leads. We're still waiting for the M.E. to give us an official cause of death. But once we get it, I've got a couple of suspects in mind we'll pick up ASAP."

Hardwick's eyes brightened. "Really? Suspects?"

She nodded in reply.

"Can I let the press know..."

"No. No way. You can't tell anyone anything. Not yet. Not until we know more. I know you're worried, but you've got to trust me. It's why you hired me in the first place." She gave his shoulders another reassuring squeeze. "We'll catch whoever did this. I promise."

He dabbed his forehead with his handkerchief and nodded. "Okay. Good enough." He let out a relieved breath. "I'll trust you, but you've got to keep me in the loop. Understand?"

"Absolutely. When I have something concrete, you'll be the first to know."

He smiled at her, then turned and began ambling his way across the street to the unassuming little brick building that acted as Summer Haven's town hall. As she watched him go, she was suddenly struck with regret for not asking to hold onto the newspaper.

"I've got to get a subscription to that stupid rag," she mumbled to herself as she strode into the station.

# FOURTEEN

**B**ecca saw Silas seated on the edge of Linda's desk as she walked into the bullpen. He was slinging a yo-yo, that had been tucked away in the station's lost and found box for as long as she could remember, and chatting away with the older office manager. Stacks of unread papers—presumably Andrea Alvarez's medical records during the time of her psychotic break—sat next to him, unread.

Before making her way over there, Becca glanced around the office for Sergeant Jeremy Tanner. She spotted him, a moment later, over at the coffee maker, pouring himself a cup.

"Anything interesting at the autopsy?" Becca asked him as she approached.

The old veteran tugged on his uniform sleeve before taking a sip from his mug, winced from the heat, and shook his head. "Too early to tell," he said. "You were right. The stab wound was post-mortem. It didn't kill her. Doc saw signs of a major heart attack though."

"A heart attack? She's only twenty-eight."

"I know, right? And here's the weird thing. There were no

signs of previous heart problems. No plaque buildup. No clogged arteries. None of the typical signs you see in someone who dies of a heart attack."

Becca poured herself a cup of coffee too. "What's Dr. Lipkovic thinking?"

"Glad you asked," he said, scarfing down one of the donuts Silas brought in earlier that day. "He wants to meet with you tomorrow. Says he wants to mull the case over with you a bit. Wants you to look a little deeper into a few things, but he wouldn't explain it to me. He asked me to send over the prescription bottles found at her house, so I took care of that."

"Thanks, Jeremy."

There was a burst of laughter from over at Linda's desk. They both turned to see Silas, who was still playing with the yo-yo—walking the dog, if Becca wasn't mistaken—and in the middle of telling what must have been a boisterous story from the way the handful of personnel were reacting.

"So, how was working with Mr. Death?" Jeremy was smirking as he said it.

"Knock it off. He's not Death. He was just joking about that," she lied. "And he's really not that bad. Smart, actually, if a bit eccentric."

"Well, I did some more diggin' on him when I got back from the medical examiner," Jeremy said. "Chief..." His eyes narrowed as he looked over at Silas. "There's no record of the man. Except for the crazy number of false-positive hits we got on his fingerprints, there's no record of a Silas Mot ever existing. Even Googled his name. Only 'Mot' that popped up was the name of some punk goth band and the Canaanite god of death." He shivered. "Kind of creepy, eh? Especially since he was just 'joking' and all."

"He's probably aware his last name is the same as the mythological god or something. He probably plays it up every chance he gets." Becca wasn't sure she was comfortable with how well she was beginning to lie to her most loyal officer. But if Silas' story was true, she had no choice. "Besides, Governor Tyler vouched for him. Part of some statewide taskforce or something. Could be an alias he uses for the job."

"Mighty bleak alias, if you ask me. All I'm sayin' is to watch yer back. I don't think I rightly trust that guy much."

"Noted and appreciated, Jeremy." She winked at the officer, then looked down at her watch. "Okay. It's getting late. Think I'll be heading out. You should go home and get some sleep too. We've had a long day."

"10-4, Chief. Have a good one."

Becca made her way over to Linda's desk. "Ah, Chief Cole," Silas said, wrapping the yo-yo up and tucking it into his pocket before patting the medical records sitting next to him. "Haven't had a chance to review this stuff yet. We were all just enjoying a bit of a chat."

"I can see that." The others milling around the desk understood the subtle hint and disbanded to their respective workstations. "The records can wait though, Mr. Mot. I'm exhausted. Only thing I want to do right now is go home and hit the sack."

He offered a sympathetic smile and a nod. "Of course, Chief. And please, call me Silas."

"Thank you, Silas."

There was a pause.

"And may I call you Becca?"

She scrunched her nose. "Hmmmm. I'd rather you didn't."

Silas's jaw dropped.

"Don't take it personal. It's just that I worked really hard to get where I am. To get past the 'darlings', 'sweeties', and 'pretty ladies' men around here still insist on using. I try to keep it professional with all my colleagues. I hope you understand."

Of course, she didn't want to tell him she wasn't sure how she felt about being on a first-name basis with the Grim Reaper. To her, it seemed a little on par with being pen pals with Hitler or something.

"Sure." His face reddened, but he tried to hide his obvious disappointment. "I understand completely." He clapped his hands together and gave them a good rub. "So, we'll get a fresh start tomorrow then?"

"Absolutely. Eight o'clock sharp."

He pushed the medical records to Linda, who immediately filed them away in her desk drawer, and offered a little wave before turning toward the door and walking out.

"Oooh, that was kind of cold, Chief," Linda said, logging off from her computer.

"I know." She felt a lump form in her throat. A symptom she always associated with guilt. "I'll make it up to him though. Somehow."

Linda stood from her desk and gathered her things. "Better do it fast. He's good looking. Crazy, but hot. He might just be a keeper."

"You know I'm seeing Brad." Becca wasn't about to tell her receptionist the zillion reasons why Silas Mot was definitely not a keeper.

"Oh yeah. Well done." She offered a sarcastic clap. "You nabbed the absolute dullest doctor in all the Southeast." Linda returned her gaze out the plate-glass window and watched Silas saunter through the parking lot outside. "One thing about that Mot...I bet he's never dull."

*Linda, you have no idea.* "Go home, Linda. And thanks for your hard work today."

"Ta-ta!" the receptionist said with a wave as she picked up her purse and keys, and glided from her cubicle to make a beeline toward the door. "Think about what I said." She let out a devious little laugh and walked out of the building.

*Yeah. Right. I've had some pretty bad judgment when it came to guys in my life, but at least I'm smart enough to give Death a wide berth.* She glanced down at her watch again. It was now almost five o'clock. Brad Harris's shift at the Summer Haven Urgent Care Center would be over soon and they'd made plans for dinner. He wouldn't like it, but she was going to have to cancel. Her bed was calling. She only hoped once she got there she could settle her mind enough to fall asleep.

*This is the craziest day I've ever had in my life*, she thought as she stalked out of the building and headed to her car. *Here's hoping for a better tomorrow.*

# FIFTEEN

GARRETT & HISLOPE FUNERAL HOME
SAINT AUGUSTINE, FLORIDA
WEDNESDAY NIGHT, 11:45 PM

The front lobby of the funeral home at 325 County Road 207 in Saint Augustine sat empty of life. Lit only by a handful of inset lights in the ceiling, spectral shadows invaded most of the interior like dark ghosts feeding on whatever illumination they could crawl their way to. The filtered air—pumping the scent of chemical flora that only funeral homes use—wafted through each room, tickling Silas Mot's nose as he looked around.

His keen eyes scanned the darkness, landing on a plaque above a door marked 'EMPLOYEES ONLY'. He let his yo-yo spin along its line as he stepped forward, entered the forbidden hallway, and looked for the Preparation Room.

Fortunately, Garrett & Hislope didn't occupy a very large building. Being a rather new institution in the nation's oldest city, it hadn't quite developed the clientele the other two mortuaries had and was able to operate in modest, yet opulent surroundings. Still playing with the yo-yo, he strolled along the plush mauve carpeting, poking his head in each room until he found what he'd come here for.

He stepped into the Preparation Room, slipped the stringed toy in his pocket, and approached the large metal door that opened to the business's walk-in cooler. He took hold of the handle and pulled. The door swung open with a squeak and a hiss of air and Silas looked inside. The cooler itself was small, capable of holding only around ten bodies at a time, so it didn't take long for him to find the one he'd come here for.

Double checking the toe tag on the cadaver to be sure, he pulled on the metal tray in which the body lay and rolled it out into the warmer air of the Prep Room. After he locked the tray's wheels in place, he moved up toward the head of the table and looked down at the deceased occupant.

The man lay naked on the table. A standard stitched autopsy incision trailed down from both his collar bones to his navel in a 'Y' pattern. His face was already caked with makeup and his hair had been expertly fashioned in preparation for whatever funeral his loved ones had chosen for him.

Silas reached out a hand and took hold of the man's bare arm. The skin and muscles beneath were firm. They were far stiffer than those of any living man. He knew, of course, that it was not a result of rigor mortis. That condition would have passed after twenty-four hours from death. No, the thick rubbery epidermis now covering the man was a result of his body being completely drained of its natural fluids and replaced by preserving fluids of embalmment.

It was a slight problem, but no more than a hiccup in his plans for the man.

With a smile, Silas patted the dead man on the shoulder. "Well now, Mr. Elliot Newman," he said. "It's a pleasure to finally meet you."

# CHAPTER
# SIXTEEN

SAND DOLLAR MOTEL
THURSDAY MORNING, 1:23 AM

"Last call!" the bartender shouted from underneath the grass pagoda of the Sand Dollar Oasis, a quaint outdoor motel bar right on the beach. She didn't need to be so loud. There were only a handful of people haunting the place at that hour. In fact, since Silas Mot had arrived an hour earlier—after stashing Elliot in his room—there'd only been the same handful of people there.

Whether it was because the strange murder was keeping people secured in their safe little homes or the fact that Summer Haven's population was disproportionately comprised of mostly elderly people whose bar-hopping days had long since passed, Silas wasn't sure. The only thing he was certain of, as he reclined in the beach chair and watched the waves crash down on the white sand, was that the fruity little drink with the umbrella he was sipping was probably the most exquisite thing he'd ever tasted. He hadn't even known what the alcoholic concoction was called. He'd simply seen one of the other patrons drinking from the coconut tiki mug and knew he had to have one.

Granted, he'd also known that never having consumed any alcohol in his entire existence, it might have been prudent to take things a little slower than he had. This temporary material body of his was still subject to many of the same frailties as any mortal, to a certain extent, and was more than capable of becoming inebriated. But he'd only been 'mortal' for a little over twenty-four hours and figured he was due a few unwise decisions here and there.

"Mr. Mot?" The lovely blonde bartender in the tight tee shirt and short shorts had sauntered up to him without him realizing it. "Would you like another one before we close up?"

Her lips curled up as she whipped her hair out of her eyes with a brush of her hand. If he wasn't mistaken, the young woman was flirting with him and he couldn't help but wonder what the implications of possibly flirting back might be.

*No, Ankou. A mistake or two is one thing.* That *mistake, however, would be disastrous.*

"Thank you, yes," he said, holding out his now empty tiki mug to her. "I most certainly would."

Taking the mug, she went back to the pagoda and began mixing the strawberry, pineapple, and vodka-filled drink, while he returned his gaze back to the moonlit sea and pondered the case some more.

There had to be an explanation for Andrea Alvarez's death. Something that didn't involve curses or the like. Truth be told, mortals didn't quite understand that magic—as they knew it —didn't exist. Curses simply didn't work. Certainly, there were beings, such as himself, who could, and often would, manipulate the material world in such a way that it seemed like magic. But mortals, by their very nature, were incapable of causing such things to happen. And barring some entity—perhaps that insane Sango himself—personally getting involved in Alvarez's death, Silas was convinced that there was a more mundane solution to it.

*But what could it be?*

The bartender was suddenly at his side again, handing him his drink, as well as the bill and a folded slip of paper.

"It's just my phone number," she said, winking. She seemed cheerful, but there was something in her eyes that concerned him. They kept glancing around as if she was nervously searching for someone. "In case you get bored or lonely during your stay here."

He held up the note with a nod of thanks before tucking it into his inside jacket pocket. Then, he rifled through his wallet and handed her a wad of cash as payment for the delightful beverages she'd served him. Her eyes widened when she saw how much he'd given her. In truth, he had no concept of monetary value and wasn't sure whether he'd even given her enough. From the look on her face, he must have done well. "Keep the change," he said, giving the lapel of his jacket where he'd tucked the note a good pat with his hand. "And thank you for the number."

She blushed, then hurried back to the bar, but by the time she'd got there, he'd already long forgotten about her. His mind was already back to working through the case. Back to magic and curses.

Of course, the Hand of Cain might be considered a magical item. Of sorts. But it wasn't like a gun. Its wielder couldn't just point the thing at someone and cause them to die. Rather, it was more like a toss of a coin, setting into motion a chain of events that would lead to someone's death in the most unexpected ways. Silas doubted Andrea was even on the wielder's radar when she died. She'd more than likely been a random victim of the coin toss—to stick with that metaphor.

He sipped the fruity drink from the straw, savoring its taste as it swirled in his mouth and wondered why such divine concoctions were relegated to the realm of mortals. *Life truly is wasted on the living*, he thought. He sucked down the very last bit of liquid until the straw hissed with growls of thirst, then he sat the mug on the table next to him and stood from the beach chair.

It was getting late. Or early, depending on how one looked at it. The body he'd generated really didn't need to sleep, but his plans for Elliot would take a little more time, and he figured he might give rest a try simply to stave off boredom. Just in case. Which meant it was time to get back to his rented room at the Sand Dollar Motel.

The crash of the waves against the beach arrested his attention, however, and he decided to spend a little more time walking its sandy pathways. He was beginning to appreciate this world a great deal and he could sort of understand why Esperanza had spent so much time in it with the mortals. There was a great deal to like in the land of the living, and the ocean and its swirling breezes and coconut tiki mugs with fruity drinks garnished with umbrellas were becoming some of his favorite things. And Warheads, of course. Warheads made his mouth feel tingly and he found he rather liked that sensation a lot.

*Yes*, he thought as he slipped out of his shoes, rolled up his pant legs, and began strolling along the beach. *I can understand why these mortals are always so reluctant to leave when their time is up.*

He walked for miles, musing on the case, the beauty of the

landscape, the living world, and even Becca. *Excuse me, Chief Cole*, he thought smugly. He wasn't sure how far he'd walked or for how long but soon decided it best to turn around and head back to the Sand Dollar Motel. Thirty minutes later, he saw the shape of the bamboo and palmetto façade of the little tiki bar and began making his way west toward the main thoroughfare.

One sodium streetlight illuminated the parking lot of the motel's bar. The shadows surrounding Silas were long and menacing. He was getting a bad feeling, though he couldn't quite put his finger on what was wrong. He moved up to the curb. His motel stood like a squat rectangular shadow to the south of the bar with only a handful of lights along the sidewalk to guide his way. A few more yards and he would be secure in his roach-infested, yet temporary abode.

A scrape of a shoe against gravel arrested his attention. He stiffened. Sniffed the air. Something was stirring in the pit of his stomach. It was a new sensation—this fight or flight instinct that mortals required to survive. Silas didn't like the feeling at all.

He turned his head, looking over his shoulders, but no one was within sight. The bar was behind him, shrouded with a blanket of night. A row of palm trees, a single parked car, and a cluster of trash cans were the only things visible in the dim light.

*Okay, Ankou, old boy. You're getting what the humans call 'the heebie jeebies'. You need to relax.*

But his ectoplasm-constructed lizard brain didn't believe his rational one for a second. Someone was out there. Following him. Waiting in ambush for him.

He tensed, stopping mid-stride and looking around once more.

Another rustle of gravel. A distinct position. Behind him

and to his left. He spun around just in time to make out the shadow of a man moving away from the single car in the parking lot. Then, from the other side of the vehicle, two more men emerged. Silas couldn't make out much about them other than that they were big with meaty shoulders and arms underneath black tee shirts and covered with tattoos—each armed with semi-automatic pistols and each wearing black balaclava masks.

*Okay. I'm dealing with a couple of Mensa members here. Wearing masks but showing off their tattoos. Brilliant.*

Uncertain what to do, he readied his finger gun, then rolled his eyes at the very thought. He'd been trying to show off with Becca yesterday. He hadn't needed to simulate a gun with his hand to put those goons down. He could have done the same thing with a mere thought. But he hadn't been lying to her earlier. His power was waning. The longer the Hand of Cain remained in a mortal's possession, the less power he could employ. At the moment, he doubted he could do anything more than a street corner magician and nothing against the hooligans now approaching. Fortunately, he didn't believe he'd need powers for his attackers here. Having witnessed untold numbers of wars, battles, and fights through the centuries, he had developed an understanding of various other sets of skills he could employ if necessary. Granted, for the moment, he thought flight would be more prudent than fight if he could manage. At least until his supernatural abilities had some time to recharge a little anyway.

"Good morning, gentlemen," he said, as the three men lumbered to within a few feet of him. "It's a glorious night, isn't it?"

They didn't respond, but the first man made a show of pulling the slide back on his weapon and pointing it directly at

Silas. The man's balaclava wrinkled across the chin and fore-head, giving Silas the distinct impression of a sneer.

"Do you not even have the decency to tell me who sent you?" Silas asked. At first, he thought the strangers might be part of Garcia's crew. An unexpected surprise from Esperanza, maybe. It was something she would do and they certainly looked the part. But he doubted she would risk their lives for her own petty revenge scheme. She'd been genuinely distraught when he'd brought them each to the point of death earlier. It had been a demonstration of his power for her benefit as much as for Becca's. She would certainly think twice before sending members of Garcia's gang to tangle with him after that.

But now that they were closer, he had a better look at his accosters' tattoos and none had the telltale signs associated with a Hispanic gang or followers of Santa Muerte. Instead, they depicted Nordic runes and Celtic crosses. Irish possibly? Or Norwegian.

"No," said the first man. His two partners hung back a few feet, their guns held casually at the ground. They didn't expect too much trouble. "But I was told to tell you this...you ain't ever gettin' what you're looking for, pretty boy. Your time is up and someone else is in charge. That's what I was told to tell ya."

Silas tensed, keeping his eye on the man's trigger finger. "I see. That's rather enigmatic. Does your employer not trust you or something?"

The thug cocked his head to one side. "Huh?"

"Well, it just seems to me that if he really did trust you, he would have given you permission to tell me who he is. Since you can't tell me, he obviously didn't think you'd get the job done."

"That's how you're going to play it? Our pride in our work?" This came from one of the two goons in the back. And obviously, the smartest of the three and the only one wearing a long sleeve shirt. His voice was familiar to Silas, though he couldn't place it.

"It seemed clever at the time." Silas rolled onto the balls of his feet, preparing to do whatever instinct told him to do next. "I presume you're the real brains behind this little gang of Rhodes Scholars?"

The smarter thug stepped forward, tapping the first out with a pat on the shoulder. He then raised his gun and leveled it at Silas. "They're my brothers. What'cha gonna do?"

Silas nodded at this. "Most definitely. Have a few inept brothers myself. I feel you." Silas' eyes swept over each of the thugs. They were tensing. Preparing themselves.

He figured he had three decent options. One was a real showy 'Grim Reaper' deal that would probably scare the trio literally to death. He didn't want to do that, however. He needed these guys alive. They were his link to whoever had the Hand. The second option was worse. He could simply run away. But it would make these thugs think he was afraid of them. Both pride and pragmatism ruled against doing that because they would just continue coming after him and might accidentally hurt an innocent in the process.

The third option had its problems too. First, it would tip his hand. If there was any doubt as to his real identity, it would be completely gone when he pulled this stunt. However, in hindsight, that might a good thing. Maybe the mastermind behind all this would begin to truly appreciate the danger he was in. Besides, this way was just going to be too much fun to pass up.

*Okay. Option C it is.*

He smiled at the lead goon. "Any chance for a head start between two brainier brothers?"

The leader shook his head. "Sorry, Mot."

His gun arm tensed, then he pulled the trigger. A blast of

fire and smoke exploded from the barrel from just a few feet away from Silas. The loud blast of the gunshot echoed out into the darkness, ringing ear drums of anyone nearby.

The smoke cleared and the three gunmen stood fixed to their spots, unable to move. Their target, Silas Mot, had simply melted away in front of them, as if he'd never been there at all.

# CHAPTER
# SEVENTEEN

CHIEF BECCA COLE'S RESIDENCE
THURSDAY MORNING, 4:45 AM

The shrill ring of her cell phone woke Becca from the dead of sleep. She snatched the phone up and looked at the time.

"Sonuva..." She practically punched the talk button with her finger. "Becca Cole," she said.

Dispatch was on the other end. An incident had been reported. Shots fired in the parking lot of the Sand Dollar Motel. Silas Mot was somehow involved.

"I'll be right there." She tossed her phone back onto the nightstand and pulled back her bedsheets with a growl. "Silas." Another growl. "Ever since that guy came into town, my sleep cycle's really taken a hit."

She didn't bother to shower. There was no time. Instead, she brewed a small pot of coffee, got dressed, poured the fresh pot into her Yeti thermos, and headed to the scene as fast as she could. She was there in twenty minutes and greeted by Sergeant Tanner the moment she got out of the car.

"What happened?" she asked. Her voice sounded harsher than she would have liked.

Tanner smirked, then thumbed over in the direction of the bar's beach chairs. "Your boy happened, that's what."

She followed the officer's thumb and saw Silas Mot lounging in one of the chairs, feet crossed, and drinking what appeared to be some kind of tropical drink with an umbrella.

Sigh.

Becca made her way over to the chairs, picked the one to Silas' right, and sat down.

He glanced over at her and he jerked in surprise. "My dear Chief Cole, you look like *me* warmed over."

"That's what happens when we mere mortals don't get much sleep two nights in a row."

He nodded at this, then reached over to the table next to him and picked up another mug with an umbrella in it. He offered it to her. "They're delicious," he said with a sad smile. "Not quite as good as the ones they make here, but I was experimenting a bit and it turned out better than expected."

She waved the drink away. "I'm on-duty."

"Alcohol free. Turns out, I just like the fruity flavor over shaved ice."

She took the offered drink and sipped some from the straw. "Not bad. Strawberry and banana?"

"And pineapple. Mixed with fresh squeezed lemonade. It's to die for."

"Congratulations. You just re-invented a Slushy." She allowed herself a chuckle before remembering why she was there. "So, what happened?"

He proceeded to tell her of the three goons that had tried to ambush him in the parking lot. Gave her a description of the tattoos, as well as the red Camaro they drove off in. Then explained how he went to his motel room and awaited the arrival of the police.

"I didn't like it, Chief Cole," he said. "The fear I felt. I know I was in no real danger from their bullets, but I still didn't like the feeling." He gestured at his body. "This? It's not real. I created it from the ether...a substance the mystics call 'ectoplasm'. It's only a facsimile of life. I can discard it and pick it up again at will. But the problem is, I'm growing accustomed to all this. This life. And thinking of the possibility that it might end badly for me turned my stomach inside out."

She nodded. "Welcome to our world, Silas. Sounds to me like you're developing real human survival instincts." She took another sip from the drink and paused. "And by the way, you can call me Becca. It might be weird for me to be on a first name basis with the supreme overlord of death, but for now, I figure we're partners and need to start acting like it."

"Thanks." He stared into the tiki mug he was holding, as if it contained all the answers to the universe. "At least we know I made a horrid blunder yesterday...announcing my identity to anyone within earshot. Naturally, for the average mortal it would have seemed the ramblings of a lunatic. But the one who possesses the Hand. That one would have reason to believe. And be concerned."

"So, you think that's why you were targeted? Not because of our investigation into Andrea's death?"

Another nod. "The thugs pretty much told me as much, though they were careful not to reveal too much about their employer."

"What makes you think they have a boss? Why couldn't one of them have this...this Hand thing?"

"Well, first of all, whoever has it, has power enough to use it. Part of that power requires above average intelligence.

While the leader of my assailants was indeed smart, I don't believe he is smart enough to learn the Hand's secrets." He took another sip. "Also, they pretty much told me they'd been instructed by someone else. That's a dead giveaway."

The two turned to stare out at the ocean's horizon. A purple and orange ribbon of light stretched for as far as the eye could see. The early radiance of dawn bloomed in the distance. The palm trees around them swayed in the steady wind coming in from the sea and, for a moment, Becca's troubles seemed to disappear.

"You know, I don't do this enough," she said after a few moments of silence. "Just sit and watch the sun come up."

"It's my experience that most humans tend not to take advantage of the gifts they've been given. Their lives are cluttered with the bric-a-brac of day to day mundanity. They're too preoccupied with yesterday or tomorrow. Rarely today. Unless, of course, they know they're soon to meet me."

Becca slurped down the last of the fruit drink, then placed the empty mug on the table, and stood up. "All right, Mr. Mot. My guys will be looking for your assailants. Right now, we've got an investigation to get back to."

Silas seemed to leap from his chair with a clap of his hands. "Excellent. It's time to solve this mystery once and for all and, hopefully, lead me one step closer to figuring out who now possesses the Hand of Cain."

She laughed. "One step at a time, partner," she said as they crossed the parking lot to her patrol car. "One step at a time."

# CHAPTER
# EIGHTEEN

OFFICE OF THE MEDICAL EXAMINER
SAINT AUGUSTINE, FLORIDA
THURSDAY MORNING, 8:10 AM

"Dr. Lipkovic only has a few minutes," the receptionist at the Medical Examiner's Office told Becca and Silas. "He's got a full day today and needs to get started on the autopsies as soon as possible."

"I understand," Becca replied. "But he did ask to speak with me."

"Of course. Follow me." The short woman with close-cropped hair and pristine blue scrubs led them down a short hallway, then knocked on an open door to their left. "Dr. Lipkovic, Chief Cole is here to see you."

"Send them in, please." The voice carried with it a thick Slavic accent. From past meetings with the medical examiner, Becca knew the doctor hailed from former Czechoslovakia, by way of Prague.

The two entered into a large office with an immense Lshaped desk in the center of the room. A large microscope and two flatscreen monitors, depicting microscopic slides of unknown human tissue, sat just to the doctor's left.

Dr. Peter Lipkovic himself was in excellent shape for a man close to seventy. His hair was light gray—almost white—but full, and his eyes bright and friendly. As Becca and Silas entered, he set down a file folder, stood and extended his hand in greeting. "Good to see you again, Chief."

She shook his hand. "Likewise, Doctor." There was an awkward moment in which Lipkovic glanced over at Silas. "Oh, my apologies. This is a colleague of mine helping with the investigation. Dr. Lipkovic, this is Silas Mot."

"Mot," the doctor said, after gesturing for them to take their seats on the other side of his desk. "That's an unusual name."

"Is it? I hadn't noticed," Silas said, brushing an invisible fleck of dust from the lapel of his jacket.

"Ancient Palestine, if I'm not mistaken. Canaanite, more specifically," Lipkovic said, then returned his gaze over to Becca. "But I digress. Chief Cole, thank you for coming. I wanted to discuss Andrea Alvarez's death with you."

"Please. Any help you can give me will be greatly appreciated."

He opened the file in front of him and thumbed through several sheets of paper until he came to the one he was looking for.

"Look, I can't give you a cause of death yet." He tapped his pen against his notes as he looked at each of them. "Truth is, this is one of the weirdest cases I've ever worked. If there wasn't a knife found in her back—inflicted postmortem, by the way, and actually rather superficial in nature despite how gruesome it looked—I would more than likely rule it a natural death. Her heart showed signs of a myocardial infarction."

"Yeah, Sergeant Tanner told me that. And you saw no signs of previous medical problems?"

He shook his head. "Her arteries looked good. There was no scarring from previous heart attacks. No previous strokes. Not even any old lacunar infarcts in her brain. Nothing to indicate hypertension or anything else that would lead to what I'm seeing. Thought maybe it could be from an embolism, but there was no evidence of that either. At least, nothing older than a few weeks, that is."

"Pardon me?" Becca asked.

"I did see signs of recent bleeds," he explained. "Serious signs of some sort of hypertensive crises in her brain and heart...but they were all recent. Like, just a few weeks. Two or three weeks at the most. Nothing chronic to indicate a long history of these issues. These were acute. Very acute, which makes me think something was introduced into her life that caused these problems suddenly." Lipkovic paused, scanning his notes. "Of course, I can't rule out drugs yet. Cocaine and other narcotics can cause sudden cardiac death. We won't get the toxicology results back for another few weeks yet, but the preliminary urine screen was negative for the most common recreational drugs."

"Any way to speed the official tox results up?"

"A few weeks *is* speeding it up. I've marked them highest priority with the lab we use. Normally, they can take up to three months." Dr. Lipkovic sighed. "But I have a few ideas. That story about her erratic behavior at the restaurant a few days before her death...that intrigued me a great deal. The paranoia. The manic, almost violent outbursts. It's all rather suggestive and most likely part of whatever killed her. Almost definitely part of those recent hypertensive events I mentioned anyway." He paused, scanning a sheet of paper with a body diagram scrawled across it. "Her stomach contents were pretty much empty. She probably vomited prior to death. But her blood smelled of alcohol. Nothing really unusual at all. So, at the moment, I'm a bit stymied."

"Understood," she said. "So, what can we do to help?"

Dr. Lipkovic reached under his desk and withdrew a brown paper bag sealed with red evidence tape and sat it on top of his files. "These are the medications crime scene collected at Ms. Alvarez's house. Unfortunately, I suspect they're not all here. There's nothing in here that would cause the phenomenon we're seeing in our victim."

"So, what does that mean?"

"If you could, I'd appreciate you returning to her house and doing a more thorough search. Maybe the CSU missed something. Maybe she had a stash somewhere the crime scene technicians didn't think to look. I just have a feeling that if you turn that place apart, you're going to find something that'll point us in the right direction on this case."

"Are you thinking this is some kind of poisoning?"

Lipkovic shook his head. "It's far too soon to speculate on that. Granted, we know someone stuck that knife in her back and dumped her body on the beach, but for all we know, this could have originally been a suicide. Loved ones of suicide victims have been known to tamper with a scene to avoid the stigma of a suicide. In their eyes, they might think it's better for her to be a murder victim than someone who takes their own life. There are religious implications to this as well. Catholics, for instance, see suicide as a mortal sin, so the pressure is on the family to do what they can to conceal the true nature of the death."

"A suicide?" Silas laughed. "You can't seriously believe this was a suicide."

"Mr. Mot, I'm a scientist, first and foremost. If you haven't noticed yet, I'm not prone to speculation. I go where the evidence takes me and keep an open mind to all the possibilities. I'm not saying this is a suicide. I'm not saying it's a homicide. I'm simply stating that right now, based on the information we have, it could pretty much be anything and we need to approach it as such," Lipkovic said. "That being said, I do believe her death is probably related to a drug of some kind. Somehow. But that's as far as I can go. That's why I need you to dig deeper into medications, illicit drugs, or any other items in her residence that might have been missed. Dig, Chief Cole. Dig deep. It's how we'll solve this case."

With that, Becca stood and shook the doctor's hand. "Thank you. We'll look into what she has in her house and get back to you."

# CHAPTER
# NINETEEN

TATE & NEELY ADVERTISING
THURSDAY, 9:20 AM

From the Medical Examiner's Office, Becca turned onto I-95 and drove north another twenty-five miles until she came to Jacksonville. She then navigated her cruiser through the city's grid-like roads until she found herself in the heart of downtown. Within minutes, she'd located the Jenkins Building, the business complex that housed Tate & Neely, the ad agency in which Andrea worked as a graphic artist.

"How long do you think we're going to be here?" Silas asked as she pulled into the parking garage adjacent to the building. "I have a rather important experiment going at my motel and I'd rather not leave it unattended for too long."

"An experiment?" Becca wasn't sure she liked the idea of that at all. "What kind of experiment?"

"Oh, nothing to worry yourself over. Just working on something to help me find the Hand of Cain. That's all." He coughed, clearing his throat. "Then, of course, we have the matter of searching Ms. Alvarez's house again for your medical examiner."

"Well, we're already in the city," she said, winding her way up the circular drive until she found an empty space on the third level. "I thought we might as well talk to Andrea's co-workers before returning to Summer Haven. It's the next logical step in the investigation." She pulled into the spot and put the car in park. "It shouldn't take very long."

"Detective work really is tedious, isn't it? Not at all like the movies. It's not about observation and deduction and brilliant minds connecting the dots. It's more about following standard operating procedure from point A to point B."

Becca nodded with a smile. "There's been some pretty brilliant minds before us who have turned investigations into an art form. While there is a lot of deduction involved, the best detectives follow the procedures. That way, they don't miss any key pieces of information. Then, after all the data's been collected...that's when we put two and two together in a logical, deductive process."

"Seems rather dull."

The two of them slipped out of the patrol car and started making their way toward the third-floor entrance to the building.

"It can be," she said, opening the door and holding it for Silas until he walked through. Then, she followed him. "It's the payoff at the end that's the real thrill. The hard work, culminating in finding justice for the victim."

"The victim's dead. What does she care about justice?"

Becca shrugged. "It's also for the family. And if there is no family, I guess it's about justice for society, as well."

They walked up to a placard on the wall detailing the different businesses housed in the building and on what floor each could be located. Tate & Neely was on the eighth floor. Suite 815.

"So, no thrill of the puzzle itself?" Silas asked after they stepped onto the elevator and pressed the button for the eighth floor. "Seems to me, if I were mortal, it would be about the game itself. Cat and mouse. The twists and turns. The Rubik's Cube of Murder."

She laughed. "Have you been watching television?"

"A little. Once I checked into my motel. Watched a few episodes of Barnaby Jones before heading to the bar last night."

"And the Rubik's Cube?"

"I suppose some kid who had stayed there left it in one of the drawers and forgot about it. It really is a rather remarkable puzzle game. Managed to get three sides of matching color, but so far that's all."

The elevator dinged and the door spread open. "Well, keep at it. It takes practice. Me? I used to just peel the stickers off and re-apply them."

"That's cheating!"

She grinned. "Yeah, I know."

They found Suite 815 and entered to be greeted by a pleasant-looking young woman with long blonde hair and a figure you typically only see in magazines. "Welcome to Tate & Neely," she said. "How can we help you today?"

"I'm Chief Rebecca Cole with the Summer Haven Police Department."

The woman at the front desk looked at her with a dazed expression. "You're who now?"

Becca figured her blue uniform and gold badge should be enough to identify her to most people, but some people just weren't that bright.

"I'm with the Summer Haven Police Department. I'm here

to speak with someone about an employee of yours. Andrea Alvarez."

The receptionist's eyes lit up with understanding. "It's so horrible what happened to poor Andrea. I still can't believe it. Yes, of course. Let me get you Mr. Neely." She picked up her phone, dialed an extension, then proceeded to tell whoever answered that the police would like to speak to them. There was a pause and the receptionist nodded as she hung up the phone. "Mr. Neely will be right with you." She gestured toward the comfortable looking waiting room chairs. "Please, have a seat."

They took their seats. Silas picked up a two-month-old Cosmopolitan magazine and riffled through its pages while Becca looked around. The office in which they found themselves was posh, with thick white carpeting, white walls, and white pedestals with an assortment of statuary displayed along the walls. Several framed images—display advertisements presumably developed by the company from the looks of them—hung in alcoves up near the ceiling, drawing the eye of anyone sitting in the waiting room.

From the looks of things, there was quite a bit of money in the advertising business and Tate & Neely had no problem flaunting it. She was just about to mention that very thing to Silas when her phone pinged with a text message. She took a look at her phone to see that Jeremy Tanner had sent the artist composite drawing of the woman who'd hired Jacinto Garcia to place the death curse on Andrea. The Babalowa had kept his word and had reported to the station earlier that morning. A few hours later, the sketch was completed.

The woman in the drawing was attractive. Probably in her early forties with light colored hair. The hair itself was long and straight, pulled back in a ponytail. She was heavier set, with the slightest hint of jowls—but not enough to undermine her natural beauty. She looked like a typical housewife, really, if Becca wanted to stereotype her.

Satisfied with the drawing, she texted Jeremy back and instructed him to head to the college to show the picture around campus. Hopefully, someone in administration or one of the teachers would recognize her and they'd have a name.

"I'm sorry to keep you waiting," a man said from the corner of her periphery. Becca glanced away from her phone to see a handsome man, dressed in business casual attire, walking over to greet her. The man was roughly six something in height with a lean, athletic build. He had a Romanesque nose and a broad, prominent chin. The only flaw that Becca could see in him was that he showed signs of male pattern baldness that had caused him to simply shave his head entirely. Still, bald was a good look on him. "I'm Terrance Neely, one of the partners of this firm."

Becca and Silas stood, each shaking the man's hand.

"I'm Chief Cole. This is Silas Mot," Becca said. "I'm sorry to bother you, but we have a few questions about an employee of yours...Andrea Alvarez."

"Oh, it was such horrible news," he said, sounding astoundingly similar to the receptionist's own declaration of dismay. Becca wondered if they'd all been instructed by some P.R. guru on how to express grief over a colleague. Before she could ponder the question further, Neely beckoned them to follow him to his office. Once inside, they each took a seat and Neely continued. "We're all quite devastated to hear about her death. But I'd like to get something straight up front, if that's okay."

"Sure."

"Ms. Alvarez was no longer employed with Tate & Neely. We let her go a week or so before her death."

*This is new. Not a single person we've talked to has even mentioned this.*

"May I ask why she was fired?"

"Well, legally, we're supposed to keep the specifics of the termination of our employees private, but since she's deceased, our legal department says I can share whatever you need to know for your investigation." He swiveled in his chair, opened up a cabinet drawer behind him, and pulled out a file. He handed it over to Becca and proceeded to explain. "That's her employment record. As you'll see, she'd worked for us for about three years. An exceptional employee for most of her time here. As a matter of fact, we'd just promoted her to the head of the art department last month."

Becca thumbed through the file, following the paper trail corroborating Neely's account.

"Andrea was going places," he continued. "Her talent and imagination were only matched by her drive for success. Even as young as she was, there was no one better in our firm to run her department. John Tate, my partner, and I had no qualms about offering her the position when the time came."

"So, what happened?" Silas asked. "If she was such an up-and-comer, why fire her?"

Neely shrugged. "We had no choice. Her behavior had become so...so disturbing in the last few weeks. Her quality of work diminished. She flaked out on meetings and would leave for lunch and not come back until the next day. The worst of it was her anger. She'd fly into fits of rage without the slightest provocation. She had simply become too much of a liability. We had to let her go."

Becca shifted in her seat and placed the file folder back on Neely's desk. "Were you aware of the personal issue she'd been going through for the last month?"

"The curse?" He laughed. "Everyone in the office knew

about it. She wouldn't stop talking about it. Don't get me wrong. I'm horribly distraught over the news of her death, but the very notion of a death curse was just too much. It was probably the biggest factor in our decision to fire her actually. After all, such talk didn't do a lot to evoke the kind of confidence in our business we want our clients to have in us."

Terrance Neely was rapidly becoming less and less attractive to her the more he spoke.

"Oh, and of course, I can't forget about the hallucinations."

"Hallucinations?"

"Oh, yes. In the last few weeks, she'd report seeing the most ridiculous things in the office. Monsters. Ghouls. A few times, she even screamed out that the Grim Reaper was trying to kill her."

Becca looked over at Silas, who rolled his eyes at the unspoken jab.

"Mr. Neely, was there anyone here in the office that was close to her?" Becca asked. "Someone she might have confided in? Someone she could have told about any enemies she had?"

"Well, she burned a lot of bridges around here. I can tell you that. But if she was close to anyone, I'd say it was Elaine Shepherd over in the art department. Those two had been thick as thieves together for the three years Andrea worked here." He pressed his intercom button and the pretty receptionist from the lobby answered. "Ms. Simmons, do you know if Elaine Shepherd has come back to work today?" He paused and looked over at Becca. "News of Andrea's death hit her pretty hard. She's taken a couple of days off to grieve."

"She's still requested another couple of days off, Mr. Neely," the receptionist answered. "But she just came into the office a few minutes ago to gather some things from her desk. She said she wants to do some work at home."

"Excellent. Thank you." Neely rose from his chair and

motioned toward the door. "Come with me and I'll take you to see Mrs. Shepherd."

Neely led them through the office, which seemed to be designed with one large square hallway with the various rooms sprouting off to the left and right. When they'd reached the southeast quadrant of the office, the bald man stopped, and gestured toward the door marked 'ART'. The door was currently closed.

"We have a staff of six graphic designers," he said, as if it was important for them to know. "Right now, they're busy working on a project for a car dealership out of Daytona."

He opened the door and they stepped into a large office space filled with six cubicles. Four of them were occupied with designers staring at computer screens and drawing with electronic pens on tablets. A fifth artist was to their left at the copy machine.

Neely ignored everyone and began moving toward the other side of the cubicles where a second closed door was located. When they came to it, she noticed a placard that read 'ART DIRECTOR'.

"Wait," Becca said. "Is this Andrea's office?"

Neely shook his head. "Not anymore. Elaine got the job after she was terminated." He knocked on the door. "Elaine, are you in there?"

There was no response. Another knock.

"Elaine?"

A second later, the door opened and a middle-aged woman with blonde hair appeared from the other side. She was wearing a tee shirt, fashionably ripped jeans, and sneakers.

Becca gasped when she saw her. She was the spitting image of the composite sketch of the woman that hired Jacinto Garcia to perform the death curse.

# CHAPTER
# TWENTY

"I'm sorry, detectives," Elaine Shepherd said, as they stepped into her office. "I'm technically off today. I'm pretty shaken up over Andrea's death and needed some time off. I don't want to be here any longer than I need to be."

"That's okay," Becca said. "This shouldn't take very long. I just have a couple of questions for you."

Elaine sat down at her desk. Silas followed suit, taking a seat across the desk from her. But Becca remained standing at the door, her hands on her hips, close to her sidearm.

"Sure. Andrea and I were pretty close. I'll help however I can."

Becca's mind raced, searching for the best way to proceed. In the end, she opted for the direct approach.

"So, the two of you were close?"

"Oh yes. We were like sisters." She pulled a tissue from a box on her desk and dabbed her eyes.

"Sisters?"

"Oh heavens, yes. Everyone here said so."

"Any sibling rivalry between the two of you?"

Elaine shifted in her seat, pulling her chair closer to the desk, then pushing it back as if she was unable to get comfortable.

"I'm sorry?"

"I'm just trying to think of motive. If you two were like siblings, it's more than likely sibling rivalry that made you kill her."

"What?" Silas asked, standing to his feet.

"What?" Elaine echoed Silas. "I, uh, don't know what you're talking about."

"There's no use lying about it, Mrs. Shepherd." She pulled out her cell phone and opened up the text message with Garcia's sketch. "Jacinto couldn't tell us your name, of course, but he certainly had an eye for detail. This is the person he says tried to hire him to perform the death curse on her."

The woman's eyes widened.

"How much you want to bet that when we ask the college, they tell us you're a student there? Or maybe a professor in their art department?"

"I...uh..."

"I'm willing to bet it all had something to do with this job. She made art director here before you. Maybe you thought you deserved it more. With her out of the way, the job would be yours."

"But I didn't need to kill her!" Elaine was shouting now. "Her getting fired took care of that for me. As a matter of fact, I was promoted Thursday. The day before they officially terminated Andrea."

"And six days before she died," Silas said to no one in particular.

"But you did try to hire Jacinto—Omo Sango—to perform the death ritual?" Becca asked, ignoring his comment.

"Yes! I'll admit it. I did try to get him to do the curse." She looked from Becca to Silas. "You can't arrest me for trying to have a curse placed on someone, can you?"

The question wasn't sarcastic. She really had no idea. The answer, of course, was no. Wishing someone to death wouldn't exactly hold up in court. At least, not without any physical evidence to support she'd taken the curse one step farther. Of course, there could be a precedent for conspiracy to commit murder if Becca wanted to push it.

"Okay, so where were you Tuesday night through early Wednesday morning?"

Elaine closed her eyes, as if scanning her memory for the dates. "Well, I would have been home. It's a school night. I think I fixed tacos that night—Taco Tuesdays, you know? Put the kids to bed around nine and my husband and I watched movies until bed."

"What time was that?"

"Around eleven-thirty."

"And your husband will verify this?"

She nodded, then winced. "Does he really have to find out about..."

"About?"

"He's a corporate lawyer. Very straight-laced. He wouldn't approve of me associating with that drug dealer."

"Of you associating with a drug dealer or asking a Babalowa to place a curse on a co-worker?" Silas asked.

Elaine shrugged. "Either one."

"If your alibi checks out, I don't see any reason for him to find out anything more," Becca said. "But if you didn't kill her, we still need to find out who did."

"Of course. I was serious when I said I'd help however I could. I didn't really want her to die. I just wanted her..."

"Out of the way?" asked Silas.

133

She nodded but refused to look them in the eyes.

"If you were as close as you say, did she tell you of any problems she was having with anyone in her life?" Becca asked.

Still averting her eyes from them, she thought about it for a moment. "Mmmm, I can't think of anyone. Most people really liked her and...oh."

"What? Did you think of someone?"

She nodded. "Yeah. But..."

"Mrs. Shepherd, if you know someone, now's the time to share."

"Well, it's odd. For the most part, she gets along with him. Considering they haven't been together in five years, they had a pretty great friendship. Ya know...for exes."

"Are you talking about the father of her child?"

She nodded. "Yes."

"What was their relationship like?"

"Well, he has full custody of little Jamie. She only had supervised visitation rights. And it had to be at the ex's place, never at hers. But they made it work. They were closer than most people would be in their situation."

"But Andrea started having problems with him recently?"

She shrugged. "Not so much with him. Like I said, they got along great. But his girlfriend? Now that's another story."

"What do you mean?"

"Well, this girl—I think she was Jamie's nanny or nurse or something—Andrea used to joke that she was just a glorified cook for the kid—she just kind of swooped in and snatched James up right after Andrea and James split." Elaine sighed. "It was pretty sad. Almost ended their friendship."

"But it didn't?"

"Not so much. Andrea decided she wouldn't let the girl ruin a good thing with James. They still remained friends, for little Jamie's sake, more than anything else. But Andrea always felt a little betrayed about how James had let that woman drive a wedge between them like that. Especially so soon after the breakup. She always wondered if they weren't already seeing each other before, ya know?"

"You said Andrea joked about this woman being a glorified cook. But she's a nurse? What do you mean by that?" Silas asked.

Elaine shrugged. "Oh, she's a nurse and a nanny, I suppose. Certified and everything. But I think she spent most of her time just cooking for little Jamie. She's apparently crazy about cooking for him. Won't let anyone else do it."

Silas scratched his head. "Huh? Why's that?"

"Well, the kid's got autism. Really bad from what I hear and he has a lot of emotional issues—Andrea always blamed herself for that, I think. Anyway, only certain medications seemed to do any good with his mood swings, but from what Andrea said, they're pretty serious meds. He has to be very careful what he eats. Poor thing can't eat chocolate. Can you imagine? Or anything fermented like cheese slices or yogurt. Things kids love. I think this nurse spent more of her time planning Jamie's daily meals than actually taking care of the kid, if you could believe Andrea's stories."

"Do you know this woman's name?" Becca asked.

"She never told me. Just always called her *las puta*...the whore," Elaine responded.

"And the ex?"

"James Andrews. A decent guy, really, though he's had a pretty rough life. In and out of prison for most of his youth."

"And the courts gave *him* custody of their son?" Silas asked.

"Well, he'd really turned his life around. Started a used car business down in Daytona and is doing pretty well."

"That wouldn't happen to be the same car dealership your art department is doing a project for is it?" Silas asked.

"Actually, it is. Andrea's the one who convinced him to use us actually." Elaine wiped her nose with a tissue. "She was so proud of the man James had become. So proud of his business and the success he had with it. That's why she volunteered to give him Jamie. She said her son deserved a better life than she could provide, so she let James keep the boy."

"But she had to be doing pretty well here, right?" Silas continued with his questioning. "I mean, this place...looks like you all are doing well."

"We are. Very well. But I don't think it was about the money with Andrea." She leaned forward, conspiratorially. "I think it had to do with her issues."

"Issues?"

"Oh, I hate to speak ill of her...especially now that she's gone."

"Just tell us what you know, Mrs. Shepherd. You tried to have her cursed to death. Now isn't the time for mock sympathy." Silas was losing his patience with the woman.

The art director gasped at his outburst but managed to compose herself enough to answer. "It was a matter of some embarrassment for her." She was now looking directly at Becca, as if Silas no longer existed in her world. "She had...um, mental issues."

"We're aware of her mental illness." Becca thought it was time to take back the interview before Silas' temper ruined it. "But for the record, just so we cover all the bases, could you highlight them for us?"

"Sure." She nodded. "Extreme anxiety, for starters. She'd had it ever since she was a kid. On top of that, she suffered from bipolar disorder, depression, and a very mild form of schizophrenia."

*Pretty much lines up with what Ceci told us*, Becca thought.

"Tell me something," she said. "Andrea recently started a new kind of therapy a few months back for her mental illness that seemed to be working well for her for a while. Did you know about that?"

Elaine nodded her head. "Yes. She was so excited about it actually."

"So, before she started on this program, did Andrea ever have any hallucinations associated with her schizophrenia?"

"Not to my knowledge. Like I said, it was a mild case. Maybe sporadic auditory hallucinations from time to time, but nothing like what she'd been experiencing lately."

"Anything introduced in her life that might have triggered them so suddenly?"

"Besides curses of death, she means," Silas added. He really didn't like this woman.

"Look, Mr. Mot, you don't really believe a curse can kill someone, do you?"

"Not at all," he replied. "But you obviously did. Or else you wouldn't have paid to have a working done on her."

"Of course, I didn't believe it." Her face was reddening. They were losing their witness. "But I knew Andrea did. I just figured having her Babalowa curse her would get in her head. I was just hoping it would affect her work a little. That's all."

"Exactly. She believed in it. And it might have driven her mad with fear."

"Look," Elaine said, her face growing from red to purple. "I already told you. I never actually got that Babalowa to perform the curse. I don't know where the rumor even got started that a curse was placed on her, but I had nothing to do with it!"

"Enough!" Becca shouted. "Both of you." But she was glaring at Silas. "Let's get back to the real investigation here."

She turned to face Elaine. "Back to this James Andrews...any idea where he lives?"

Elaine's face returned to her normal color and she started pilfering through the top desk drawer. "Andrea had it on a Rolodex card she kept in here. In case of emergencies. Just a second." It took a little longer than a second. The drawer was nearly overflowing with candy wrappers, rubber bands, and Post-It notes. It was a wonder the woman could find anything at all in there. "Ah! Here it is."

She pulled out a bent Rolodex card and handed it to Becca. The writing on it was in pencil and faded, but she could just make out the address.

"You said he had a car dealership in Daytona, but this says he lives in Hammock Dunes. How up to date is this?"

"As far as I know, he hasn't moved. Andrea said he just commutes. It's only about thirty minutes north of Daytona, after all."

Becca stuffed the card into her notepad. "Thank you, Mrs. Shepherd. We'll look into your alibi and if it checks out, you won't hear from us again." She paused. "Unless, of course, we have any more questions about Andrea."

The graphic artist smiled, then glared at Silas. "You won't bring him with you next time, will you?"

Becca laughed. "That's becoming a standard request, I'm afraid. But you have my word. If we need to talk again, I'll make him sit in the car."

With that, they left Tate & Neely and headed back to Summer Haven.

# CHAPTER
# TWENTY-ONE

SAND DOLLAR MOTEL
THURSDAY, 12:34 PM

"What are we doing here, Mot?" Becca asked as she pulled into the closest space near Silas' motel room. "We don't have time for this."

He slipped from the car and leaned in through the passenger window before holding up a finger. "This will only take a minute or two. Just wait here and I'll be back in a flash. Promise."

He trotted up the sidewalk to his door, glanced over his shoulder to ensure the police chief wasn't following him, then removed the DO NOT DISTURB sign from the handle and let himself into his room.

The body of Elliot Newman still lay on the bed in which he'd left him, now clothed in a gaudy red and yellow Hawaiian shirt and a pair of cargo shorts he'd picked up from the local Goodwill store.

"How are we doing this morning?" Silas asked, moving up to the side of the bed and lifting the man's arm to take his pulse. It was faint, but present—which was infinitely better than what could have been said for him before his visit to the funeral home last night.

Elliot's eyes shifted, moving unfocused in Silas' direction. He tried to open his mouth to speak, but soon gave up.

"Easy. Easy," Silas said, patting the man's hand before laying it back on the bed. "Don't try to recover too soon. Your body is still breaking down the embalming fluid flowing through your veins. Your muscles and skin are still far too rigid for much movement, but you're getting there. Slowly, but surely."

Elliot let out a pitiful groan.

"Oh, I know. It's frustrating. I know. But you're not in any pain, are you?"

The man's head moved slightly to the left.

"I'll take that as a 'no'."

Silas laughed. Not at the sad condition the previously dead man was currently in, but in the brilliance of his plan to begin with. He wished he'd thought of it sooner. There was no doubt that a man with Elliot Newman's knowledge would help lead him to the Hand of Cain far faster than he ever could on his own. He was now going to be approaching this problem from two fronts—first, the investigation into whatever strange deaths happened upon the citizens of Summer Haven, and second, from an archaeological angle. Whoever has the Hand of Cain would have had to use some tangible method for recovering it and Elliot was the perfect person to track that method down.

"All right, my friend. I need to leave you again. But only for a little while." He reached for the TV remote and turned the flatscreen on, which happened to be tuned into the Cartoon

Network. "I'll just leave this on for you so you won't become unbearably bored." Silas glanced at the screen to see an Animaniacs marathon showing on the network. "Oh, one of my favorites! I believe you'll find this to your liking. Who doesn't get tickled by the Warner Brothers' antics?"

Elliot's eyes moved from the television to Silas without any visible reaction.

"Ah! A man of excellent taste, I think. Good."

Silas patted the man on the shoulder, then walked out of his room, placed the DO NOT DISTURB sign back on the knob, and returned to Becca's waiting car.

# CHAPTER
# TWENTY-TWO

ANDREWS DREAM CAR AUTOMOTIVE
DAYTONA BEACH, FLORIDA
THURSDAY, 1:27 PM

T he drive down I-95 was surprisingly fast. Traffic, once they left the St. Johns County line, was light and flowed easily enough for Becca to pull off onto International Speedway Boulevard in record time. As an added bonus, Silas had been uncharacteristically silent during the drive and had opted, instead, to watch the cars drive by with childlike wonder.

A rustling of plastic in the passenger seat jarred her from her thoughts.

*Okay. So, I spoke too soon*, she thought, turning her head to see Silas ripping open a brand-new bag of Twizzlers.

"What are you doing?"

"Snack time." He pulled a strip from the block of red licorice, bit down on one end of it, and ripped a piece from the stick.

"Where did you get that?"

"In the Circle K. When you were getting gas." He held up a plastic bag filled with an assortment of candies, gum, and other treats of the confectionary variety.

"You know, you're going to need to start looking out for cavities if you keep going this way."

"Have no fear, Chief. These teeth are spectacular." He grinned at her and her heart thumped against her chest at the sight.

*You can say that again.* "You also need to be concerned with diabetes."

He shrugged, offering her the bag. "Want one?"

"No, thank you." She finally decided to ask the question that had been on her mind since leaving the Sand Dollar Motel. "So, what's this 'experiment' you're working on, anyway?"

Silas bit off both ends of the Twizzler and chewed for a moment. "That'd ruin the surprise if I told you."

"I'm a cop. I don't really care for surprises."

He waved her off. "Don't worry. I'll be happy to show you when it's all ready. As a matter of fact, I'm looking forward to it. For now, I just ask that you trust me."

She cringed. That was a request that was far easier said than done when it came to Silas Mot, but for the moment, she figured she had very little choice in the matter. Short of forcing her way into his motel room, she knew she could do nothing but wait on him for when the time was right. For now, all she could do was concentrate on the drive to James Andrews' car dealership and hope for the best.

"So, how do we know Mr. Andrews is at work right now?" Silas asked, pulling another piece of licorice off with his teeth.

"We don't. But at this time of day, I don't think he'll be home. Not if he's the savvy businessman Elaine made him out to be. And I didn't want to call ahead to check either. It'd put him on the alert to our visit. Give him too much time to either come up with pat answers to our questions or just make a run for it if he's our killer."

She made a right on South Palmetto Avenue, drove another three blocks, and pulled up to the curb in front of the dealership.

"And you think he's a good possibility? Shepherd seemed to think they had a decent relationship."

Becca put the car in park and turned off the ignition. "Everyone's a good possibility in this case. I know you like Spenser Blakely for it, but the truth is, I haven't ruled out a single suspect yet." She got out of the car. Silas did the same and they began making their way toward the dealership's big white office and showroom. "And statistically, husbands, boyfriends, and exes are usually the culprit, so yeah. He's a good possibility."

They stepped into the cool air-conditioned showroom and looked around for someone to help them find Andrews. Probably half-dozen customers milled around, kicking tires and checking out the price stickers in the window. Despite the crowd, they didn't have to wait long. Three seconds after entering the building, they were approached by a smiling man with a thick head of golden hair and a pastel green Polo shirt with the name 'Stu' stitched on the left chest. Above it was a stylized logo of a car with the words 'Andrews Dream Car Automotive'.

"Welcome, welcome!" the man, presumably named Stu, said, taking Becca by the hand and giving it a good shake. "Welcome to Andrews Dream Cars, where we're always excited to put you in the car of your dreams. My name is Stu, and you can just think of me as your very own Dream Counselor." He chuckled at his own goofy sales pitch, then looked Becca up and down. "We do offer fantastic discounts for our protectors in blue, I might add."

"Thank you, Stu." Becca had to practically pry her hand away from his. "But we're not here to buy today."

For a moment, his face looked crestfallen, then he took a breath and smiled. "Nonsense. We have the best selection of pre-owned cars on the First Coast. You might not think you're ready to purchase the car of your dreams, but she's out there somewhere." He waved his hand toward the lot outside. "Just waiting for you to find her. Give me just a few minutes of your time to introduce you to her. You won't be sorry."

"Trust me, Stu," Silas said with the only grin in the world larger than Stu's. "The only dream she has at the moment is the one where she catches a ruthless killer."

"Huh?" Stu's mouth went slack. "What?"

"I'm here to speak with James Andrews," she said. "Can you point us in his direction?"

Stu glanced around the showroom. "Oh, well, let's see..." He stood up on his tiptoes, making a show of searching for his boss. "I don't actually...um...nope, I don't see him." He looked back at Becca. "I don't think he's here at the moment."

"Oh, Stu," Silas said, clapping him on the back with a laugh. "You really are a delight. Come, Becca. Stu showed us exactly where his boss is."

"Wait. I did?"

But the two were already walking away toward the back of the room.

"He did?" Becca whispered the question. "How?"

He chuckled and pointed to an office in the back with one-way mirrored glass. "It was the one spot in which Stu didn't look. Obviously, it's where his employer—the person who signs his paychecks, mind you—is."

She rolled her eyes at this. "Yeah, right. Or you're going to be so embarrassed when you find out it's the facility's bathroom."

She knew, of course, that it wasn't. The glass should have been a dead giveaway.

They strode up to the door and knocked.

"Just a second," came a voice from inside.

"James Andrews? This is Chief Becca Cole from the Summer Haven Police Department. We're here to ask you a few questions about Andrea Alvarez."

The door swung open almost immediately. "I'm so sorry," the man behind the door said, chewing on something. "I had no idea it was you. I was just eating my lunch." He wiped his hand on the back of his trousers and held it out to her to shake. "I'm James Andrews. Come in, please."

Silas cast Becca a look that seemed to say, "This is a surprise. Our suspect seems like a nice, open guy."

Remembering her manners, Becca shook his hand and walked into his office. Silas followed after and Andrews shut the door behind them. He gestured to some chairs before walking to the other side of a small desk and sitting down himself.

The office itself was sparse, containing a small metal desk, complete with computer monitor, keyboard, and mouse, and a handful of photos hanging on the walls of the man's son, Jamie. Two more framed pictures sat on the desk beside his monitor, and a mess of papers and invoices sat neatly stacked to his right. There was no window and, for a moment, Becca got the claustrophobic feeling of incarceration. If not for the one-way glass, she was sure Andrews would have certainly gone mad if he was forced to stay in here for any length of time.

Becca took a moment to get a good look at the used car salesman and father of Andrea's son. He was slightly over-weight, with the build of a former football player. Probably a lineman of some kind or a fullback. He had close-cropped brown hair with a receding hairline and a neatly trimmed mustache and goatee. Like Stu, he wore khaki pants and a Polo shirt—though James' was blue—with his name and business logo stitched above its pocket.

"Thank you for taking the time to talk with us, Mr. Andrews," she said, taking the seat he gestured toward. "It looks pretty busy out there, so I'll try not to keep you too long."

Andrews waved the comment away. There was a half-eaten bacon, lettuce, and tomato sandwich and some chips laying on a paper plate in front of him, but he pushed them aside and gave her his undivided attention. "No, no. I'd like to help however I can. I've been so heartbroken since hearing about Andrea's death." He paused. "Anything you can tell me on how the investigation is going?"

"It might have gone smoother if you'd let someone know you even existed," Silas said, his eyes narrowing at the car salesman. "It's been over twenty-four hours since your son's mother was found dead of suspicious circumstances. You'd think someone who genuinely cared would have reached out to us by now."

"Silas!" Becca snapped. She was going to have to have a talk with him about his abrasive manner with their suspects. Good cop, bad cop might work in the movies, but it was poor policing in the real world. She looked over at Andrews. "I'm sorry for my partner. He's a little on edge."

"Oh, no apology necessary. He's right. I should have come forward from the start." He absently stroked at the goatee covering his chin. "But I know spouses and exes are always the first on the police's suspect list. Given my criminal history... well, I'll just say it, I was afraid you guys would take my son away from me."

"Okay," Becca said. "I can understand why you might be

afraid we'd finger you for a prime suspect, but why would you think we'd go after your son? I mean, right away. That's something that takes time. Hearings. Judges' rulings. And that wouldn't happen unless you actually *did* kill Andrea Alverez."

"Or if it was believed you were an unfit parent," Silas chimed in. His eyes suddenly lit up. "Hold on. Was Andrea trying to get back custody of your son?"

James' shoulders sagged. "We'd been good for so long. Best friends. Even after we broke up, we'd always been tight. She had no problem with me having full custody of Jamie since our separation." He straightened up a handful of pens on his desk as he spoke. "Until a couple of months ago anyway."

"What happened a couple of months ago?" Becca asked.

"You have to understand, Andrea had given Jamie up voluntarily. She was concerned about her mental illness. She didn't want the boy growing up around someone who could have a mood swing at the drop of a hat. Didn't want him to see her if she had some type of schizophrenic hallucination."

"So, she offered him over to you with the promise of supervised visitation."

James nodded. "She'd been seeing this doctor. Dr. Emil Fruehan."

"Yeah, we're aware of that. He had her on some sort of special treatment or something."

"Exactly. He'd been treating her for her disorders for a few years now. Working closely with her. During his treatment, he worked at perfecting a medication regimen. It really seemed to be doing the trick. She was getting better. Her mood swings had dwindled down to nothing. She'd stopped having auditory or visual hallucinations. She felt as though, as long as she kept taking the medicine, she would be fine to share Jamie."

"But you didn't?"

"Dr. Fruehan didn't. I went to talk with him after she came

to me about her desire for joint custody." He threw up his hands. "Look, I had no problem with sharing Jamie with her. She was a good mom. She loved Jamie dearly. But I wanted to see what her doctor thought."

"And?"

"He told me that it was too soon to tell if it was working," Andrews said. "He said, like a lot of medicine, that Andrea could develop a tolerance for the treatment. The effects could wear off over time. He wasn't convinced her condition would improve over the long term."

"What did you do after he told you that?"

"I had no choice. I had to refuse her request," he said. "It broke my heart to do it. It really did. It broke hers, too." He gave a little shudder as if remembering something unpleasant. "You should have seen the look on her face when I told her. I'd crushed her, which crushed me. I'm telling you, I loved that woman. Not in a romantic way, mind you. But we'd been together for a long time. We shared a child together. The last thing I ever wanted was to see that look on her face."

Silas held up a finger to interrupt them. "Mr. Andrews, I'm curious. Where is the photograph that is missing from your desk?"

The man's eyes widened. "Huh?"

Silas pointed to the two frames beside his monitor. "Well, it's just odd to me," he said, looking at Becca first, then back to Andrews. "You're kind of a neat freak. Maybe a little OCD. I mean look at those pens you just corralled. Look how neatly aligned they are." He motioned to the papers on the left side of the desk. "And those. Not a page out of place. You've even folded your bag of potato chips up and sealed them with a clip. You can't stand anything out of place, I believe."

"Well...yeah." James Andrews shrugged. "Lots of people are. I don't understand."

Silas directed their attention back to the framed pictures on his desk. "Well, they're improperly aligned. If there had only been two photos there, you'd have them closer together. Perhaps angled differently. The gap between them gives the impression that there was another photo sitting there. Maybe one you didn't want us to see when you saw us coming from that one-way glass behind me?" He thumbed back to the mirror.

Becca looked from the photos to Andrews.

"Is he right?"

The car salesman's face turned several shades of red. "It's not what you think."

"I'm getting kind of tired of people telling me that," Becca said. "So, what am I thinking?"

With a sigh, Andrews reached into a desk drawer and pulled out an 8x10 picture frame and held it up for both of them to see. It depicted a professionally photographed image of Andrea Alvarez, standing on the beach in a flowing white dress. Wind whipped at her hair as she appeared to stand on one foot in a ballerina's pirouette.

"I don't understand," Becca said. "Why hide this from us?"

He shook his head. "I wasn't. At least, I wasn't hiding it from you." He carefully returned it to the top drawer of his desk. "I've had it out since I heard about her death. Honestly, I can't stop thinking about her now that she's gone, wondering if we made a horrible mistake by breaking up."

"Ah," Silas said. "I see. You weren't hiding it from us. You were hiding it from your girlfriend."

James Andrews nodded. "I really didn't see you guys from the window when you approached. When you knocked, I was afraid it was my girlfriend." He gave a sad smile. "I love her, but I know she wouldn't understand."

Becca cleared her throat. "I understand," Becca said. "I just have one more question for you. If you had to guess, who would be the most likely person who'd want to see Andrea dead?"

He leaned back and looked up at the ceiling for a moment, thinking. Then, with the most serious face Becca had probably ever seen, he said, "Spenser Blakely. No doubt in my mind."

# TWENTY-THREE

SAND CASTLE CONDOMINIUMS
THURSDAY, 3:40 PM

Becca pulled her cruiser into the parking lot of the Sand Castle Condominiums and parked it in the same spot she'd pulled into yesterday. Officer Sharron's car was once more parked a few spaces over, but no one was inside the vehicle.

"Strange," Becca said as they climbed out of the patrol unit. "Tim should be here."

"Unless he's making one of those random rounds he told you about yesterday."

"Good point."

"I hate to say I told you so," Silas said, as they started making their way for Andrea's front door.

"Then don't."

"Yeah, but James Andrews seems to agree with me that Blakely is our guy."

"True, but neither of you are cops, are you?" They turned

onto the sidewalk leading directly to Andrea's door. "There's a little thing we need called evidence before we can start accusing people of murder."

"Well, that's why we're here isn't it? To see if there's anything we missed that might tie Blakely to her death?"

She nodded. "Keep in mind though, until the medical examiner rules this a homicide, we're only conducting a death investigation. Nothing more. So, technically, we're here just to search for any medication, drugs, or poisons that CSU might have missed." She paused. "Of course, if we happen to see anything we might have missed the last time we were here, all the better."

"Personally, I'd like to take a closer look at those Santeria paraphernalia in Andrea's living room," Silas said. "I can't put my finger on it, but after seeing Blakely's collection, I know there was something off about her own."

They came to the door and Becca froze, pointing to the police tape attached to the frame—or rather, the tape that was supposed to be attached. Now, the yellow and black tape hung limply against the wood, flapping occasionally in the breeze.

"Curious," Silas said, but was cut off before he could say anything else by Becca placing a finger to her lips.

She withdrew her sidearm and flicked the safety off, then motioned for Silas to sneak around to the back of the property in case someone was still inside and decided to make a run for it out the sliding glass door. Afterwards, she pointed to herself, then held up a hand with all five fingers sticking out, closed the hand into a fist, and opened it again.

*Wait for my signal before entering*, she silently ordered him.

Nodding his understanding, he left her, disappearing around the corner of the building. Of course, she'd only done that to get him out of the way. Grim Reaper or not, she still wasn't convinced that he was immortal now that he was in human form. She wasn't sure how it all worked and wasn't willing to take any chances. To the public, he was a civilian and she was going to treat him that way. She couldn't have him traipsing into dangerous situations if she could help it. It was bad enough he'd been attacked by three thugs earlier that morning. Like it or not, he was her responsibility and she would do what she needed in order to keep him safe.

Once he was out of sight, Becca reached for the knob and turned it. Unsurprisingly, it was unlocked. Her eyes made a quick scan of the door jamb, but there were no marks of any kind. It hadn't been jimmied, so whoever had entered had done so using a key.

The landlord had been given explicit instructions not to enter the residence. She had no idea who had keys to Andrea's place other than him and Ceci. Then again, Andrea had been found nude on the beach. No personal effects were anywhere near her, so it's possible the killer had taken the keys after the murder.

*And where on earth is Officer Sharron?*

She didn't have time to worry about it right now. She had more pressing matters to deal with, like sweep the condo for any potential intruders still lingering around. And she had to do it quietly.

Knob still in hand, she eased the door open inch by inch, praying the hinges wouldn't squeak as she did so. Then, there was a crash from inside. The sound of glass shattering and an angry yell. Throwing caution to the wind, she burst into the house, gun ready, and ran toward the commotion. She came up short when she peeled into the living room to find Silas on the floor, holding his bleeding head, and the shattered remains of an Orisha statue crumpled on the floor around him. The sliding glass door was wide open and there was no sign of the intruder.

*Geez,* she thought as she looked down at Silas. *That's a lot of blood.*

She crouched down, placing a hand on Silas' shoulder. "Hey, are you okay?"

He groaned, still rubbing the back of his head, but managed to look up at her and nod. She stood, ran upstairs and grabbed a couple of towels from the linen closet before returning downstairs to tend to him. By the time she returned, he was seated on an ottoman in front of the reading chair and looking at the blood covering his hands.

"Here." She handed him a towel. "Hopefully that will stem the bleeding. But head wounds bleed more than anywhere else, so we might need to take you to the urgent care clinic for some stitches."

"Not to worry," he said, pressing the towel to the back of his head. "Looks far worse than it is. I can feel the ectoplasm already closing the wound as we speak."

"Forgive me if I don't take your word for it. Ectoplasm or not, that still looks an awful lot like blood. You're still going to get checked out." She looked around the room. Besides the broken idol and the open sliding glass door, it pretty much looked the same as it did yesterday when they were there. "So, what happened?"

"Came around back, like you asked." He winced as if he'd pressed down too hard on his injury. "I found Officer Sharron unconscious over on the side of the building." He stopped his story and held up a hand to wave the statement away. "Don't worry. He's okay. Just knocked out. Anyway, I came around to the back and found the door wide open, just like it is now."

"You came inside then? Before I gave the signal?"

"Signal? You didn't mention a signal."

"I most certainly did." She pantomimed the hand signals again.

155

He let out another groan. "I'm sorry," he said sarcastically. "I've never bothered to learn police sign language. My bad."

She gave him a playful scowl.

"Anyway, yes. I let myself in and just started to look around when someone came at me from behind and slammed poor *Eleggua* down over my head." He glanced around the apartment as well, though he looked dazed. Possibly had a concussion. "Next thing I know, you're standing over me with your gun out."

"I'll call for a rescue unit to come check you and Tim out," she said. "I'm assuming you didn't get a good look at whoever attacked you?"

He shook his head. "Sorry. My eyes were too busy rolling into the back of my head."

"Okay. Just sit tight for a second."

Becca walked out the back door and gave a cursory examination of her unconscious officer. She checked his pulse and respiration. Everything seemed within normal parameters. She then rolled him over onto his back to ensure he got enough oxygen. As she did so, she noticed the faint trace of solvent in the air. A familiar odor. She leaned closer toward Tim's face and the world around her began to spin. She backed off, inhaling a lungful of fresher air, and stood over the officer a minute to collect her thoughts.

"Chloroform." She pulled out her cell phone and dialed 911, providing the details to the operator and returning to Andrea's apartment. Silas was already up and searching the living room. "What are you doing?"

"Looking to see what our mystery visitor was up to." He was still holding the towel to the back of his head.

"You should be sitting down. Resting."

"I'm fine." He stood in front of the antique travel chest in the corner of the room, his fingers hovering over the lid as he prepared to open it. "But so far, I haven't found a single thing we missed yesterday, nor anything our intruder might have taken."

"EMTs are on their way," she told him. "I'll go upstairs and look around. You stay down here and keep an eye out for them. Show them where Officer Sharron is once they get here."

He nodded, swinging the chest's lid up.

"And don't bleed on any evidence," she joked, before taking the stairs to start her search in the master bedroom of the two-bedroom townhome. Very little had changed in the room since the last time she was there. The king-sized bed was still neatly made and devoid of any clutter or clothes Andrea might have tossed on it prior to her death. The vanity mirror in the corner still had the same creepy writing in blood scrawled across it, though now it was dry and chipping away from the glass. There was an overturned nightstand to the left of the bed.

She opened the drawer of the nightstand next to the bed and found the usual odds and ends. An adult toy, hair scrunchies, a couple of paperback romances, and a miniature version of one of the Orisha statues at the front door—she couldn't remember which one it was—the one with the cross-bow, she thought. In the center drawer, under a pile of socks, she found three pill bottles. Becca, of course, couldn't pronounce the name of any of the medications, but she'd seen enough of them in her time to know they were psych meds of some type. She set them aside to collect later and resumed her search.

From the nightstand, she moved into the adjacent bathroom, pulling open drawers and cabinets, but found nothing particularly interesting inside any of them. On a hunch, she moved over to the toilet and lifted the lid to the water tank. Often, drug users would place contraband inside Ziploc bags and hide them in toilets in case the police came knocking on their doors. However, this didn't seem to be the case in Andrea's home. All that was inside was water.

She moved back into Andrea's bedroom, stopped, and just took the whole place in. She searched with her eyes, hoping to see something that caught her attention. But unless she just wasn't seeing it, there were no signs of drugs, apart from the few bottles she'd found a minute ago. Nothing appeared missing or disturbed. No sign of what the intruder had been there for. She was just about to look through Andrea's dresser for the second time when Silas shouted from downstairs.

"Becca? EMTs are here," he said. "And I think I just figured out who our intruder was and what he was doing here."

# TWENTY-FOUR

By the time Becca came down the steps, one of the EMTs was already examining the back of Silas' head, while two others were rolling their stretcher through the sliding glass door to the backyard. Two of her officers were also now on scene, assisting the paramedics with their unconscious comrade.

There was a quick knock on the front door and Dr. Brad Harris, Becca's 'kind of' boyfriend, as she liked to think of him, appeared. He was dressed in his customary sky-blue scrubs and white lab coat that hugged his muscular frame in a way that always worked to dissolve her uncertain reservations about him. His blonde surfer hair and perpetual five-o'clock shadow covering his square jaw only helped to accentuate the bronze tan covering his well-sculpted face and arms.

Of course, despite his gorgeous looks, her office administrator, Linda, was right. Brad Harris was one of the most boring men on the planet. But he was dependable, practical, and kind to a fault.

"Brad?"

"Becca, are you okay?"

"Of course. I'm fine." She nodded toward Silas. "He's the one that got knocked silly."

"Serious," Silas said. "I got knocked serious." He looked the doctor up and down. "I was silly before. Now I'm seriously irritated."

She rolled her eyes. "His ego's hurt more than anything, I think."

Brad eyed the black-suited man being attended by the EMT. "Who's that?"

Becca shrugged. "He's a consultant, of sorts. He's helping me with this investigation."

"And you were attacked?"

"He was. The officer I had watching the place was knocked out with Chloroform." She smiled up at him. "I was still out front before I knew what was happening."

"Dang it, Becca, we've talked about this."

"Yes, we have. And as I've told you before...it's my job."

Brad walked over to Silas, politely nudged the EMT away, and began inspecting his head.

"Um, hi," Silas said, looking up at the newcomer. "Who are you again and why are you poking around my head like some lunatic phrenologist?"

Brad leaned back a bit and offered a polite wave. "Dr. Brad Harris," he said before resuming his examination of Silas' head. "Uh." The doctor paused, then leaned back with a puzzled expression on his face.

"What is it?" Becca asked.

He blinked, then bent forward for a closer look. "A second ago, this was a serious laceration. It was going to need stitches." He dabbed the spot on Silas' head with clean gauze. "Now, I can't find it. It's just gone."

"I tried to tell her I was a fast healer, Doc," Silas chuckled. "But she wouldn't believe me."

He wiped more blood away; his movements were almost frantic. "But, this isn't possible. No one heals that quickly." Brad looked over at Becca. "It literally closed in front of my eyes."

Becca glared at Silas, who only grinned back at her. He'd done that on purpose. He'd healed himself in front of Brad as a matter of mischief. *More showing off.*

"I'm sure it was a trick of the light," she said. "Probably wasn't as bad as you first thought. You cleaned the blood up more and voila."

Brad nodded. "Yeah, I guess." He looked down at the bloody gauze in his hand. "Though I can't figure out where all this came from if that was the case."

"Ah! The mysteries of the universe," Silas said. "Some things just aren't meant to be understood." He stood up and clapped the doctor on the shoulder. "Or maybe you really do have that special healer's touch."

Brad shivered while trying to pull himself together. "Well, truth is, we still need to take you back to the urgent care center," he said. "Doesn't look like you have a concussion, but a blow like that...I'd prefer to keep you under observation for a while, if I can."

Silas looked over at Becca. His brows furrowed. "Chief Cole?"

She struggled to contain the smile threatening to form across her face. Truth is, it would be the perfect opportunity to get rid of him. At least, for a few hours. She hadn't worked with a partner in almost a year. She'd grown accustomed to doing investigations alone. Add to that the fact that the sharp-dressed man was also Death Incarnate and the temptation doubled.

"Becca?" Silas asked again. His voice squeaked a little. He was getting nervous.

When it was all said and done, as wild as his presence was, she was growing to like having him around. He thought outside the box and didn't let politics or social graces interfere with getting to the truth. And his almost childlike wonder at the living world—its candies and yo-yos and the beauty of the ocean itself—was infectious.

"Brad, can you just let this one go?" she finally said. "As much as I hate to admit it, I do kind of need him. If he starts acting weird, I'll take him straight to see you. I promise."

The doctor shrugged. "I'm not sure. Like I said, he doesn't seem to have a concussion or anything, but I can't rule out a subdural hematoma without a CT scan. He might have some serious injuries internally." He looked at Silas. "You under-stand that, right?"

Silas smirked. "Sure thing, Doc. But I'll be all right." He swirled his index finger dramatically in the air. "I've got a good feeling about my chances."

Brad gawked at him, then glanced over at Becca as if to say, 'Is this guy for real?'

She grinned back with a nod.

"Okay, I think you're crazy for not getting checked out, but..."

"You're not the first to tell me that." Silas nodded toward Becca. "She thought I was crazy too, but I won her over."

Brad hesitated, giving her a look of concern. "What I was going to say is...I can't make you get checked out. But if you get dizzy or lightheaded, come see me as soon as possible."

Silas shot him a salute, but if Brad caught the sarcasm in it, he made no indication. Instead, he turned and walked over to Becca, and placed his hand on her shoulders. "You be care-ful," he said, leaning forward and planting a kiss on her forehead. "I can't imagine what I would do if anything happened to you."

Her stomach churned. She was such a horrible person. Brad cared so much for her, yet she could only see him as a temporary thing. More a way to pass the time than anything else. Yet one look in those gorgeous baby blue eyes of his and she could never find a way to tell him how she really felt. Instead, she just let him go on believing they had a future together, which was just about as evil as you could get, in her opinion.

"I'll watch my step," she said, giving him a light kiss on the lips. "Promise."

He smiled, then nodded at Silas, and walked out of the apartment with the EMT.

Silas sat in silence for several awkward moments. Becca stared unmoving at the front door. The clock above the television ticked in rhythm to her heartbeat.

"Wow," Silas finally said. "Just wow."

His voice interrupted her train of thought. She wheeled around and glared at him.

"What?"

"Oh, nothing."

"It's not nothing." She placed her hands on her hips and squared off in front of him. "Say what you've got to say."

He patted the back of his head gently, testing the spot where the injury had been. When he winced, she knew at least that it was still sore. "So where did you find Captain America?"

"Oh, there it is! The jokes. I had a feeling you'd have something to say about Brad once you met him." She laughed. "And how do you know about Captain America anyway."

"Kid left a few comic books in my motel room along with the Rubik's Cube. Read a couple of issues. A real goodie-two-shoes that Cap."

"Brad is a good guy. He's a lot of fun."

"Brad," he said, as if tasting the name on his tongue. "Brad. Of course, his name is Brad. He looks like a Brad actually. Bet he drove a Miata in high school and wore his Polo shirt collar turned up."

"How would you know? You never even went to school."

"Besides reading comics and watching Perry Mason reruns, I also managed to catch a few episodes of *Welcome Back, Kotter* and *Saved by the Bell* since I've been in town. I got the gist."

She shook her head but found herself smiling anyway.

"Brrraaaad," he said again. He smacked his lips after saying it. "Such a weird name, if you say it enough times."

"All right. Enough."

He laughed, but then his smile faded as he gently tapped at the goose egg on the back of his head.

"What? What's wrong?" she asked.

"Not sure," he said with a shrug. "But this?" He pointed at his head. "It shouldn't have happened."

"Oh, don't beat yourself up over it. We all get ambushed at some point in this business."

He shook his head. "No, that's not what I'm talking about. You don't understand. This..." He waved up and down at his body. "...this isn't a real body. There's no blood running through its veins. Actually, no veins for blood to run through. No organs. And no brain to get a concussion or a subdural hematoma." His eyes snapped up at her. "No jokes."

Becca chuckled.

"Point is, like I told you earlier today, it's a body I constructed myself to be visible to humans. An ectoplasmic shell made of ethereal matter. It's how I was able to slip through your handcuffs and walk out of the jail cell without being seen." He rubbed his head again. "It's how I disappeared when those thugs tried to shoot me. I just disposed of it, returned to my spirit form, and constructed a new one after. Because of that, this injury shouldn't have happened."

"So, what do you think it means?"

"Not sure, but it's concerning. I'm afraid that the longer the Hand of Cain stays in the hands of whoever has it, the less power I'll have. My throne is being usurped, Becca, and there are beings out there that would love nothing more than to see me gone. This injury is an indicator of my power. The more I lose, the more human I'll become."

She pondered that for a second, then nodded. "Well then, we'll just need to solve this mystery all the sooner, right?" She turned and scanned the living room again. "Before we were interrupted, you said you found something and that you thought you knew who our intruder was."

"Oh yes!" Silas exploded from the ottoman and instantly regretted it. His legs wobbled and he was forced to hold out both arms to balance himself. "Whoa."

Becca lunged forward, grabbing hold of his arm before he fell backwards.

"Thanks," he said. He took a series of concentrated breaths and steadied himself. "Okay. I'm fine now."

She let go and he eased himself over to the travel chest. "Take a look."

He pointed down at the collection inside. She walked over and crouched, searching through the contents. Besides an assortment of multi-colored candles, there were a couple of handmade dolls constructed of palm fronds and other vegetation wrapped together with twine to form a human figure. She saw a few more miniature Orisha idols, two ceremonial daggers, and an open notebook with hand-drawn symbols scrawled over the pages. That was it.

"What am I looking at?"

He pointed down again. "You don't see it?"

"What am I supposed to see?"

He crouched down beside her and pointed to the two daggers. One of them looked very familiar to her.

"That dagger." She pointed to the one on the left. "If I'm not mistaken, it's a match to the one found in Andrea's back."

"Well, of course it is," Silas said. "I noticed that yesterday. But that's not what I'm talking about."

"Wait. You noticed it yesterday and you didn't think to mention it to me?"

He cocked his head inquisitively. "Why would I? It was obvious. Plus, it's not like the knife killed her."

"It's still important for me to know."

"More important than the fact that the dagger on the right doesn't match the dagger on the left?"

Her nose twitched.

"Or that the right dagger wasn't here yesterday?"

She looked up at him, waiting for what she suspected was next.

"Or that the right dagger matches the set Spenser Blakely had in his display case at his office?"

And there it was. A connection they could use. She stood, made a phone call to the sheriff's office CSU team and waited for them to show up to collect the new evidence. She was going to stay and personally supervise the process until every vital clue was collected by the book.

While they waited, they continued to search the downstairs. A few minutes later, Silas called out from the kitchen.

"Becca? I think you should probably see this."

She placed the book she'd been looking at back on the bookshelf in the living room and went to see what he had found. When she stepped into the kitchen, she found Silas, holding an empty trash can, and standing over a pile of garbage he'd strewn all over the linoleum floor.

166

"What are you doing?" She noticed her voice sounded weary. "Besides making a mess of our crime scene?"

"Found..." He crouched down and sifted through the debris. "...something." A second later, he let out a joyful shout, stood, and turned to her with a closed fist. "I think this might be the clue Lipkovic was hoping for."

He opened his fist to reveal an entire handful of oblong white pills.

"What are they?" she asked.

"Have no idea. There's no bottle in the trash that I could see. But it looks like Andrea, or someone else, dumped almost an entire bottle out in there." He waited for Becca to open a small evidence bag and he tossed the pills inside. "Now that's something I find curious, don't you?"

She had to agree that she did and the two soon found themselves sitting in the living room discussing the implications of the pills while they waited for CSU to arrive.

# CHAPTER
# TWENTY-FIVE

SAND DOLLAR MOTEL
FRIDAY, 12:05 AM

S ilas leaned against the tower of pillows he'd placed against his bed's headboard, careful not to place too much pressure on the lump left over from his blow to the head. He grabbed a handful of buttery microwaved popcorn and tossed a few pieces in his mouth. He giggled at the television screen, which was playing *Big Trouble in Little China* at the moment while he kicked his shoes off his feet.

"Want some?" He held the bag out to the adjacent bed where Elliot now sat, propped up by his own pillows.

The archaeologist slowly moved his head back and forth but didn't answer verbally. Of course, Silas knew he couldn't. Not yet anyway. He had improved a lot since his earlier visit. All of Elliot's fractured bones were now healed. The Formalin permeating his muscle and other tissue was almost entirely purged. But his joints and ligaments were still pretty stiff with the stuff. In another day, he'd be as good as new, but for now, he was immobilized in his rented motel room bed.

"Your loss," Silas said, returning his attention to the movie just as the protagonist, Jack Burton, caught a knife being hurled at him from the gigantic Lo Pan.

He was trying hard to put the events of the day behind him. They had learned a great deal. Yet with every answer they discovered, two more questions popped up. He was certain Spenser Blakely was the one who'd attacked him in Andrea's house...certain he'd broken in to replace the dagger from her set. But did that mean he killed her? What was his motive? Seemed to Silas that the cursed woman was his ticket to better newspaper sales. Then again, if he knew the curse had been lifted, his gravy train was about to dry up.

*Gravy train?* He thought. *Geez, maybe I really am watching too much television.*

Granted, he was finding the distraction of the rectangular screen to be something of a miracle. A method of allowing the swirling chaos of his mind to ebb. To 'veg', as he'd heard it called on one show. A wondrous means of escape from the pressures of the real world. He could see why so many mortals turned it into the altar of their familial abode.

But it was becoming concerning. As his eyes stayed riveted on Jack Burton's antics, he found it harder to pull away. It was like he had no control anymore, and if there was one thing that defined the Grim Reaper, it was control. Discipline.

No. It seemed the longer he pretended to be a mortal, the more he found himself changing. The longer he pretended, the more mortal he was actually becoming. Part of him rather liked that notion. The other part of him—the one that took his responsibilities as Death with utmost respect—was mortified by the prospect. Where would the world be without his sacred station?

He sighed, turning his attention back to the adventures of the truck driver in a mystic-filled Chinatown and up to his neck in Chinese black magic. He laughed at a one-liner the oafish hero made to Lo Pan and nearly choked on a kernel of popcorn when his room's telephone began to ring.

He sat up instantly, moving the bag of popcorn aside and staring at the phone. Only Becca knew he was staying in this particular room at the motel. If his phone was ringing, it would have to be her. But if that was the case, why was every instinct in his gut screaming at him not to answer it.

*Come on, Ankou. It's probably Becca. She might have some new information about the case.*

His hand hovered over the receiver. Something in the back of his mind screamed at him not to pick it up. He looked over at Elliot, who was eyeing the ringing phone as well.

"Oh, stop looking at me like that," Silas said. "I'll answer it when I'm good and ready." He snatched the receiver from its cradle and brought it to his ear. "Silas Mot here."

There was a pause on the other end. Some static. A rustle of something rubbing against something. Then...

"Hola, mi esposa."

His gut twisted into knots at the sound of Esperanza's voice.

"Stop calling me that," he said, his tone flat and threatening. "What do you want?"

"To see you. To talk. Maybe some other things as well."

"I'll pass. Thank you."

"Ah, come on, *mi amor*. For old time's sake?"

"My recollection of our old times involved a lot of backstabbing and plots against me."

She giggled. "Oh, pish-posh. That was part of the fun of our love for each other, was it not?"

"What do you really want Esperanza? You're interrupting one of Kurt Russell's best movie roles."

He glanced over at Elliot. Whatever happened, he knew he'd have to keep Essie from finding out about the archaeologist. She couldn't know he'd revived him. At least, not until the little guy was back to his old self anyway.

"Meet me," she said. Her voice now sounded hushed, as if she was trying to avoid being heard by someone. "At the tiki bar across from your motel in ten minutes. I have information about the Hand you need to hear. I promise, it's not a trick."

He hesitated.

"You know who has it?"

"You'll have to come see me to find out."

"The last time I walked that beach at night, I was attacked and shot at by three goons." He cringed. He might have said too much. The only thing keeping Esperanza from going for an all-out takeover of his position was the fact that she had no idea just how weak he currently was at the moment. "Notice they weren't successful, mind you."

*Hopefully, that covered my mistake a little.*

"Well, I didn't send them. I swear."

He'd already guessed as much. The Celtic tattoos didn't seem appropriate for one of *Los Cuernos del Diablo*. It still didn't mean she was completely innocent of it either. There were other gangs out there that Santa Muerte could get her hooks into.

Silas sighed. "Fine," he said with a sigh. "I'll be there in five minutes. But this better not be a waste of my time."

"I swear. You won't be sorry."

He could have sworn she was nearly purring as she hung up.

"I already am." But the line had already gone dead as he balanced the receiver on his fingertips in thought.

A moment later, Silas cradled the phone back in its place. He then slid from the bed, put his shoes back on, and knotted his tie before slipping on his jacket. After glancing in the mirror to make sure the tie was straight, he turned back to Elliot.

"I'm going out for a while, my boy." He placed the remote on the bed next to him. "Feel free to watch all the TV you want. I'd tell you that you should get some rest, but you've pretty much been doing that for the past few days." He walked over to the door and started to open it. "And whatever you do, don't let anyone in until I get back."

He chuckled at this, knowing full well the man still could hardly move a muscle. Then, he was hit by a wave of remorse that twisted at his insides and weighed his shoulders down like a giant boulder had been placed on top of him. It was a sensation he'd never experienced before.

Silas had ripped Elliot Newman from his eternal slumber. He'd selfishly pulled his soul from his final reward—the ecstatic taste of bliss only death could bring—and plopped him headfirst back into the world of pain, suffering, and fear. Add to that the poor guy's immobility and inability to speak a word—yet—and Silas had essentially thrown him into the prison of his own body without explanation.

All because the man might have some insight into the whereabouts of the Hand of Cain.

Yes, he felt bad. A distinctly human trait he didn't particularly care for.

"You know what you need, Silas, old boy?" he asked as he strode casually over to the motel bar. "One of those delicious fruity drinks with the umbrella in it. That'll make you feel much better."

# TWENTY-SIX

SAND DOLLAR OASIS BAR
FRIDAY, 12:33 AM

T he beach was even less crowded tonight than it had been yesterday. Only two or three patrons were drinking away their blues at the Sand Dollar Oasis. Silas looked, but the pretty bartender he'd met didn't seem to be working. Instead, it was a young guy, barely in his twenties, serving the poor schlubs at the bar. Silas walked up to him and tried to order the same drink he'd had the night before but had never learned its name. He tried to describe it as best he could, but the bartender couldn't figure out what he was referring to.

"It's in a freaking tiki mug," Silas shouted. "It's fruity. It has an umbrella in it. And I'm pretty sure it's filled with a whole lot of vodka."

"I'm sorry, dude," the bartender said. His speech pattern had the typical surfer lilt he'd seen in a couple of movies he'd watched earlier that night. "This is a *tiki* bar. Lots of our drinks come in those mugs. I'm not sure what it is. But I can throw something together for ya if you want. Maybe a Mai Tai or something."

"A what?" He thought about it, then reached into his coat pocket and withdrew the sliver of paper the bartender from last night had given him. She'd left him her number. He could just give her a call and find out more about the drink.

Silas scanned the note and his throat tightened. There was no phone number. Only a hastily scrawled note that sent chills down his spine.

"You're in danger," the note read. "Meet me at your room as soon as I close up the bar. ~ Courtney."

Had she been trying to warn him about the three goons that had tried to kill him? Or was it something else? He hadn't returned to his room afterwards. Instead, he'd gone with Becca to continue their investigation. He hadn't seen the girl since she closed down the bar.

Silas leaned forward and glanced at the bartender's name tag. "Look, Sam. I was wondering...Have you seen the girl who worked here last night?" He looked at the note again. "Courtney was her name."

Sam shook his head. "It's weird too. She missed her shift. They had to call me in to cover." He wiped down the bar top with a wet cloth. "Guess she's fired now. A shame. That girl was hot."

Silas' heart raced. "Do you know where she lives?"

The bartender shook his head. "Even if I did, I wouldn't tell you."

"Blast," Silas said, wheeling around and nearly bumping into Esperanza in the process.

She leapt back just in time and giggled. "Whoa, *mi amor*. I know you're frustrated with me, but you don't have to hit me."

He waved her comment away. "Do you have a car?"

"Si, but..."

He grabbed her wrist and started for the parking lot. "Good. You're driving."

"But Ankou..."

"We'll talk in the car," he said, then skidded to halt and scanned the lot. "Um, which car is yours?"

She nodded over to a shiny red convertible Mercedes and he proceeded to pull her toward it until they came to the driver's side door.

"Where are we going?" she asked.

He had no idea. All he knew was that he had to find Courtney. He hoped he wasn't too late. "Do you happen to know Courtney?" he asked.

"Courtney who?"

He was beginning to realize just how much he didn't know about this world he'd entered. Mortals don't all know each other. He was embarrassed he'd even asked it.

"Ankou, what's going on?"

"A bartender I met last night," he said. "I thought she was flirting with me. Said she was giving me her number, only I just looked at it."

He handed Esperanza the note. "So?"

He blinked. "So? What do you mean 'so'?"

"*So*, she might or might not have known something. She might have been aware of those hooligans that came after you last night. *So*, what?" Her face twisted into a mask of indifference. "She's probably dead now, anyway."

"Exactly! But if there's a chance she's not, I've got to find her. Protect her if possible."

Esperanza laughed. "Save her? You're Death, *mi esposa*! You do not save. You take. You harvest. What are these mortals to the likes of us?"

"Says the megalomaniac that fawns over any humans that

bow down to her." He pointed to the driver's side door. "Now get in."

"And do what? Drive around Summer Haven in hopes we bump into her?"

"Preferably, we don't bump into her with your car." He narrowed his eyes at her in warning. "And I have an idea. I need a diviner."

She hesitated for a moment, then shook her head. "I don't think Omo Sango wants to see you again anytime soon. Especially after you humiliated him the way you did yesterday."

"I don't have a choice. I need to find Courtney. He's a Babalowa. Divination is part of his schtick. He has to help me."

Esperanza shrugged. "Only if the Orisha, Sango, tells him he should." She leaned in close to him, running her fingers through his hair. "And you and he don't exactly see eye to eye."

"Well, right now, he's my only option, so please. Take me to him."

With a smile, she leaned in and kissed him on the lips. "Your funeral." She chuckled as she said this and got into her car. Silas climbed into the passenger seat and soon, they were off, speeding toward the seedy district of Gruenwald Commons.

# CHAPTER
# TWENTY-SEVEN

THE PIER
GRUENWALD COMMONS
FRIDAY, 1:57 AM

They talked as Esperanza drove toward Gruenwald Commons. They had a lot to catch up on, and Silas had to admit, much of it wasn't bad. Like him, she wasn't evil per se. Amoral would be a more appropriate term. But she had always been ambitious. Self-centered. Her Purpose had never been enough. She always wanted more. And like her namesake of legend, Lilith, she was hungry for it, ready to devour anything that got in her way.

Still, through the millennia, the two of them had had good times.

"By the way, we never got around to it at the bar," Silas said. "What did you have to tell me earlier?"

"Tell you?"

"You wanted to meet me. Said you had some information you wanted to share."

"Did I?"

He rolled his eyes. They'd had some good times, sure enough...but that didn't mean he could believe a word that came out of her mouth.

"So, it was just a ruse to see me?"

She laughed. "Ruse? Who uses 'ruse' anymore?" She turned on the blinker and turned right, in the direction of the harbor. "What if I was just wanting to see you again, *mi amor*? Is it so wrong for a wife to miss her husband?"

"You know we're horrible together."

"I thought we were wonderful." She almost squealed with sensual pleasure as she spoke the word 'wonderful'.

"I'm sure the victims of the Bubonic Plague didn't think so. We got a little carried away."

"We were merely distracted by our love for each other. Nothing more romantic than only having eyes for one's mate."

Silas pinched the bridge of his nose, shaking his head.

"You always did invest too much in these humans, you know," she continued. "None of us ever understood it. You actually pitied them."

He didn't say anything for a few moments, reflecting on the centuries. "It wasn't pity," he finally said. "In fact, I think it's more like envy. Many of those we've taken departed for their Reward—something we'll never experience. Others, sure. Some were downright pitiful. But in the end, the only thing I've ever done is follow my Purpose. Nothing more. Nothing less."

"Purpose." She scoffed at the word. "That's all you ever used to talk about. You never looked toward the horizon. Never saw the bigger picture."

She pulled the car up to a long metal warehouse and put it in park. Silas could hear water lapping up against wooden pylons on the other side of the building. The gentle creaking of the pier swaying under the harbor's current.

"Omo Sango? He's not at the storage facility?" Silas asked, intentionally changing the subject. Last thing he needed was for them to get into a full-blown argument in Narco gang territory.

"He doesn't spend all his time there," she said. "He does run a business, you know."

She opened the door to get out, but Silas grabbed her arm like a striking viper. "Wait."

Esperanza looked at him in surprise.

"Before we go see him, tell me what you wanted to tell me."

She eyed him up and down, as if contemplating her options.

"I know you didn't just want to see me for old time's sake, Essie. There was a purpose to reaching out to me. What was it?"

She hesitated a moment. "I wanted to warn you."

"About?"

She brushed a stray hair from her eyes but wouldn't look at him directly. "They're gathering, Ankou."

There was no need for her to elaborate on who 'they' were. Silas had been expecting this.

"No big surprise. You're in town, too."

"Water is wet."

"And I assume *they'll* be calling for an enclave soon?"

She nodded. "They're all drawn to the Hand. Just as you were. It calls to them. Soon, there will be a gathering of our kind. A motion for a vote of no confidence has already been issued."

"By who?"

"I don't know. They won't discuss it until the time of the meeting."

Silas figured as much. An enclave was the next logical step to the dilemma. His rule and ability to deal with the mortal in possession of the Hand of Cain would be called into question. He'd be forced to defend his position...and someone—one of their own kind—obviously had their sights set on his throne.

"And you swear this isn't your doing?" he asked her. "You're not the one to make the motion?"

She shook her head. "Never. You know I'd never stab you in the back like that. When I take you down, you'll see me coming all the way."

She smiled mischievously at him and he could do nothing but grin back. She was right. Essie was all about open attack. She wasn't averse to using subterfuge from time to time, but a play at the throne...she would want it to be a fair fight.

He let go of her arm and they got out of the car. Esperanza led him around the other side of the building to a chain-linked fence topped with razor wire. A gate stood just a few feet away with two gangster thugs standing guard. Automatic weapons rested snugly in the crooks of their arms.

She strode up to the gate and said something in Spanish to them. They opened the gate with bowed heads and let the two of them pass without a word.

Once past the guards, they strode casually down the pier toward a large yacht moored to the dock. Workers busied themselves removing crates from the craft and loading them into a waiting Mercedes Sprinter. A few of the workers tensed when they noticed their approach, then resumed their activity once they saw Esperanza.

Silas watched, scanning each person carefully as they walked. None of them appeared to have the same tattoos he'd seen his attackers wearing the night before. It didn't mean they weren't part of the crew, but he didn't think so.

Without talking to any of the workers, Esperanza stalked up the gangplank to the top deck of the yacht and Silas followed without concern. As far as he knew, he was still under his bride's protection and had no need to fear any of them. Besides that, he'd managed to put the fear of God into their leader, Omo Sango, yesterday and he doubted the big man would test fate by trying to kill his fabricated body during their meeting now.

As he stepped on deck, he had no trouble picking the Babalowa out from the rest of the crowd. With the man's sheer enormity, he stood out from the crowd like a beach ball amid a set of children's building blocks.

"Omo Sango," he said, walking up to the leader of *Los Cuernos del Diablo* and extending his hand.

The big man accepted the offered hand and they shook in greeting.

"What can I do for you tonight, Senior Muerte?" Omo Sango said. He looked curiously down at Silas as he spoke. "You name it and it's yours."

"I have a favor to ask you."

"He's hoping you will perform the *Diloggon* for him," Esperanza interrupted. She was getting impatient. "He is missing a human and needs you to divine her whereabouts."

"She's a bartender." Silas handed the Babalowa the note he'd been given. "Her name is Courtney, not 'human'. And I think she's in danger."

Omo Sango looked at the note, then back at Silas. "Sure. I will see what the Orisha tells me about her, but nothing more."

"I understand."

Omo Sango instructed everyone onboard to form a circle around him and he sat down on deck, crossing his legs. Then, he reached into a pouch attached to his belt, withdrew sixteen cowry shells, and tossed them on the ground in front of him. The big man began chanting under his breath, eyeing the patterns the shells made. He scooped them up in his meaty paw, gave them another shake, and cast the shells again.

Silas watched, taking in everything. His muscles tensed. It was a long shot this would work. He knew from personal experience that the Orishas were fickle spirits. And a few of them were no friends of his. He held his breath, waiting for the Babalowa to speak.

"This is ridiculous," Esperanza whispered in his ear. "The girl is mostly likely long dead. You're wasting our time."

He gave her a sideways glance and growled. "Quiet. Let the man work."

Omo Sango tossed the shells a third time, then let out a deep breath. "I see something." He looked up at Silas, then at Esperanza. There was a pause, then she nodded her assent. "The girl you seek is alive, but in danger. On the run even now. Hiding. Hurt."

"Where? Where is she?"

The big man looked down at the shells and squinted. "At the beach. Near the place where you first met her. She thinks it's safe there. There's a hiding spot she's using among the dunes. But she's about to be found."

"Thank you," Silas said, grabbing Esperanza's wrist and dragging her off the boat. "Come on!" They ran down the pier, around the warehouse, and leapt into her car. Esperanza, irritated with his desperation, started the car and began to drive back to Summer Haven. "Do you have a mobile?"

"A phone," she said. "They just call it a phone here." With one hand on the wheel, she reached into her purse, pulled out a cell phone, and handed it to him.

Unsure how to operate the device, he held the device out from his face, turning it over and over in his hand. "I, uh..."

"Oh, for goodness sake," Esperanza said, snatching it from his hand and punching at the screen. She handed the phone back to him and he put it to his ear.

"911," a voice on the other end said. "What is your emergency?"

# CHAPTER
# TWENTY-EIGHT

SUMMER HAVEN BEACH
FRIDAY, 2:40 AM

S ilas flew out of the car the moment Esperanza came to a stop and ran as fast he could past the now-closed tiki bar and onto the beach. He looked right and left, searching for the slightest trace of the bartender or anyone who might be in pursuit of her. Fortunately, he had exceptional night vision and within minutes, he caught a glimpse of upturned sand a few yards to his left.

Foot prints. From the looks of them, there were several. The sand had been churned in a way that could only be from someone running, stopping, then running again.

"Ankou, wait!" Esperanza shouted from the wooden stairs leading down to the beach, but he ignored her.

He bolted in the direction the footsteps led. North, toward the less populated region of the ocean front. There weren't as many houses or businesses this way, which would have made it a good place for someone to hide. At the same time, it was also a good place to murder someone if necessary. There'd be fewer chances of witnesses.

He ran at full speed for nearly five minutes until the footprints disappeared in the rising tide. He stopped, trying to catch his breath. He turned, glancing around for anything that might put him back on Courtney's track again.

Silas wasn't sure why he was so desperate to find the woman. His rational mind argued it was purely pragmatic. It was because she knew something about his attackers from last night and, by association, something about the person who had possession of the Hand of Cain. But as his heart pounded against his ectoplasmic ribcage, he knew that reason was a lie.

She was a mortal in danger. There was nothing more to it than that.

For millennia, he had taken countless lives in the name of his sacred commission. He'd never once pondered the emotional turmoil he caused on a daily basis for these fragile humans. These beings that were little more than spoiled celestial infants in the grand cosmos. He had taken them. He had sent them to their reward—good or bad. And he'd never once concerned himself with what it all meant.

Until now. Until he'd spent a few days as one of them. Until he'd experienced the pain of getting hit in the head with a statue. Until he felt the raw surge of fear coursing through his veins when being shot at by criminals. Until he had tasted candy for the very first time or had enjoyed the simplistic wonder of physics in the form of a child's yo-yo. He had a much better appreciation for these mortals now. For Life as they knew it.

Plus, Courtney had tried to help him when he hadn't even known he needed help. That said a lot about the woman's character. She deserved to be saved if he was able, no matter what she did or didn't know.

His eyes darted toward the distance, but even with his uncanny sight, it was far too dark to see for any real distance. There was no sign that anyone had turned back, so he had to assume they had continued northward.

Silas took a deep breath.

Of course, there was one thing he could do, but he was loath to try it. The moment he left his fabricated body, it would dissolve in a whiff of smoke and ectoplasm. He could make a new one soon enough, but it wouldn't be the same—just as the one he currently wore wasn't the same as the one he'd used the night before to escape the gun-wielding goons. His memory was near-perfect, but not flawless. He simply couldn't remember all the minute details enough to precisely replicate Silas Mot exactly.

But, he also knew there really was no other choice.

He moved away from the shoreline, stalking over to the dunes covered in cattails, sawgrass, and other vegetation, and found a secluded spot. He'd been foolish last night. He should have never tried this stunt in front of witnesses. Now, he wanted to ensure no one would see what he was about to do.

He lay down in his spot, taking a few more, deep breaths and he was released from the material form he had worked so hard to construct.

Back to his immortal spirit form, he looked down at his body. A single crab, disturbed by the sudden nocturnal intruder in its domain, scurried up from the sand and onto his jacket sleeve.

"Shoo, you vile invertebrate!" he shouted at the animal, knowing full well it couldn't hear him.

Silas hovered there a moment longer, lingering over his body, and watched as it began to melt—suit and all—into a pinkish-brown smoke that evaporated into the air.

If his spirit form had a mouth, he would have sighed at the

sight. A perfectly good body...wasted. But there was no time to mourn its loss. He had to find Courtney. With that in mind, he rose higher into the air and continued his search for the woman.

THE MOMENT he was far enough away from the mortal realm, his 'knowledge' returned and he knew without a doubt that Courtney the bartender was doomed. It was, he instinctively recalled, her Time. As a matter of fact, she was dying even as he hovered miles above the earth.

And he also knew precisely where she was.

With a small effort of will, he found himself hovering over her bleeding body on the beach. She was only about a hundred or so yards from where Silas had hidden his own body away. The water rolled up to her legs, soaking her shorts and tank top as it crawled up the sand underneath her. A large red stain soaked through her top, just below her left breast. A ring of black powder could be seen within the blood. A gunshot wound.

Courtney sucked in a labored breath. Her eyes roved into the night sky until they settled on him. There was no fear in them. Only acceptance.

"I...I know you. Don't I?" she asked. Her voice was little more than a rasping whisper.

He wasn't sure how she would. In his Grim Reaper spirit state, he no longer looked like Silas Mot. In truth, he didn't look like much of anything. He was formless. Invisible to all but the dying. He wore no robes and carried no scythe, despite the artistic masterpieces of old.

"Yes, child," he said. He had no lips or mouth to speak, but he knew his words were as clear as if he did. "Yes, you know me. Everyone eventually does."

She gasped. A trickle of blood leaked from her mouth. Slowly, she shook her head. "No. At work." She coughed. "Last night." She reached out a hand toward him, but he backed away. He wasn't ready to take her. It didn't seem right. "Mr. Mot, right?"

If he had eyes, they would have widened at her inquiry. There should be no reason for her to recognize him in this state. No way for her to associate him with the fabricated body he used as a vehicle to move among the mortals.

"Tell me, child," he said, knowing she was running out of time. "Who did this to you? Help me avenge your death."

Seventy-two hours earlier, the concept of avenging anyone's death would have seemed preposterous to him. Death was a natural order of life. It was part of the Creator's plan. Part of the nature of the universe—cursed though it may be—and not something to be shunned or reviled. Then, the Hand of Cain was rediscovered and lives began to be taken far too soon. But Courtney's life was being taken according to her own Time. This was not an unnatural occurrence, despite the manner in which she was killed. His former self would have scoffed at the very notion, but it was obvious he was an altogether different being today than just a few days earlier.

Courtney shook her head, coughing uncontrollably as she did. "Be careful," she whispered. "They know..." Her words faded. Her lips moved, but no sound would come. Then, her eyes, still staring up into the stars, dimmed. One final breath was expelled and she was gone.

The Reaper glanced over a few feet to his right. One of his nameless minions hovered there, unspeaking. A brilliant orb of spectral light, known throughout the universe as the Shakina Glory, materialized from within the spirit being—the 'light at the end of the tunnel', as humans called it—and, beckoned for her to come. A moment later, Courtney's spirit entered the light, ready to be escorted to her reward, whatever it may be.

He nodded at the minion, who returned the greeting, and watched as it, and the light, faded from sight.

The bartender was dead. And Silas' gut twisted inside him over her loss—which was strange, given that in this form, there was no gut to twist. But the woman hadn't deserved this fate. She—who had no way of knowing his true nature—had merely tried to warn him of the danger he was in and she had paid for it with her life.

He gave her body another glance. Mentally tipped his hat to her and disappeared.

# CHAPTER
# TWENTY-NINE

SAND DOLLAR OASIS
FRIDAY, 3:25 AM

Becca Cole cursed as she got out of her patrol car and headed toward the group of uniformed officers gathered around the thatched tiki bar of the Sand Dollar Oasis. Third night in a row she'd been interrupted in the dead of night. Third night in a row of very little sleep. It was wearing her down.

"What have we got?" she asked as she approached Sergeant Tanner. Of course, she realized, her most stalwart officer wasn't getting any more sleep than she was.

The older officer turned when he heard her approach. His face looked grim. "We have another one," he said, glancing down at his notepad. "Your new pal Death called it in." He nodded in the direction of the beach. Portable high-powered lights, running on generators, had been set up a few hundred yards south of the bar. Something lay flat in the sand, covered by a sheet. Yellow crime scene tape flapped in the

190

ocean breeze around the body. Two uniformed officers guarded the tape. Silas Mot and—*Is that Esperanza? What is she doing here? With him?*—stood solemnly outside the perimeter.

"What happened?" she asked Tanner.

"Still piecing it together. Got a 911 call from Dead Boy over there. Said he suspected the girl was in trouble and that we needed to send someone to the bar ASAP. By the time we got here, he and that woman were already down there standing over the body."

"Who is she?"

"The hot brunette he's standing with?"

"No. Our victim."

"Name's Courtney Abeling, twenty-two years old. Works here nights and weekends while going to college in the city."

Becca nodded, patted Jeremy on the shoulder as a thank you, then began making her way toward Silas. He looked different somehow. She tilted her head, looking him up and down as she approached the police tape. Then she saw it.

"Is that a goatee?" she asked. It was indeed a goatee, neatly groomed, and attached to a Clark Gable-like mustache just under his nose. "How the heck did you grow a goatee in just a few hours?"

He reached up and felt his face. His eyes widened as if he had no idea it was even there.

"Blast!" he said. "I knew that was going to happen."

Becca decided to let the comment go and her attention turned to the dark-skinned Latina by his side. He noticed her gaze and offered a sheepish smile in an attempt, no doubt, to distract her from the woman's presence. Esperanza offered nothing more than a scowl.

"And another thing...are you ever going to let me get a full night's sleep?" she asked.

"Sorry. I was hoping to get to her before...well, this." He motioned to the sheet covering the body.

"Want to tell me about it?" It wasn't a request, but from his expression, she knew she needed to at least try a little diplomacy.

"Met her the night I was attacked," he said, holding out a strip of paper. "She gave me this while I was enjoying one of those delicious drinks she made for me. I thought she was flirting with me, but apparently, there was more to it than that."

Becca read the note. It was a little vague.

"Any idea what she wanted to talk to you about at your motel room?"

He shook his head. "I assume it has to do with the Hand."

Esperanza's head whipped toward him. "You told her?"

"I enlisted her assistance to help me find it," he said. Becca had never seen him so serious. Maybe even remorseful. "She couldn't very well help me without knowing what it was I was looking for."

"Which begs the question," Becca said. "What is *she* doing here? She's a known associate of one of our suspects, for crying out loud."

"We both know that Omo Sango didn't do it. And she was helping me track the bartender down. That's why she's here."

"And now that I've done that, I'll be taking my leave," Esperanza said, before turning to walk away.

"Hold it right there," Becca said. "You still need to give a statement."

The Hispanic beauty sneered. "I'm leaving. That's my statement." Her brow furrowed. "Just try to stop me."

Becca readied herself to do just that but was stopped by Silas' strong hand on her shoulder. "Let her go. It's not worth the hassle." He looked over at his ex. "Besides, anything she tells you would be a lie. Just out of spite."

Esperanza giggled at this, then sauntered toward the parking lot where her Mercedes still waited for her.

"Here's what happened. We learned that Courtney was hiding somewhere near the bar, so we came straight here. I called the police, hoping they'd get here before we did. But that didn't happen. We started searching and a few minutes later, we found her here." He looked down at the sheet. "No sign of whoever did this. Besides a ton of indistinguishable footprints in the sand, there was nothing to point to the killer."

Becca ducked under the tape and pulled the sheet away. The bartender, who was lying face up in the sand, was dressed in a tank top and shorts. No shoes or flip-flops, but that was to be expected if she was running from someone on the beach. She had been pretty. Young. Petite, though obviously had work done on her breasts. Regular beach-goer type. The girl was probably one of those who almost lived there, if Becca had to guess.

Unfortunately, her beach-going days were over. The small round hole in her chest took care of that.

Becca looked at her officers. "Any signs of shell casings?"

They shook their head.

"So, either the killer picked them up or used a revolver," she said. "I don't see an exit, so the bullet's probably still there." She pressed the radio transmitter clipped to her lapel. "Dispatch, this is Unit 101. Contact the M.E. and the sheriff's office CSU and have them en route as soon as possible. Then see if the S.O.'s major crimes division can work this one. I've already got my hands full with Alvarez's death." She waved Sergeant Tanner over. When he walked up, she pointed to the body. "Wait for crime scene and the M.E. Mr. Mot and I have to go take care of some business."

"We do?"

She ignored the question and waited for Tanner to respond. The moment he agreed, she waved for Silas to follow her and they left the beach, making a beeline for her car.

"Mind telling me where we're going?" he asked.

She held up her keychain fob and unlocked her car doors remotely. "Get in and shut up."

She was being a little harder on him than perhaps she would like, but she was annoyed. Her homicide rate had doubled in a matter of days since his arrival in her town and she didn't like it. Once again, probably not his fault. But then again, how did she really know that? Assuming everything he'd told her was true. Assuming he really was the Grim Reaper, Lord of All Things Death...then wasn't it his responsibility to keep a crazy artifact like something called the Hand of Cain out of the paws of psychotic humans? Was he that inept?

They slipped into her car and she pulled out of the parking lot, her tires burning rubber in a shrill screech.

"You're angry."

"You bet your creepy hoodie, I'm angry," Becca growled. "You've turned my town into a regular shooting gallery and I don't know how to fix it."

"I had nothing to do with any of this! This is on a mortal. A human. The whole lot of you are depraved. Greedy. Nuts." He threw his hands up in the air. "I came here...wearing this ridiculous human body like the world's least comfortable suit... to try to save you from yourselves."

She pressed down on the accelerator, speeding down A1A like a bat out of hell. This time of night, the roads were generally clear and she needed to clear her head. Speed always helped do that for her.

"And for your information, I feel horrible about the bartender," Silas continued. "She had been nice to me."

"You mean 'flirted' with you, don't you?"

Why did that bother her so much?

"She had been *nice* to me. She obviously was warning me. Obviously was trying to protect me from someone and ended up dying for her troubles. That's not a thing I take lightly. If I die, I can come back...eventually. It might take some time, but I can return to continue my work. She, on the other hand, can't. It's not fair and I am angry about it. The rub of it is, I've been in this body for so long, I'm beginning to empathize with the lot of you. And trust me...that doesn't make my job any easier."

She listened to his tirade and eased up on the gas. Her knuckles were white against the steering wheel, so she loosened her grip as well. She hadn't even considered how this all might affect Silas. He was Death, after all. She never imagined a Grim Reaper with emotions before. At least, not very real, very human ones.

"I'm sorry," she finally said. "I hadn't thought about how this whole thing might make you feel. Still, now we have two dead women. The question is whether they are related."

"Possible, but somehow I doubt it," he said, looking out the passenger window at the night enshrouded trees as they zoomed past. "Andrea Alvarez, I still believe, was a random casualty of the Hand of Cain. Courtney Abeling, on the other hand, was a deliberate assassination. Probably because she knew the person in possession of it."

"Swell. So, we have two killers to hunt down now. It would have been nice if the person who killed Andrea was the same as the one who killed Courtney."

"The M.O. isn't even close. Whoever killed Andrea was going for the sensational. Nude on the beach with a knife sticking out of her back that didn't kill her. This new murder was the spitting image of efficiency. There was no showmanship to it at all. Two murders by two very different hands."

She had to admit, his logic was sound.

"Okay. Are you sure you can't just divine up answers to this stuff with your magic Death powers?"

He offered a sad laugh. "If I could do that, there would have been no need to enter your world and solve these murders. I could have used my 'magic', as you call it, and simply removed the one who possesses the Hand. Even in the spirit realm, my knowledge is limited. Here, in this form, I'm mostly just like you. Only difference is I have knowledge of the spiritual world and its inner-workings that you don't."

"So that's a no."

He smiled. She really did like that smile. It was a good smile, even when it was sad.

She glanced at the clock on her dashboard. Almost five in the morning. Spencer Blakely would be at the newspaper by now preparing for deliveries of the morning edition. She slowed to a near stop in the road and made a careful U-turn to head back to town. Time to make Mr. Death a happy camper and go talk to their number one suspect in the Andrea Alvarez murder.

# CHAPTER
# THIRTY

THE SUMMER HAVEN CHRONICLER
FRIDAY, 5:33 AM

"Are you saying we can arrest him, even though we still don't know exactly how Andrea was killed?" Silas asked as she pulled into the parking lot of the newspaper.

The building glowed from the inside; its glaring fluorescent lighting shined through the large pane windows like a lantern in a pitch-black cavern. A swarm of moths and mosquitoes hovered in thick clouds near the entrance.

"We can't charge him yet. I have to wait for the state attorney to give me authorization for that." She smiled and hoped it looked devious. "But that doesn't mean we can't take him down to the station for a few hours to sweat him out while we search his office and residence for evidence."

"You think we have enough for warrants?"

They got out of the car and started making their way to the front entrance.

"I was thinking about this last night before bed. You and I both know what we'll find when we take a look in that display case in his office. I think that'll be enough to convince a judge."

His perpetual grin widened. "So, you do like him for the murder?"

"He's the one who makes the most sense." She took hold of the front door and pulled, but it wouldn't budge. "Crap. Locked."

She placed her hands against the glass and peered inside. No one, not even the spritely elderly receptionist was within view.

"Chances are they're in the back at the loading bay," she said, walking toward the corner of the building. "Delivery drivers and such would be back there for their morning paper run. I'm betting that's where we'll find Blakely."

The two crept toward the back of the building. When they'd been inside the newspaper two days earlier, Becca had noticed security monitors in his office, watching the exterior of the building with electronic eyes. If the journalist had been anywhere near the monitors when she and Silas pulled into the parking lot, there was no doubt in her mind he'd know why they were there.

Becca kept her hand near the holster of her weapon, just in case the journalist decided to surprise them. As they approached the rear of the building, something dashed out from the corner of her eye. Instinctively, she drew her gun, but it was unnecessary. A shadowy figure bolted away from the loading bay, running toward a privacy fence on the far end of the property. Becca took off after him, running at full speed.

"Becca, wait!" She heard Silas calling after her but was too focused to process the words and continued her pursuit.

It was too dark to get a good look at whoever was fleeing from her, but she guessed it was Blakely. He came up to the fence and went into a running slide, feet first, and scrambled under a gap between the fencing and the ground. It was a move she would have never imagined an overweight middle-aged man like Blakely capable of making.

"Crap, crap, crap!" She hated runners. She ruined more uniforms because of them.

She followed the figure under the fence, came to her feet, and looked around to see a cozy little residential neighborhood nestled behind the newspaper's office. She recognized it.

*Clairmont Heights.*

But knowing where she was offered no benefit to her. The runner was nowhere to be seen.

Becca had patrolled the little subdivision a few times. She knew the roads, but not well enough to be aware of all the potential hiding spots an absconder might use to elude the police.

"Dispatch, this is Unit 101." She breathed heavily into the radio mic fastened to her collar. She'd let herself get out of shape since taking over the chief's position. It was something she'd need to rectify. "I need two units to respond to Clairmont Heights." She looked around for street signs, then added. "Have them meet me at the corner of Lexington and Hamilton."

"10-4," replied the dispatcher. "Units are 10-50x to you now."

Units were en route with emergency lights running for a faster response time. Good.

She tried catching her breath as she searched the sleeping neighborhood. A dog barked somewhere to the south. Motor vehicle traffic rumbled from the Interstate a few miles to the west.

She turned in place, searching for any sign of the runner, but he was nowhere in sight. Neither, for that matter, was

Silas. She looked back at the fence from which she'd crawled, but he wasn't there.

*Great. Way to have my back, partner.*

Keeping her gun at the ready, she paced the length of Lexington Street, peering into every deep shadow she could find. Moments later, the area was lit up by a swath of brilliant red and blue lights and two patrol cars—one of hers and one from the sheriff's office—pulled up beside her.

"Drive around," she told them. "Look for anyone out and about. We're looking for Spencer Blakely, the owner of *The Chronicler*." The two patrolmen took off in opposite directions, shining their spotlights into yards as they passed. They, along with Becca who was still on foot, continued the search for another thirty minutes before calling it quits. She ordered the officers to go to Blakely's residence and to stay there in case he turned up. When they drove off, Becca crawled under the fence again, and headed to the newspaper building.

"And then I told him, 'That's not a gun in my pocket. It's a rabbit!'," Silas said to the Hispanic-looking delivery driver as she stepped onto the loading dock. They both burst out in raucous laughter at the punchline, which only worked to annoy Becca even more than she already was.

*Jokes. He's telling jokes. That's just great.*

Silas Mot, her so-called partner, had abandoned her when she might have needed him most. He'd flaked while she risked her own life in pursuit of a suspected killer and now she found him hanging back, trading one-liners with their suspect's employee.

"Ah, Becca!" he said, when he noticed her approach. "You're back."

"No thanks to you."

His head tilted curiously, then he seemed to shrug the comment off and gestured to the driver. "I'd like to introduce you to Pedro. Pedro Gonzalez. He's one of Blakely's drivers."

Pedro, a rotund man of Mayan descent with a wide, genuine smile, wore a brown jumpsuit with his name patch stitched just above his left breast pocket. His thick head of jet-black hair was covered in a matching brown baseball cap with mesh backing. A typical trucker's hat.

"*Buenos dias*," Pedro said to her cheerfully.

She nodded a polite hello, but kept her reply directed at Silas. "I kind of figured he was a driver. His uniform was pretty much a dead giveaway." She glanced around the loading bay. Several trucks sat idling at the docks with the other drivers lounging around smoking, drinking coffee, and chatting with one another. "Question is, why aren't they driving now? Why aren't they delivering the papers?"

"Because," Silas said with the dramatic flair of a sideshow magician, "there are no papers to deliver! Apparently, Blakely didn't come to work this morning to run them. The drivers, being union, get paid whether they drive or not, so they decided to hang here for a while and just enjoy their morning." He patted Pedro on the shoulder. "Gave me some time to chat with Pedro here, who has some wonderful stories to tell about his employer, don't you, Pedro?"

"Si, si," Pedro said, nodding enthusiastically.

"In fact, he's seen a few interesting things around here lately. Like Blakely and Ms. Alvarez arguing a few nights before her murder." Silas rubbed his hands together as he spoke, his excitement for the case renewed after his somber demeanor over the death of the bartender earlier that morning. "And..."

201

"Silas, hold on..."

"And..." He interjected, not allowing her an opportunity to speak. "...it apparently turned violent at one point. Pedro saw Blakely hit Andrea in the heat of it all."

Becca's protest evaporated. She looked at the driver. "Really? You saw him get violent with her?"

"*Si.*" The man continued to nod like a life-sized bobble head. "*Es muy mal.* Senorita Andrea, she was sad after. *Estaba llorando.* She crying very much."

"Would you be willing to testify to this?" Becca asked.

The driver squinted and she got the distinct impression he didn't understand the question. Silas said something in perfect Spanish and the man's eyes widened. He shook his head emphatically and offered a string of unintelligible words in response.

"He's afraid of losing his job," Silas explained. "He assures me that he and his family are here legally. However, he's the only one working right now and the only one able to support his wife and eight—" His train of thought broke off and he looked back at Pedro. "*Ocho?*" The driver nodded cheerfully once more. "His eight children. If he testifies, he's afraid he'll be out of work and his family would starve."

She sighed. "Well, it doesn't really matter. Not that you seem to care, but Blakely got away." Becca nodded to the fence. "He slipped underneath and I lost sight of him."

"Well, I yelled at you to stop. You were wasting your time."

"First of all, I wasn't paying attention to you. I was too busy chasing down a suspect," she said, folding her arms across her chest. "Second, wasting my time? Really?"

"Yeah, really. My powers might not be as potent as they normally are, but one thing I have in spades is excellent night vision. I could tell right from the start the man you were chasing wasn't Blakely."

"What?"

Silas chuckled. "Yeah. That was Jorge." He looked over at Pedro and winked. "And he *was* here illegally. He saw you and your uniform, thought you were the INS coming to deport him, so he took off."

Becca felt her blood begin to boil. Granted, she was still miffed at having been awakened for the third night in a row. She also might still be harboring an unjust grudge against Silas for all three of those nights. But for crying out loud, why did he have to be so infuriating?

"So, does Pedro have any idea where his employer is at this moment?"

"Not a clue. But I'm not finished telling you all the awesome stuff Pedro has seen around here." He was practically popping with excitement. "You'll never guess who has been a regular visitor to *The Summer Haven Chronicler* since around the time of Andrea's supposed curse."

"Who?"

Silas scowled, shaking his head. "Ah, come on. Guess."

"Silas, just tell me."

"Okay, fine. Pedro said he started seeing a pretty, but plump blonde lady coming by here late at night a few weeks ago. She'd always come in the early morning hours, after Blakely had finished with the morning press run and the two would go back into his office with the door closed. No one knows what they were up to, but all sorts of speculation about a torrid affair were flying around."

"A blonde? What blonde?"

Silas was practically beaming. He held out his hand. "Let me see your phone."

She hesitated, then tentatively handed the phone over to him. A moment later, he was flipping through her text messages until he came to the one he was looking for and held it up for Pedro to see.

"Is this the woman you were talking about?"

Pedro's eyes widened as he nodded his head adamantly. "Si. Si! Es ella! That is her."

Becca's mind reeled at the information. The photo Silas had showed the driver was the sketch of Elaine Shepherd, the woman who'd tried to have the death curse placed on Andrea.

# CHAPTER
# THIRTY-ONE

SUMMER HAVEN POLICE DEPARTMENT
FRIDAY, 8:05 AM

Awaiting the warrant to search the newspaper, as well as Spencer Blakely's residence, Becca and Silas returned to the police station to catch their breath as they planned their next move. Becca had left Silas sitting at Linda's desk while she went over to the break room to fill up her 'World's Greatest Chief' mug with the sluggish brown liquid her officers had the audacity to call coffee.

Silas reclined in a chair next to Linda White's desk with his feet up on another chair. He knew Becca was exhausted. The human body needed sleep to function. And though he had no way of truly understanding the effort of will she must have been enduring just to keep her eyes open, he nevertheless sympathized with her.

Then, he was struck with a pang in his chest. A heaviness he'd never experienced before, but he knew with no uncertainty that the humans called the feeling 'guilt'. His mind had drifted from Becca's arousal prematurely from bed to that of the murder of Courtney Abeling, which, in turn, had twisted his gut like a pretzel. It was because of him the lovely young woman was dead. So much potential, now evaporated into the ether like his body had just a few hours before.

Of course, he knew the guilt was misplaced. First, it was, indeed, her Time. There was nothing he could have done to prevent it. But also, he had not pulled the trigger on her himself. That had been someone else. He assumed it had been the same thugs that had attempted to kill him, which meant that the ultimate culprit was the one trying to usurp his throne. The one who held the Hand of Cain.

He sighed, staring up at the florescent lights of the institutionalized ceiling and absently flicking his wrist to send his yo-yo into an 'Around the World' move.

"Did you grow a goatee?" Linda, who'd just walked into the station, said as she sat down at her desk. "I like it. It totally gives you that refined British gentleman look."

He gave her a weak smile of thanks. He was in no mood to be charming at that moment, but he did appreciate her compliment. He supposed he would keep the facial hair a little while longer, just for something different.

"My dear Linda," he said, spinning the yo-yo back up into his palm and pocketing it. "You are a ray of sunshine in an otherwise gloomy day."

She blushed in response, then proceeded to boot up her computer to prepare for the day of work. As she did so, Silas let his eyes roam around the bullpen, taking in the organized chaos buzzing around the room. He watched as cops, from both the police department and the sheriff's office, entered and exited, answered phone calls, and chatted with each other while drinking fresh coffee. It was shift change and the night crew were working at filing their reports while the day crew busied themselves with briefings of the previous night's activities and gathered the necessary gear required to tackle the coming day.

It was, as they say, a hotbed of activity and, for a brief moment, Silas enjoyed just a moment of reprieve to 'people watch'. The department was impressive in its diversity. Of the five uniformed officers coming on duty, two were Hispanic and one was African-American and a woman.

Silas watched as they came out of the briefing room, chatting with each other while making their way toward the exit and to the back-parking lot where most of the cruisers were kept. Most wore the standard blue uniform of a typical patrolman. Two, however, wore more formal attire comprised of long sleeves, shining black leather shoes, and gold bars on their sleeves. Supervisors, obviously. Though Silas wasn't sure how, as mortals, they could tolerate being out in the hot Florida sun wearing such attire. For him in his jet-black suit, it was no big deal. His body wasn't real. It didn't get hot or cold, sweaty or chilled.

But for these police officers, the heat could be brutal and he pitied them.

"Tell me, Linda." He nodded to the officers wearing the long sleeve shirts. "Aren't they allowed to wear short sleeves in this weather? Their subordinates can. Why not them?"

Linda looked up from her computer screen and turned in the direction of the men he'd indicated. She smiled. "Oh, yeah. The chief allows all the officers to wear short sleeves. Some of them, when on bike patrol, even wear polos and shorts. But those guys can't. They've got tattoos."

"Huh?"

"Tattoos. Department policy says that any tattoos must be covered while on duty. It's unprofessional. The citizens around here are kind of conservative. Older. They're still pretty suspicious of anyone who has things like tattoos or piercings."

Silas let that information sink in for a minute as he watched the two supervisors heading out the door.

"And how many officers here have tattoos?" he asked.

"Oh, I'd say more than a handful." She pointed over to Becca, who was standing next to Sgt. Tanner. "Even old timers like Jeremy are all tatted up these days though. Won't be long before the old long sleeve policy goes the way of the dodo, if you ask me."

Silas looked at the senior officer. He'd never noticed it before, but he too was decked out in the more formal, long sleeve uniform.

As he stared, Becca glanced over at him and waved him over.

"Pardon me, Linda," he said, getting up from his chair. "But the boss is beckoning."

He walked over to the chief and sergeant, pondering what he'd just learned about the office policy. Tanner gave him a casual, but suspicious, nod of hello, then turned to Becca.

"Okay," he said to her. "I'll have her brought into the interrogation room now."

With that, the sergeant walked away toward the holding cells, leaving Silas and Becca to themselves.

"Bring who to the interrogation room?" Silas asked.

For the first time since he met her, Becca offered a full-blown grin. He would never consider her a dour woman, but for the most part, she was deadly serious. As she smiled, he took her in, not for the first time, and decided he rather liked this look on her. He hoped he could continue to see it more often.

"Well," she said. "While you've been lounging around here

distracting my employees with your impressive displays of yo-yo tricks, I've been busy."

"You mean the search warrant for the newspaper and Blakely's home?"

"That. But also, I had Elaine Shepherd picked up just as she was leaving for work. The sheriff's office just got here. I figured you'd want to be part of the interrogation."

"Oh, trust me," he said, rummaging through his pockets and finding a Warhead candy he'd nabbed from Becca's candy jar earlier. "It'll be a pleasure to be on the other side of that table this time."

"Good." She started walking toward the interrogation room. But before she could walk inside, Linda waved her over.

"CHIEF," Linda said, holding up a telephone. "It's the medical examiner. Line two."

"Thanks. I'll take it in my office." A moment later, she pressed the speaker phone button so Silas could listen in. "What can I do for you, Doc?"

"Actually, it's what I can do for you," he said. "I've examined all of Ms. Alvarez's pill bottles, as well as the pills you found in her trash. I think I have a pretty good handle on what happened."

"Really?" She looked over at Silas, who had raised one of his eyebrows with interest.

"Yes." She heard papers rustling around on the doctor's end of the line, as if he was sifting through a file. "It's just a working theory, mind you. We'll know conclusively when we get the toxicology screen back. But it looks like someone has switched out some of her Ativan, a benzodiazepine, for Eldepryl."

"Okay." Her mind raced to process why that tidbit mattered. "I'm not sure exactly what that means."

"Of course. You see, Eldepryl is a monoamine oxidase inhibitor. Like the benzos, it's an antidepressant, but it's fallen out of favor by most doctors because of some pretty serious side effects."

"What kind of side effects?"

"Well, first of all, if mixed with other medications, it can cause serious complications resulting in something called Serotonin Syndrome. Too much of the stuff can cause it as well."

"Serotonin Syndrome? Isn't that a dangerous increase in Serotonin?" Silas asked.

"Serotonin?" Becca asked. She'd heard of it before. Knew it was some type of hormone, but that was pretty much the extent of it.

"Serotonin is the chemical that's released when people sleep," Silas explained. "It's what causes dreams and things like that."

"Exactly. Serotonin is what helps give us a sense of well-being. Helps ease our minds. And can increase our imagination. But an increase in the hormone could cause serious problems. Someone suffering from Serotonin Syndrome would experience a wide variety of symptoms from heart palpitations to paranoia. They'd get chills, fever, elevated blood pressure. And in extreme cases, hallucinations."

"Like what Andrea was having the weeks before her death."

"Yes."

"But would this kill her? Would someone with this Serotonin Syndrome die from it?"

"It depends on how it was ingested." Dr. Lipkovic cleared his throat. "Like I said, if she took the monoamine oxidase inhibitor, or MAOIs as they're more commonly called, it would pretty much just increase the amount of Serotonin in the brain and cause the side effects I already mentioned."

"What kind of drugs would need to be mixed?" Silas asked.

"Oh, there are too many to list. But for our purposes, any of the SSRI's would do. For instance, Lexapro, which our victim was taking regularly. Her Lexapro wasn't switched out, so I assume she was still taking them anyway. Mix an MAOI with Lexapro and you'd develop a hyperpyrexic crisis. In other words, Serotonin Syndrome."

"And that can be lethal?" Becca asked.

"Oh, in extreme cases, yes. But it's easily identifiable and treated, which is what happened at the ER on the night she was Baker Acted." They heard more shifting of papers on the other end of the line. "However, certain foods eaten while on an MAOI like Eldepryl can cause almost instant death. The food will mix with the drug, causing a hypertensive crisis, which most often leads to a myocardial infarction."

"Which is what you saw in her autopsy."

"Precisely. I only wish her stomach contents had revealed more, but unfortunately, nothing remained. I have a feeling she regurgitated her food just before she died. Emptied her stomach entirely. It's the only thing that makes sense."

There'd been no signs of vomit in her bedroom or bathroom, making Becca think someone must have cleaned it up. *But then, why leave the overturned nightstand? The empty glass on the floor?*

"What kind of food are we talking about, Doc?" Silas asked.

"Oh, alcoholic beverages would do it. As you remember, I *did* detect the smell of alcohol on her blood during autopsy. Also, several types of cheeses, cured meats, and anything with soy in it. The reaction comes from tyramine in the food, which plays havoc with blood pressure."

"And you believe someone's been switching her regularly prescribed benzodiazepines with these mono...mono..."

"Monoamine oxidase inhibitors. Yes. The pills you found in her trash can were Ativan. When I looked in her bottles of Ativan, I found the Eldepryl instead."

Silas looked at Becca. "When we searched the house, there was a block of cheddar cheese and an empty bottle of wine in the kitchen. You're saying..."

"Absolutely. If Ms. Alvarez ingested any of that, she would most definitely have suffered some type of hypertensive crisis, which could easily lead to death."

"Thank you, Doctor," Becca said. "That helps a lot."

"You're welcome. Please let me know if there's anything else I can do for you," he said. "And I'll be sure to send you my final report when I get the toxicology results back."

She hung up the phone. "Well, looks like we have our cause of death."

"Yeah, but it doesn't make a whole lot of sense," Silas said. "Seems to me there are plenty of easier ways to kill someone if that's what you intend to do."

"Unless you wanted to make it look like a death curse had finally taken its victim."

"True."

Becca let out a breath and began making her way to the door. "So, I guess there's nothing else to do right now other than interview our suspect," she said.

The two began making their way once more to the interrogation room and a sudden surge of energy for the case rushed through Becca's veins. She finally had a probable cause of death. She had two excellent suspects. And at that moment, she was very curious to find out just what business Elaine had with Blakely and why she'd failed to mention their early morning rendezvous when they spoke yesterday. It was bad enough that she had attempted to have Jacinto Garcia place a death curse on their victim—a woman Elaine claimed to be 'like a sister' to her. But the fact that she had been having secret meetings with Ms. Alvarez's current boyfriend was a twist almost too delicious not to enjoy.

# THIRTY-TWO

When they entered the small twenty by twenty box of a room, Elaine Shepherd looked up at them with wide eyes. Tears streaked her cheeks. Her mouth opened to speak, her lips trembling wildly, then she closed them as if uncertain what to say. Her wrists were shackled, chained to the table. The clink of metal echoed within the interrogation room with every nervous twitch she made.

"Mrs. Shepherd, thank you for coming," Becca said, taking the seat opposite their new suspect. Silas, for his part, moved over to the corner of the room, just out of view from the one-way mirrored glass and doing his best to look menacing.

"I...I don't think I had much of a choice, did I?" she asked. "They arrested me in front of my kids."

"I'm truly sorry about that, but some things have come to light in our investigation that warranted it." Becca set a manila folder down on the table in front of her, the same tactic she'd used when interrogating Silas, as well as just about any other suspect. She wasn't certain why, but the official nature of the innocuous folder carried with it a great psychological power when questioning people. It was a trick she'd learned when first starting out that now had become a habit.

"What do you mean? What has come to light?"

"For starters, the fact that you weren't very honest with us yesterday," Silas said. He was now leaning against the corner of the room, his arms crossed over his chest and one foot up against the wall. "Actually, I'm not sure how honest you are with anyone...including your so-called best friend, Andrea Alvarez."

Elaine's eyes darted from Silas to Becca.

"W-what's he talking about?"

Becca sat quietly, studying the woman across from her. Silence was another invaluable tool in interrogations. People tended to abhor silence. It's why most people could rarely go ten minutes without the radio playing in their car as they drive to their local grocery store. Why public speakers tended to insert 'um' in the space between pauses in their sentences. Silence, she'd learned, had the same screeching effect on a person's psyche as nails going down a chalkboard.

"We have a BOLO out now on Mr. Spenser Blakely," Becca finally said when she felt her silence had conveyed the necessary affect she was going for.

"Huh?"

Interrogation Trick #3. Try to throw a suspect off balance by saying the most unpredictable thing possible as your opening salvo. It created confusion. Built tension. And made it difficult for them to deduce what direction the questioning would take.

"A BOLO," Becca reiterated. "Means 'Be On the Look Out'. Essentially, Spenser Blakely is about to be arrested for Andrea Alvarez's murder."

Elaine's eyes lit up. "But...that's wonderful. You've found

her killer!" Then her brow furrowed. "Wait. Then why am I here?"

"I'm curious, Mrs. Shepherd," Becca said. "What do you suppose Mr. Blakely will say about you once we get him in this room?"

She stared back at the chief, unable to move. Unable to speak.

"Mrs. Shepherd? What do you think he's going to tell us about his relationship to you?"

"I...we...we don't have a relationship. I don't even know the man."

"You're lying, Elaine!" Silas was suddenly standing at the table, slamming the flat of his hand down on it. The percussive force of the blow echoed through the confined space of the room. Elaine flinched at the outburst. "Lies. Lies. Lies. That's all you seem to know to do."

"I'm telling the truth!" she shouted. "I don't know him. I only know about him from the things Andrea told me."

"Mrs. Shepherd, we have a witness who puts you with Blakely several times in the last few weeks," Becca said. Her voice was calm. Even. Soothing. "These meetings were always in the dead of night when the rest of Summer Haven was asleep."

Their suspect stammered. Fidgeted in the metal seat bolted to the concrete floor. "I...um...maybe your witness is wrong. Maybe they're the one who's lying. I've never so much as seen Blakely in person. I swear."

"Swear?" Silas leaned in with a salacious grin stretched across his face. "Cross your heart and hope to...die?"

"Silas!" Becca barked, grabbing the man by the wrist and squeezing. "Enough."

Elaine was sobbing now.

"Mrs. Shepherd, do you really think that Blakely will

corroborate what you're telling us when we have him in custody?" Becca continued now that Silas had moved back to his corner. "Do you really trust him that much not to turn over on you? Now's the time to come clean. We might be able to work out a deal."

"I'm telling you...I had nothing to do with Andrea's death!"

"Then tell us about your relationship with Spenser Blakely. If we're satisfied, you might be able to go home."

Elaine sniffed, looking up pitiably at Becca. "I...I think I want my lawyer now."

The words out of the woman's mouth, Becca glanced back at Silas and stood up. The interrogation was over.

217

# THIRTY-THREE

THE SUMMER HAVEN CHRONICLER
FRIDAY, 10:35 AM

"We have a warrant to search the premises," Becca said, holding up the signed document as they strode into the front office of *The Chronicler*.

Mrs. Hamilton, Blakely's receptionist, stood from her desk with a gasp.

"W-what?" she asked. "What's going on?"

"I'm sorry, ma'am, but I'm going to have to ask you to vacate the building while we conduct our business."

"But, I need to call..." She reached for the phone on her desk, then pulled her hand away a moment later.

"Call who, Mrs. Hamilton?"

"I-I-I'm not sure." The old woman blustered about, indecision painted on her face. Becca was sure she had been in touch with her employer and would probably know where he was.

She'd be sure to sit her down for a chat when they finished their search.

"Mrs. Hamilton, this is Sergeant Tanner." Becca gestured to the senior officer. "He's going to walk you outside and sit with you until we're finished. Is that *okay*?"

The way she'd emphasized the word 'okay' could leave little doubt that she was only being polite. The woman really had no other choice. To leave now would make her an accessory to murder if they found enough evidence to convict her boss.

Shaking, Mrs. Hamilton nodded and shuffled across the tile floor over to Tanner, who led her outside. After she was gone, Becca, Silas, and four uniformed officers made a quick sweep of the building to ensure no one else lurked inside—including Spencer Blakely himself. But the place seemed to be deserted.

"Okay," she said to her officers. "We'll do a systematic search of each room. Ellis, you and Wood take the main lobby and reception area. Robinson and Gilmour, you handle the print shop, and Silas and I will take Blakely's office."

As the teams of officers split up to carry out their assignments, Becca handed Silas a pair of latex gloves. "Put them on before you touch anything."

She waited until he'd complied, slipped a pair on herself, and the two entered Blakely's office before heading straight to the glass display case. Silas frowned the moment he looked inside.

"I don't understand." He looked at her. His forehead creased in confusion. "They're both here. Both daggers are here. I thought for sure he was the one who'd broken into Alvarez's condo and clocked me in the back of my head."

"He might still have," she assured him. "Maybe it has nothing to do with the daggers themselves. Maybe he was there for some other reason."

He stood staring at the display case, his jaw slack as he puzzled over its contents. He hadn't heard a word she said.

"All right. You just stand there gawking at that case. I'll search the rest of the office."

She left him and turned around to survey the room. Not much had changed since she'd last been inside its polished cherry-wood walls. She walked over to the bookcase, perusing the numerous books ranging from classic pieces of literature to Julius Caesar's writings on the Gallic Wars. Becca removed a few books at random, looking for anything that might have been tucked within their pages. Many of them were old. Some were first editions. None of them contained anything remotely useful.

She moved over to the desk, obviously a matching set with the bookshelves, and sat down in Blakely's chair. She hoped to get a feel for the man simply by occupying the same space as he. From the height he'd set his chair, she suddenly realized just how short the man was. The chair itself tilted slightly to the left and the cushion squished at an odd angle that often occurred with overweight people.

What on earth did Andrea see in the guy? She chastised herself for being so shallow, but she still couldn't get over the vast age difference between the two. Andrea herself had been a fetching woman. Perhaps not a head-turner, but attractive nonetheless.

Returning her attention to the task at hand, she pulled on the center desk drawer and found it locked. Undeterred, she reached into her breast pocket and withdrew two paperclips she immediately bent into picks and set to work unlocking the drawer. Within fifteen seconds, she heard a satisfying click and pulled it open.

Silas was now bent over the display case, eyeing the contents even more carefully.

"Would you give that a rest and look somewhere else?"

He offered a response, something akin to, "Grmph" and continued his examination. She decided her best retort would be to ignore him and look through the desk drawer she'd just opened. If her memory served, this was the drawer Blakely had opened to retrieve the bilongo doll that had been used to frighten Andrea.

She shuffled through the debris inside—little more than an assortment of pens, notepads, and paperclips—then pushed the drawer closed with a groan. She had no idea what she was looking for. Even though they now had a method for Andrea Alvarez's murder, they still had no clue as to motive. No physical evidence at either the dump scene or the victim's home other than the medications dumped in her trash. Without anything more to go on, searching for evidence within Blakely's office was a hopeless cause. Any object in here could be potential evidence. Nothing in here might be evidence as well. In all her years investigating murders, this might be the first time she'd been truly stumped.

"Aha!" Silas shouted, craning his head to beam at her. "We've got him."

She got up from the warped chair and strode over to the display case. "What are you talking about? Both knives are there."

He shook his head. "No, no. No. That's where you're wrong. *Two* knives are there, not *both* knives."

"Huh?"

Maybe it was from the lack of sleep, but the man wasn't making any sense.

He pointed to the knife on the left. "Take a closer look."

She leaned forward, examining the weapon as best she could. It was long, about nine inches, and curved in a serpentine pattern toward the middle. The handle was wooden, wrapped from top to bottom in red and black beads. A single short-stemmed feather hung by a red piece of twine at the hilt.

"Okay, what am I looking at?" She looked at the other knife. They looked pretty much the same to her.

He pointed emphatically to the metal blade.

It had a chrome finish and was scarred by nicks and scratches along its surface from wear. The other blade was similar, with many of the same signs of wear as the first.

"I repeat my question," she said, looking up at his gleaming smile.

He ran a gloved finger along the side of the blade. "These nicks and scratches? They're artificial."

"What do you mean artificial?"

"I mean they didn't get there from regular use. He's spent some time aging the knife. Dragging it behind his car maybe. Or throwing it against the wall. Something like that. To make it look older than it really is."

Her nose crinkled. "That's a bit of a stretch, isn't it?"

He shook his head. "Not at all. Look at the other one. See how the scratches here seem a little more faded than these?" He pointed to two different sections of the blade with two distinct sets of wear. "And look here...a little oxidation can be seen in this groove here. That's because these blemishes happened over time. Different incidents occurring throughout the knife's existence." Silas changed focus back to the first knife. "But the blemishes on this one...they're all pretty even. They're all about the same age. And there's not the slightest trace of rust on it. This is a newer knife."

Becca shrugged. "It doesn't mean anything. Maybe one was used more than the other."

But he wasn't done. "Then there's the blood."

"Blood?"

"He pointed at the second knife's blade. "It's been cleaned, of course, but see the slight discoloration along the ridge here? That's from dried blood—presumably from animal sacrifices practiced by followers of Santeria. There's no signs of blood on the other knife."

"Like I said, one knife could have been used more often."

"True. But how much you want to bet that the knife we found in Ms. Alvarez's back match one of the knives in her apartment and the other one we found in her apartment matches the older one here much better than its current mate?"

Now that was something she hadn't thought of. Forensics could show which blades belong to which set.

"So, you're thinking Blakely killed her, then used one of her own knives to stab her in the back?" she asked. "That would make it seem like a crime of opportunity. But that doesn't add up. We know she didn't die from the stab wound. She died from a myocardial infarction caused by an interaction with the medication—both prescribed and switched, as well as the cheese and alcohol. It was almost the perfect murder. We might not have suspected a thing if not for the knife in her back. If he went to all that trouble to plan the perfect murder, why screw it up with a stab wound?"

She shook her head. The more they figured out about this case, the more confusing it became. Nothing was adding up, which usually meant they were missing a major piece of the puzzle.

"I don't have all the answers," Silas said. "But I'm pretty confident about the knives. Blakely used one of hers and replaced it with one of his."

"Then replaced his missing one with a newer one? Why not leave the newer one in Andrea's place if he was going to go to all that trouble?"

"He probably figured the knives in her apartment would be

scrutinized pretty close. He wanted to make sure the one he replaced was authentic. These knives, as far as anyone knows, are just souvenirs. Props, more than anything. So why would anyone pay close attention to them?"

Just then, Officer Gilmour appeared at the door. "Chief, we found something. You really need to see this."

# CHAPTER
# THIRTY-FOUR

Officer Gilmour led them into the print shop, around the giant press and to the southeast wall where Robinson stood, guarding a door to what looked like a storage closet. When the officer saw them approach, he opened the door and Becca saw the closet was bigger than she'd imagined—nearly eight by ten feet and cluttered with an assortment of ritualistic bric-a-brac, artifacts, and black magic paraphernalia.

"Dear Lord," she hissed as she approached the door.

"Hardly," Silas said, poking his head through the door for a better look.

The room was painted black, from ceiling to floor, and contained a blood red pentagram painted on the wall directly across from them. In the center of the room sat an iron cauldron, filled with numerous sticks of assorted sizes and what looked to be a handful of human bones.

"What the heck is that?" she asked.

"An *n'ganga*," Silas answered. "A kind of altar for those who practice Palo Mayombe—Santoria's much darker cousin." He visibly blushed when he looked at her. "They kind of have a thing for...well, me." He pointed to the bones in the cauldron. "Chances are, you've had some recent grave robberies in nearby cemeteries. Those bones probably came from one of the graves."

Her head swiveled as she took in more of the room. A small table stood in the far-right corner. A statue of some kind of saint, painted in vibrant colors, stood on the table and was surrounded by jars of pennies, a bottle of whiskey, and pipe tobacco.

"Are all these...these things part of the same religious disciplines?" she asked. "It looks too eclectic for some reason."

"It is." Silas stepped cautiously into the room and made a full three-hundred and sixty-degree turn. "I see representations of neo-paganism in here. Wicca." He pointed to the table with the saint statue on it. "Vodun. Palo Mayombe. Santeria. And a few things I don't recognize at all."

"What do you suppose it all means?"

He looked at her. His face was grim. "He's covering all his bases. He's trying to amass as much power as he can by dabbling in as many magico-religious practices as possible."

"To what end?"

"Only thing I can think of...he's trying to gain enough power to control something of immense power."

"Like the Hand?"

Silas glanced at the two officers standing at the door with a suspicious eye, then noticed their short-sleeved uniforms. No tattoos. He returned his gaze back to the room. "Possibly. Most of these religious practices originated within the same part of the world...the same culture. Their syncretic malleability is a matter of historic record. It's not unreasonable that Blakely's been trying to combine them to create some kind of mega-discipline and I can't see why anyone would try it unless they needed an exceptional amount of power."

"You're talking about this stuff like it's real. Like magic is real."

He shook his head. "It's not. It's all an illusion. A twisted game some of the nastier groups from the spiritual realm play on mortals. But that doesn't mean there aren't some of those same spiritual beings that would love to see someone as bitter and dark as Blakely get control over the realm of Death." He sighed. "I've got a lot of enemies, Becca. A lot of ambitious beings vying for my spot on the food chain."

"Like your wife."

He pinched at the bridge of his nose. "My ex-wife. *Ex*. And yes. Exactly like her. Only, there are beings out there far worse."

"Chief?" Officer Robinson interrupted. "Did Gilmour tell you about the other thing we found?"

Becca glanced at her two officers and shook her head. "No, but if it's anything like this, I'm not sure how much I want to know."

Robinson's brow creased, but he waved for them to follow. They were led back to the farthest corner of the print shop, leaving Gilmour to stand guard at the newspaper man's magical inner sanctum. When the officer finally stopped, he pointed to three large plastic containers that were advertised on the labels to contain five gallons of black ink each.

She looked at the officer, waiting for him to explain the significance of the containers. Instead, he just nodded to them nervously. His eyes round with worry.

Impatient, Silas stepped forward, took hold of one of the containers' lids, and lifted it away. But the thick liquid inside was anything but black. Instead, it was a swirl of deep reds and darker maroons and filled nearly three-fourths of the way to the top.

"Blood?" she asked.

Silas nodded. He sniffed the air.

"Same as the blood on Ms. Alvarez if I'm not mistaken. It has the same smell anyway."

She struggled to keep from smiling. They'd found Blakely's connection to Andrea's murder. Once forensics analyzed the blood, they could definitively link him to the body found on the beach. That was good news and the source of her strong desire to celebrate. On the other hand, as she stared down into the oily crimson pool in the container, she wanted nothing more than to go home, curl up in bed, and hide under the covers. In all her years as a homicide detective, she'd never seen anything as dark or scary as the things she'd seen on this case.

Gangbangers killing each other, she could understand. Wives killing their cheating husbands? Sure, why not. But this? Ritualistic magic? Trying to amass some mystical power? That room with its pentagrams and cauldrons filled with bones? It was beyond her limits to understand and that scared her more than anything. If Rebecca Cole was anything, it was rational, and there was nothing rational at all about Andrea Alvarez's murder.

Silas closed the lid on the container and placed a hand on her shoulder. "Are you okay?"

She nodded and pulled her gaze away from the ink containers. When she did, she noticed a set of filing cabinets sitting a few feet away next to a work bench with an assortment of tools and two large plastic tackle boxes.

She stepped over to the file cabinet. "Wonder what's in here?" It seemed strange to have them out here instead of in the administrative portion of the building. She examined the cabinets. Each drawer was marked with a strange symbol just above the thumb lever. "Any idea what these mean?"

Silas shook his head.

She opened the top drawer to discover a large row of manila folders, each labeled with a person's last name ranging from the letters A through C. She pulled the first folder out and opened it to find a handful of small Ziploc bags containing an assortment of hair strands, fingernail clippings, buttons, cigarette butts, and other oddities.

"What in the world...?" She slid the folder back in and randomly selected another name: Buchner. Like the first folder she'd examined, this also had an equally as diverse supply of garbage sealed in plastic baggies. "What is this stuff?"

Silas stepped forward, thumbed through the folders until he paused. He slid out one more folder and handed it to Becca. It was labeled 'Alvarez'. Her throat went dry as she looked at the name, then she opened it. The folder was empty.

"Wait. What does this mean?"

"Do you recognize any of the names in this cabinet, Becca?"

She scanned the labels, her mind concentrating on each name.

"Wait." She pulled out another file which contained more hairs and personal items inside. "These are all names of residents in Summer Haven." She opened another drawer and found the same in each folder. She gasped when her eyes drifted to a folder marked 'Mot'. She pulled it out, but found it empty as well. She looked up at Silas, confused. "I don't understand."

He gave her a sad smile, then closed the drawer currently opened and returned to the first. "You missed one in here," he said, riffling down the line of folders until he found the one labeled 'Cole'. Her heart was hammering inside her chest as he withdrew it and opened it in front of her. She wasn't entirely certain whether she was relieved or terrified to find it empty too. "I think I know what's going on here...and Blakely's connection to Elaine Shepherd."

Silas laid the folder on top of the cabinet and walked over to the work bench with Becca close on his heels. He then grabbed the first tackle box nearest to him, pulled it forward, and opened it. Inside, they found two small drawstring bags. He withdrew one, opened it, and emptied the contents onto the bench.

It was a doll, dressed in all black and wrapped in multi-colored ribbons.

"Th-that's you?"

He nodded. "A bilongo of me, yes." He emptied the second bag, which contained another doll in blue with a yellow star painted on its torso. "And that's you. Spenser Blakely has attempted to do a working on us, Chief Cole." He nodded over to the file cabinets. "That appears to be a collection of personal items from every citizen in Summer Haven. Items necessary to place within these dolls to create a connection with their intended target. He's probably been collecting these things for years, hoping it could come in handy sometime in the future for his political aspirations." He paused, taking a closer look at the black-clad doll. "I'm not entirely sure what he used from me, since my body isn't likely to shed any hair or skin cells, but all it takes is something closely connected with the individual."

He held out a hand to her. "Pocket knife?"

She looked down at his hand, unable to comprehend what she was hearing.

"Becca, do you have a pocket knife?"

Officer Robinson stepped forward. "I do." He dropped his knife in Silas' hand, who turned to his own personal bilongo and sliced it open. The doll was filled mostly with sand, pebbles, and a few items Becca couldn't readily identify. Then she heard something inside it crinkle. "Ah, so that's what he used." Silas reached two thin fingers inside the doll and pulled out a clear plastic candy wrapper. "Warheads," he said with a smile.

"I still don't understand," Becca said. "So, he tried to hex us. How does this connect to Elaine Shepherd?"

His smile broadened. "Because, dear Becca, when Jacinto Garcia refused her request to curse Andrea, she turned to the only other person she knew who might be able to do it."

Becca's eyes widened and she returned her partner's smile. "Of course," she said, finally seeing the pieces fall into place. "Spenser Blakely. He put the curse on his own girlfriend." Curious, she reached for the second tackle box and opened it. A third pouch was hidden underneath a plastic tray. She pulled the bag out, opened it, and dumped the doll inside onto the bench. It was nondescript with no clothing, hair, or facial features. The only identifying mark on the doll at all was a photo cut from a magazine page of a car that was pinned to the doll's chest. "And it looks like he's going after Andrea's ex now."

# THIRTY-FIVE

SAND DOLLAR MOTEL
FRIDAY, 12:03 PM

B ecca and Silas left the newspaper's office and began making their way to James Andrews' residence after calling his dealership and being told he'd taken a sick day. She'd sent Sergeant Tanner on to Blakely's house with the search warrant, trusting him to look for anything there that might link the journalist to Andrea's death.

At the moment, she and Silas were both pretty quiet as she navigated the back streets of Summer Haven. Their discoveries at *The Chronicler* had been more exciting than she had expected, and the case seemed to be finally coming together, which was why she supposed neither of them were in much of a mood to talk. They didn't want to jinx anything with words.

"HQ to Unit 101," Becca's radio squawked to life, jarring both the car's occupants from their thoughts.

She pulled the transmitter from its mount and brought it to her lips. "Go ahead, Linda."

"Um, we just got a kind of weird call from the Sand Dollar Motel." Silas seemed to tense at the news. "The whole place is kind of freaking out about a strange man running around the complex, hiding in shrubs, and peeking in windows." Becca gave her companion a sideways glance. "Just wondering if you wanted me to send a unit or to just let the sheriff's office handle this one since our guys are already stretched to the limit."

Before Becca could answer, Silas' hand shot out, snatching the transmitter from her hand. "That's okay, Linda," he said into the mic. "We're near the motel. We'll just go ahead and handle it."

Becca yanked the transmitter from his hand, glaring at him as she did so. There was a pause on the other end of the radio.

"Are...are you sure about that?" Linda finally asked.

Still scowling at the man, Becca brought the mic to her lips. "Yeah, yeah. We'll swing by the motel and have a look around." She replaced the transmitter and took the next left. "Silas? What have you done?"

"Me?" He stared out the windshield innocently. "Why do you think I have anything to do with a man in an Hawaiian shirt running around my motel?"

"Linda didn't say anything about a Hawaiian shirt." She gave her head a frustrated shake. "Seriously. What did you do?"

She flicked her emergency lights on and sped through the residential neighborhood toward State Road A1A.

Finally, he looked over at her, offering her a nervous grin. "Okay," he said. "But I think when it's all said and done, you're going to laugh."

"Spill."

He sighed. "Well, you know that little experiment I've been talking about?"

233

"Yes." The word ground its way out through clenched teeth.

"Um, yeah...that would be Elliot Newman."

"The archaeologist that was killed by a bus?"

He nodded.

"What about him?"

"Well, I think he's probably our peeping Tom."

Becca slammed on the brakes of the cruiser, bringing it to a grinding halt. Fortunately, there was no traffic behind her and she pulled over to the curb. Then she unbuckled her seat belt and turned to glare at him.

"Excuse me? Mind saying that again?" She was pretty sure a plume of smoke was rising from her ears as she spoke.

"The strange man," he said, running a hand nervously through his hair. "I'm pretty sure it's Elliot Newman."

"But he's dead."

"Yeah, well...not anymore."

She turned back to stare out the window. She took a deep breath. Then another one.

"And how, I might ask, is that possible?"

"Um, hello?" Using both hands, he thumbed back at himself. "Death?"

"Yeah, I get that. Let me rephrase my question. *Why* is a dead archaeologist now running around the motel's property?"

"I have no idea why. He's supposed to be keeping a low profile inside my room."

"You know what I mean, Mot."

He chuckled but stopped the moment he noticed her face. "Look, I thought maybe he'd be a help to us in finding the Hand of Cain. The guy was studying the pirate ship wreck on the coast, as well as its fabled treasure, before he died. I believe that's where the Hand was discovered. I figured he'd have some insight into the players around here who might have an affinity for ancient artifacts and could point us in the right direction."

"So, you can bring people back from the dead?"

He shrugged. "Sorta."

"All this time, you could bring back people who had died?"

"It's kind of my thing."

"And you never once thought to just bring Andrea Alvarez back to life to see if she knew who killed her?"

Silas shook his head. "Doesn't work like that. Alvarez isn't one of mine. It wasn't her Time. So, I've got no control over her afterlife. Elliot was a different story." Sometime during the conversation, he'd removed the yo-yo from his pocket and was absently winding the string around his right forefinger. "And before you ask, no. It's not something I would do willy-nilly. It goes against everything I believe in to snatch someone from their final reward and plop them back in their bodies. But with Elliot, I didn't think I really had much of a choice." He looked over at her. "Besides, I told you several times what I planned to do and you never tried to stop me."

"That's because I never in a million years thought you were serious about it!"

He fidgeted some more with the yo-yo string and nodded ahead. "Shouldn't we be going? If it is Elliot, he's probably freaking out right now. He's been in and out of consciousness since I woke him up and will have no idea what's going on."

With a growl, she put the car in drive and sped on to the motel. The moment she pulled into the covered turnabout, a beleaguered-looking older gentleman wearing a rumpled and sweat-stained button down ambled out into the parking lot to greet them.

"Thank goodness you're here, chief," he said, walking over to the driver's side door. "That guy is like a wild man. He's crazed, I tell ya."

Becca got out of the car and looked the man up and down. "And you are?"

"Ernest Guillespe, Chief. I'm the day manager of this place." He eyed Silas as he slipped from the car. "You!" He pointed a long, crooked finger at him. "That lunatic came out of your room! We might tolerate the occasional discreet rendezvous with our guests, but whatever you two were doing in there was unnatural. Unnatural, I say!"

"You have no idea," Silas said with a grin.

Becca glared at him. "You're not helping." She then took the manager by his shoulders to calm him down. "Mr. Guillespe, we'll take care of it. Now, where is he?"

The old man pointed toward the beach. "On the other side of the motel, hiding in the dunes. He's freaked out our guests somethin' fierce. We're not one of the fanciest places around here. This kind of thing can ruin our business." He glared at Silas. "Which I'm blaming you for, Slick. I ain't paying for whatever you've been up to, no siree."

"Thank you, Mr. Guillespe," Becca said. "Now go on inside and let us handle this, okay?"

"I've a mind to give Mr. Mot the boot after this little fiasco," he mumbled, but nodded and walked back toward the motel lobby entrance.

"I don't blame you one bit," Becca called back. "I'm of a mind to do something similar."

"Oh, for crying out loud," Silas said as they began making their way around the side of the motel. "I was just trying to give us an edge against our adversary."

"You were messing with the forces of nature."

"I *am* one of the forces of nature, remember?" he said as they made their way to the boardwalk that led directly to the beach, glancing out over the rails at the dunes on each side.

If she wasn't afraid of scaring off the previously deceased

Elliot Newman, she would have screamed. The man could be absolutely infuriating.

"I think you should be quiet now," she said. Her eyes scanned from right to left, searching for a trace of her quarry. "I swear, I may just shoot you here and now. I won't hurt you, but it'll feel really good."

"Well, that's not a very nice..."

A rustle of vegetation to the left stopped him from uttering the rest of his sentence. They followed the noise, peering into a thick patch of palmetto bushes. Becca caught the slightest hint of movement. Pink skin. Something garishly red. Something ginger as well.

"Mr. Newman, is that you?" she asked, trying to keep her voice calm and even.

"Elliot?" Silas whispered.

The pink, red, and ginger thing in the palmetto bushes shifted.

"It's okay, Mr. Newman, we're here to help you."

A ginger-covered head peaked up from the bush. Becca saw a man with a pale face, wide-bewildered eyes, and a jaw slack in confused gawk. He blinked.

"I...I don't know where I am," he said with a trembling, high-pitched voice.

"Summer Haven, mate," Silas said, offering a friendly wave. "Glad to see you up and about again."

The timid little man squinted in the sunlight, trying to catch a better glimpse of Silas. "Do...do I know you?"

"It's a bit of a long story, really." Silas straightened his tie, nervously. "If you come out, we'll talk about it. I promise I'll clear everything up."

Elliot shifted to his left, but he didn't stand. He peered around the left side of the bush now and looked at Becca. "I...I don't trust that man." He pointed at Silas.

She chuckled, raising an eyebrow at her partner. "That's because you have very good instincts, Mr. Newman. He's foolish and impetuous. I, on the other hand, am chief of police here. You can trust me."

Like a doe, uncertain of what to do, he rose from behind the bushes and Becca struggled to suppress a giggle when she saw the ridiculous attire he was wearing. He was dressed in a pair of cargo shorts, at least three sizes too big, and a bright red Hawaiian shirt with yellow floral print. Like most gingers, he was fair-skinned and was already showing signs of sunburn on his exposed flesh from where he'd been out in the sun too long. His face was thin with large, expressive eyes and a mouth that seemed to hang open perpetually.

"It's okay, Mr. Newman." She held out a hand to him over the boardwalk's rails. "Let me take you some place a little more comfortable so we can figure things out, okay?"

"Sure. Sure." He stumbled forward, like his limbs were too stiff to function normally.

"It's the embalming fluid," Silas whispered in her ear, as if reading her mind. "His body is still trying to flush it out of his system. He'll be stiff for another day or two, I'd say."

Three minutes later, the dead man scrambled over the railing and was led back to Silas Mot's motel room without any more complications.

CHAPTER

# THIRTY-SIX

E lliot Newman plopped down on the queen-sized bed inside Silas' room, wrapped a blanket around his shoulders, and shivered. "I...I just don't understand what's going on," he said. "I feel so weird."

"That's understandable," Silas said, leaning against the dresser. "You're dead."

Becca's head snapped in his direction. If she could have burned him to a crisp with laser vision, she would have.

"Um, I mean, you *were* dead. There's a difference."

"Dead? What do you mean 'dead'?"

Becca shook her head. "Don't you worry a bit about it," she said, sitting down beside him. "He's just got a rotten sense of humor." She paused. "So, what's the last thing you remember?"

There was a part of her that was far too fascinated with this conversation than she would ever admit to being. It wasn't every day that you could actually talk to someone who had been dead for a couple of days. Could he have the answers that

239

humanity has sought since its existence? Life after death? The light at the end of the tunnel? She supposed these were all things she could ask Silas about, but she also knew she could never fully trust him with the truth. She needed to hear certain things from the lips of mortals...people who understood the instinctive lure such questions held for everyone.

Elliot shrugged. "It's all kind of fuzzy," he said, scooting back in the bed until his back was pressed against the head-board. He was keeping a wary eye on Silas Mot. "I was in Summer Haven, preparing for an underwater excavation." His gaze shifted over to Becca. "You've heard about the sunken ship, right?"

She nodded.

"Yeah, so I had just booked our charter boat and scuba supplies and stepped out onto the sidewalk just outside Diver Dan's, when out of nowhere, this gorgeous brunette with a body like a Greek goddess, came up to me, said I looked sad, and started kissing me."

Becca stared at the man, uncertain where his story was going.

"And?" Silas asked.

"And, it shocked me. I'd never had anything like that happen to me in my entire life. Confused, I stepped off the sidewalk into the street and...um...that's all I remember."

*And that's when you got hit by a tour bus. Poor guy.*

"This woman," Silas said, his eyes narrowing. "Did she have an accent?"

"An accent?" Elliot wrinkled his nose, as if in thought. "Yeah, I think she did. Hispanic, I think."

Silas glanced over at Becca. "Esperanza." He sighed. "It's her M.O. She tends to like to send guys off with a smile on their faces."

"So, she killed him?"

"Not necessarily. It was his Time. We know that or I would never have been able to bring him back. But sometimes, she likes to give people a special little sendoff. Maybe a nudge in the right direction, yes."

"W-what do you mean, 'killed' me?" Elliot asked.

"Kid, I wasn't lying to you a minute ago," Silas said. "Of course, Chief Cole thinks I should coddle you and not tell you the truth, but that won't do any of us any good. You need to know everything before we can proceed."

Then, Silas was good to his word and told him everything. Told him about his death. About the bus. About the woman who had kissed him, as well as just who Silas Mot really was. He told him about the Hand of Cain and the danger to humanity it represented, and the murder investigation he was currently helping Becca with in hopes of drawing closer to the one who possessed the Hand.

And all the while, Elliot Newman, brainy archaeologist from Palatka, Florida, sat huddled on the bed—his knees pulled up to his chest—as he took it all in with a slack jaw and wide, unblinking eyes. He trembled when told about the bus running him over. His lips twitched when he learned about Esperanza. And he froze with abject terror when told that the Grim Reaper himself had raised him from the dead to help him track down this powerful artifact that could destroy people's lives at the whim of whoever wielded it.

When Silas finished talking, Elliot sat in silence. He was now rocking back and forth, his arms wrapped around his knees.

"Uh..." Rock. Rock. Rock. "I...uh..." He blinked away a few tears. Looked at Silas, then at Becca. "Yeah, I'm not..."

Before anyone could react, Elliot leapt from the bed and

dashed straight to the door, slid the security chain out of its cradle, and pulled the door open to flee. But Silas was faster than he looked. In the span of a single blink, he was in front of the frightened man, shooing him back inside the motel room.

"Hold on now," he said, grinning from ear to ear. "You haven't heard my proposal yet. Trust me. It's something you're gonna want to hear."

Reluctantly, Elliot returned to the room and Silas closed the door behind him. He then gestured for the former dead man to sit down next to Becca. When Elliot had complied, Silas sat on the opposite bed across from them.

"Look. Here's the deal. I broke about a zillion laws of nature to bring you back." He made a show of wiping his hands. "No problem. I'll take the heat. But you have two options here, Elliot, my boy. One. You help me locate the Hand of Cain. If you do that, I'll be able to justify your re-lifeing and you'll be granted a second death later down the road. Two. You flake out, ostrich your head in the sand, and pretend none of this is happening, and I've got no choice but to send you back to the morgue where I got you."

"Silas!" Becca snapped. She wasn't sure she liked the emotional hostage tactics he was using against the poor guy.

"Sorry, Chief, but those are his only options. I don't mind taking the heat for the abomination I've created by giving him life again...if he's going to help save the world as a result. If he's not, I'm sorry. But no matter how I might act, I do have rules I have to follow. I'll have no choice, but to send him back."

"What do you need me to do?" Elliot asked. He wouldn't look Silas in the eyes. Becca couldn't really blame him.

"Right now, I need you to rest. Your body still hasn't purged your post-mortem toxins yet. That's why you feel so stiff right now. Why you are so disoriented." Silas grabbed the

TV remote from the nightstand and handed to him. "Catch up on your shows. Think of it as a beach vacation."

"And then what? When I'm back to normal, what then?"

"Then, you'll proceed with your investigation into the sunken pirate ship. I think that's where the Hand of Cain was discovered and there might be some evidence that'll point us to who took it."

Elliot shook his head. "That'll be trickier than you think," he said. "The wreck's already been scavenged by several well-known treasure hunters. And last I heard..." He trailed off for a moment. "...before, ya know, I was killed...there was a deal being made to bring in that charlatan Lance Avery and his dumb archaeology show, *Mysterious Expedition*, here to televise the whole thing. Some rich widow was talking to the state to get full access to the wreck with the promise of television crews and tourists flocking to the area. I was in the process of fighting it—trying to get the state to maintain rights to the wreck—when I was...." He coughed. "...killed."

"But I thought those sites were protected from private parties?" Becca asked. "How could a private citizen get access like that?"

"Apparently, this woman's got major pull in Tallahassee. Don't remember her name though." He looked over at Becca. "What day is it?"

"April 26."

"I've been..." He swallowed. It looked like it hurt. "...dead for four days now?"

She nodded.

"There's no telling what's happened to the wreck by now."

Becca looked over at Silas, then Elliot. "I'll ask the sheriff's office to send one of their marine units on routine patrols. And I'll have Jeremy start doing some intelligence work...trying to find out who this mysterious widow is and building a profile on any strangers in town that might fit the treasure hunter bill."

"Not Tanner," Silas said abruptly.

"Huh? Why not?"

"Just trust me on this. Don't send Tanner or any of your other officers who wear long sleeve shirts. And keep this project as secretive as possible."

"Long sleeve shirts?"

"I'll explain everything when the time is right. For now, please. Just trust me."

"Okay." She nodded, but she didn't like where her thoughts were heading when she thought about Silas' sudden suspicion of her most trusted officer.

Silas turned his attention back to Elliot. "Now, like I said, the only thing you can do is rest. We're about to solve this case. When we're finished, you should be fully recuperated. We'll get started on *your* investigation then. Sound good?"

Elliot nodded, but his deer-caught-in-headlights eyes told a different story.

"I'm serious. I need you to stay here. No one can know you're alive again. No one."

"I understand."

Becca didn't think he really did, but it was the best they were going to get out of him at the moment.

Silas stood and walked over to the door. "You ready?" he asked Becca. "We need to go check on James Andrews' well-being, find Blakely, and take care of this case once and for all."

She stood up and looked down at the poor man dressed in the most God-awful Hawaiian shirt she'd ever seen. He was once more huddled up against the headboard of the bed and clutching the remote control in his hand.

"We'll be back soon, Elliot. Will you be all right?"

The nerdy little man nodded, offering her a weak smile.

"Feel free to order room service," Silas said, opening the door. "Have them leave whatever you order outside. Don't answer the door for anyone but go nuts. I highly recommend the ice cream sundae, by the way."

With that, he gestured Becca through the door and they left the recently dead archaeologist to his own devices.

# THIRTY-SEVEN

143 BRANSON STREET
HAMMOCK DUNES, FLORIDA
FRIDAY, 1:40 PM

Though technically, Oceanshore Boulevard was still considered State Road A1A, Becca and Silas had driven into one of the more upscale portions of Flagler County, the county a few miles south from Summer Haven, which demanded a more appealing street name for its affluent residents. The fact that Andrea's ex lived out here, despite his humble beginnings, was a testament to just how successful his car lot must be.

On each side of the highway, a wall of jungle-like vegetation grew, reminding Becca of the harsh primal land Florida had once been before developers mowed most of it down for resorts, condos, and beach houses. Though the ocean was just a few hundred yards to their left, the jungle foliage blocked any view of it from passing motorists, creating a whole other world of paradise that lived on the other side.

Normally, she enjoyed this stretch of road, but now her mind was at war with a flurry of conflicting thoughts and emotions. It turned over the disturbing evidence they had found in *The Summer Haven Chronicler*, which sent it careening to the mental image of the bilongo dolls she and Silas had found, ultimately leading her mind to the purpose of driving to Hammock Dunes in the first place—to find out why Spenser Blakely had included Andrea Alvarez's ex in his little bag of cursed horrors.

And speaking of horrors, she couldn't get Elliot Newman out of her mind either, nor the abominable act Silas had done in bringing him back to life. She had no real concept of what the implications such a feat might cause in the grand scheme of the universe, but she imagined it couldn't be good. Though she hadn't been to Sunday School since she was a little girl, she'd pretty much assumed that only one man had the power over Death, and she couldn't imagine he'd be too pleased with Silas' actions right now.

Still, she supposed Mot's logic was somewhat sound. In theory. If the Hand of Cain truly had been discovered in that old ship wreck, then it stood to reason that the one man tasked with officially studying it would be the best person to look to for answers that even Silas didn't seem to know. She couldn't really blame him for doing whatever he could to assure the safe return of such a dangerous artifact.

"Are you all right?" she heard Silas say, driving the myriad of thoughts from her head. "You haven't said a word since we left the motel."

She allowed herself an anxious groan as she turned left into Hammock Park, the gated community in which James Andrews lived. A moment later, she was motioned through by the guard at the security station.

"I don't know what I am," she finally answered. "I'm not

sure how I'm supposed to be if you want to know the truth. There wasn't exactly a class on how to solve a murder with cosmic destruction possibilities in the police academy. I'm pretty much holding on by a thread here."

From her peripheral vision, she could see him nod his understanding. Thankfully, it was his only response, allowing her to concentrate on navigating the maze-like roads through the neighborhood.

She hung a right on Marlin Street, then took the third left. Three-quarters of a mile later, they were pulling into the turn-about driveway of a two-story house built of coquina shell with Spanish roof tiles. The façade featured an old-fashioned wrap-around porch with white Corinthian columns and twelve different windows covering both floors.

A sporty little cherry red Mini-Cooper sat parked at the end of the driveway.

"Well, would you look at that," Silas said with a whistle. "Now where have we seen that car before?"

"Okay. That's interesting," Becca agreed.

They got out of the car and walked straight for the front door. Becca rang the doorbell and was immediately rewarded with the yapping of what sounded like two or three small dogs.

"It's only a little after one-thirty," she told him. "Even though his receptionist told me he'd taken a sick day, he might not be here."

There was a rustle of curtains off to their left and Silas nodded to it.

"Well, we know someone's home." Silas chuckled. "Oh, what I would give to have been a fly on the wall when sweet little Ceci saw your patrol car pull into the driveway behind her car."

"Relax. It might not mean a thing."

"Yes, and Marie Antoinette just asked for a 'little off the top'."

Becca shot him a look, silently ordering him to shut up. Apparently, he got the hint because he did just that. A few seconds later, they heard the lock turn and the door slowly opened up to them. In the entrance, as expected, stood the wary, makeup-heavy face of Ceci Palmer, Andrea's supposed best friend.

"Oh, hi," she said, giving them a sheepish look. "Were you guys looking for me?"

Silas, who couldn't wipe the smugness from his face, shook his head. "Oh, no, pet. Not at all. Not at all."

Ceci blinked at him, then looked at Becca.

"We're actually here to see James Andrews," the chief said. "Is he here?"

The woman with dyed cherry red hair glanced over her shoulder then back at them. A bead of sweat glistened off her brow. "Uh, no. He's working right now. I'm just here babysitting his..."

"Honey?" A man's voice called out from inside the house. "Who was at the door?"

She let out a little squeak at the sound of the man's voice.

"You were saying, Ceci?"

Ceci closed her eyes and let out a long breath. "Fine. He stayed home today. He's working on funeral arrangements for Andrea since she doesn't have any living family anymore." She waved the two of them inside. "Come in," she said. "Come in. Might as well get this over with."

Becca and Silas stepped into a marble-tiled foyer with a high vaulted ceiling. A staircase made of hardwood with rich mahogany bannisters leading to the second floor was immediately to their right.

Ceci motioned for them to follow her and she led them

through the house. A television playing cartoons could be heard from a room somewhere to their left. The sound of a child giggling and the electronic zaps of some kind of toy could be heard over the TV. They kept walking until they came to a large Florida room at the back of the house with a gorgeous view of the ocean beyond. A small dinette table sat underneath a bamboo ceiling fan.

James Andrews looked up from his laptop and offered a sad smile when he noticed Becca and Silas.

"Chief Cole," he said with a nod of greeting. "Mr. Mot. Please. Sit." He waved the two of them to the table. "Ceci, honey, could you get them some sweet tea or something?"

"Nothing for me, thanks," Becca said.

"Oooh, sweet tea!" Silas looked ecstatic. "I've always wanted to try some. Please."

Ceci nodded and disappeared back into the house.

James motioned toward his computer. "I'm doing research. Trying to find a good funeral home for Andrea," he said. "No one ever really knows what to do at times like this, do they? But I think I owe it to her...and to Jamie...to make sure she's laid to rest in a way deserving of the woman she was."

"That's nice of you," Becca said, moving from the door and sitting down at the table across from him. Silas took the seat next to her. "How has Jamie taken the news?"

"He doesn't quite understand. Not really." James looked down at the computer screen, then pushed the laptop away before turning back to them. "So, I take it your visit isn't a social one?"

Before they could answer, Ceci re-emerged carrying a tall glass of tea and set it in front of Silas. Beads of sweat glistened off the glass, trickling down on the wooden dinette. A moment later, Ceci lifted the glass and laid a coaster underneath it. She then took a seat next to James and wrapped an arm around his waist.

Silas, after taking a sip of the sweet beverage with a moan of delight, nodded at the short redhead. "So, she's the mysterious girlfriend, eh? The one Andrea believed betrayed their friendship?"

Ceci opened her mouth to protest, but James took hold of her hand and gave it a squeeze. "It's not like that, Mr. Mot. I know it might look bad to you, discovering our relationship so soon after Andrea's death. But Ceci and I have been together for several years now. There's nothing new about it. And yes, Andrea was upset at first, but they soon put it behind them and became friends again."

"Then why didn't either of you tell us about the relationship?" Becca asked. "We talked to both of you. Ms. Palmer mentioned you having a girlfriend. You talked about your girlfriend in your office the other day. Why didn't you tell us it was Ceci?"

"Honestly?"

"Oh, that would be refreshing," Silas grinned. He took another drink of sweet tea with a satisfied gasp.

"We knew how it would look," Ceci said. Tears were starting to trickle from her eyes and she wiped them away with the back of her hand. "You guys don't know us. You don't know how close Andrea and I were. It was pretty easy to figure we'd become suspects right away if you knew I was living with Andrea's ex."

"Okay, fine," Becca said. "Let's put a pin in your failure to tell us about the relationship for a moment. Let's hear more about your friendship with Andrea. From what we've heard, she really felt angry with you when you started having a romantic relationship with Mr. Andrews here. Something about the fact that you were hired to be the nanny or something and then, suddenly, you two were an item? I can see where that might upset her."

"That's not exactly what happened," Ceci said. "Like James said, it wasn't as sudden as you were made to believe."

"Enlighten us then."

The red-head looked over at James, who gave her an encouraging nod.

"Jamie is a special needs child. He has a severe form of autism." She sniffed, swiping another tear away. The woman could definitely put on the water works. "I'm a registered nurse. Before Andrea and James broke up, she asked me to come on and help them take care of Jamie. He was just too much for her, especially with her own mental problems. She'd lose her temper so easily around him. She didn't trust herself to be alone with him when James was at work."

"Okay. So, you came to work for them. And that's when you fell in love with Mr. Andrews?"

"Maybe helped their breakup along?" Silas piped in.

"No! It wasn't like that. I'm not responsible for their breakup."

"It's true," James confirmed. "Truth is, I hardly even noticed Ceci back then. I was rarely ever around when she was here. Back then, she only took care of Jamie during the day... when I was at work." He glanced from Silas to Becca. "No, our break up was pretty much what I've already told you. Her mental illness was just too much. We were always fighting. Sometimes, it would get violent. Andrea would get violent. It put too much stress on Jamie, so we both agreed it was time to end things."

"Naturally, after Andrea left, James needed me to work on a more full-time basis. He needed me here twenty-four-seven. So, I started staying in the guest bedroom. That way, I could be here at night if Jamie had one of his night terrors or what have you, prepare his food, and handle his doctor's appointments. It was a very practical arrangement at first." Ceci glanced over at James and squeezed his hand. "We didn't start anything romantic until a full year later. Sure, Andrea was angry about it when she first found out. She thought I had betrayed her. But you can't help who you fall in love with, can you?"

"Okay, I get that. But you really want us to believe that she finally got over it and you two became best friends again? After she felt so strongly about it being a betrayal?"

"I know it sounds crazy, but it's true. The two of us have been inseparable since she moved here from Colombia. Ask anyone." Ceci's shoulders quivered as she struggled to keep her tears in check. "Yes, we occasionally fought like cats and dogs. All the time. But we always made up in the end. I loved her like a sister and she loved me."

The words of Elaine Shepherd came rushing back to Becca's mind. She'd said pretty much the same thing. *With sisters like these, who needs enemies?*

"Okay, so I'm curious though. She was eventually fine with your relationship," Becca said. "But how did you feel when she started trying to regain custody of Jamie? Surely, you must have a pretty strong attachment to him. Did you have a problem with her trying to get her son back?"

"Not at first. When she originally came to James about it, I was happy for her. She was getting better. And she loved Jamie so much. I was rooting for her," Ceci said. She was holding onto James Andrews' hand for dear life. "But when it turned nasty, yeah...I sort of lost my cool with her."

"Nasty?" Becca looked at James. He hadn't mentioned anything about the situation turning 'nasty' when they'd spoken to him at the dealership.

James nodded. "After I talked to her doctor and told her I wouldn't allow her to share custody of Jamie, she tried to get an attorney to help her. Fortunately, no one would take the case. They all knew it was a lost cause."

"When that didn't work, she filed a petition for custody on her own. Then she started getting sneaky as we waited for the court date," Ceci said. "She called Children and Family Services on us. Said I was doing drugs. That I hit the boy. Locked him in a closet while I watched soaps all day. Said all kinds of horrible things about me. All in hopes of having the state take Jamie away from us."

At this, Silas put the glass back down on the table—intentionally missing the coaster—and looked at Ceci. "Which is funny since the two of you were such close friends and all."

The redhead rolled her eyes. "We were. I swear. Best friends. Even after she said all those lies about me."

"So, what happened with the accusations...to her attempts at getting Jamie back?"

"They just kind of fizzled out," Ceci said. "She eventually gave up."

"No, that's not true, honey," James said. "They need to know the truth."

Becca's heart skipped at the declaration. "What truth?"

"You already know what I'm about to tell you, but Dr. Fruehan's worst fears started happening. And with a vengeance." James' eyes glistened. He was struggling to hold back his own tears. "She started having hallucinations again. Horrific ones. Far worse than anything she'd ever had before."

"And?"

"And, she realized what she'd dreaded most of all was happening to her. Realized she wasn't getting better and called the whole thing off." James leaned back in his seat and pulled a pack of cigarettes from his pockets. "Mind if I smoke?"

Becca shook her head. He pulled one out and lit it up before taking a deep drag on it. He visibly relaxed the moment the nicotine was in his system. After a moment to let the tobacco sooth his frazzled nerves, he looked at her again. "So, is that all? Is there anything else you need?"

His hands were shaking as he pulled the cigarette from his lips.

"Actually, yes. One more thing." Becca looked over at Silas, who reached into the interior pocket of his jacket and withdrew the bilongo bag they'd found in Blakely's shop. "Do you have any idea what this is?"

James looked at the leather pouch, then shook his head. Ceci, however, fidgeted in her seat as she looked at it.

"That's a...that's what Andrea received with her curse," she said. Her wide eyes were glued to the little bag. "What are you doing bringing that thing in our house?"

"Why, Ms. Palmer," Silas said. "You don't actually believe in curses, do you?"

She glared at him. "I don't believe in Martians either, but I wouldn't invite them in my house."

Becca widened the drawstring, opening the bag, and dumped the doll inside onto the kitchen counter. Both James and Ceci stared at it as if it were a rattler ready to strike.

"Recognize him?" Silas asked them.

"Is that...is that James?" Ceci asked.

"We think so, yes," Becca answered. "We found it amid some of Spenser Blakely's belongings. It appears that Mr. Blakely was secretly involved in not only Santeria, but several other occult religions as well."

"It appears he had his sights set on Mr. Andrews here," Silas continued. "Would either of you know why that would be?"

James shook his head. "I've never even met the guy. Ceci had told me Andrea was dating him, but I've never had any interaction with him. I have no idea why he'd want to hurt me with a curse."

They turned to look at Ceci, who was biting down on her lower lip, staring blankly at the little doll.

"Ms. Palmer?"

Finally, the portly little redhead shook her head. "I honestly have no idea. I can't believe it. I thought that guy was trying to get rid of these types of people. I had no idea he was into the weird stuff too."

Becca was about to ask a follow up question when her phone buzzed in her pocket. "Excuse me a moment," she said, before putting the phone to her ear. "This is Chief Cole."

"Chief, it's Jeremy. We've got him. We found Spenser Blakely and arrested him."

# CHAPTER
# THIRTY-EIGHT

SUMMER HAVEN POLICE DEPARTMENT
FRIDAY, 3:55 PM

S ilas and Becca looked at Spenser Blakely through the two-way mirror on the other side of the interrogation room. The overweight, balding man, oblivious to their presence, looked an absolute mess. His clothes and hair were disheveled. His face was smeared with blood and dirt. His white shirt was torn at the sleeves and ripped down his torso.

He sat in his chair, shifting every so often in an attempt to get comfortable, but could never seem to find the right position. Sweat glistened down his forehead as his eyes darted back and forth in the room.

"He looks a bit nervous, don't you think?" Silas asked.

"Wouldn't you?" Becca turned to Sergeant Tanner. "The blood? Did he resist arrest?"

Jeremy shook his head. "No. He was like that when we found him. When we showed up, he practically jumped in my patrol car begging me to take him to the station."

Silas glanced down at the officer's arms. They were clasped in front of him as he stood at attention in front of his superior, those infernal long sleeves blocking any view of the tattoos that graced his skin.

"And where exactly did you find him?" Silas asked, turning his attention back to the suspect. "At his house?"

"Sort of," the sergeant said. "He was hiding in an old tree-house in back of his property. The thing was built back when the Parsons used to own the place." He chuckled. "If Larry hadn't heard something shuffling around up there, we might never have found him."

"I'll have to remember to compliment him on a job well done," Becca said. "Has Blakely said anything?"

Jeremy shook his head again.

"What about the lab work on the knives...the one found in Andrea's body and the ones we found in her house and Blakely's collection? Are they back yet?"

The sergeant handed her a file folder. "Yep. And found DNA that matched his on the dagger found in Alvarez's travel chest too."

Becca offered a conservative nod, but Silas could tell she was pleased at the news.

"Lawyered up?"

"Nope. Says he wants to talk to you as soon as possible. Alone."

Silas' eyes narrowed. "Well now, that's rather unexpected," he said.

"Not about wanting to see me alone," she replied with a half-smile. "You have a certain way of making people not want to be around you. But I am rather surprised he wants to talk at all. He's shown nothing but arrogance toward me and my father for years. If I was a betting woman, I would have laid odds on him asking for a lawyer straight away."

"Me?" He brought his hand to chest, aghast. "I'm the picture of charismatic charm."

"Yeah, right." Becca turned toward the door. "Well, let's not keep the good man waiting."

Silas began to follow, but she stopped him with her hand. "Not this time, Dr. Doom. It's too important. I don't want to spook him. That means you'll be sitting this one out."

"But..."

She gave him a look, then turned to Jeremy. "Keep an eye on him, will ya?"

The sergeant nodded, grinning. "Will do, Chief."

With that said, she exited the observation room and made her way to interrogate the suspect.

Silas watched as Becca opened the door to the interrogation room and took her usual seat at the bolted-down table. An expression of instant relief washed over Blakely's face at the sight of her.

"Chief, thank God you're finally here," he said. He tried to raise his hands as he spoke but was limited by the handcuffs chaining him to the table.

"Really? Then why were you hiding from me all this time?"

"I wasn't!" His response was instant. "Not from you. I wasn't hiding from you."

"She is rather brilliant at interrogation, isn't she?" Silas said to Jeremy, who hovered just behind him at the window, but the police officer said nothing in response.

"If you weren't hiding from me, then who?" Becca said, bringing Silas back to the interview.

"I can't tell you that. Not now anyway. Not here." Blakely's eyes drifted around the room as if half-expecting a specter to lunge from the shadows to murder him right there on the spot.

*Then again, maybe he is expecting a specter of sorts,* Silas thought, casting a backwards glance at the taciturn police sergeant.

"I'm not buying it, Mr. Blakely," Becca continued, waving her hand up and down in front of his face to garner his undivided attention. "All this. This act you've got going. We've seen your sanctum. We've found your stash of bilongo dolls in your print shop. This scared little innocent act isn't going to work on me."

"No, no. You don't understand. I'll tell you whatever you want to know," Blakely said. "But I need something in return."

Becca's brow wrinkled. "You need something from me?"

The newspaper man nodded. "Yes. Yes. I need to get away from here. As soon as possible. Prison is fine. I'd just rather not be anywhere near here while I'm incarcerated."

Becca opened her mouth to speak, then closed it before looking back at the two-way glass. She was clearly as stumped by this turn of events as Silas. It was, for a lack of a better term, unexpected to say the least.

She returned her attention back to the suspect. "Okay, fine," she said. "So, tell me. Why did you kill Andrea Alvarez?"

"I didn't."

"Mr. Blakely, you just told me you were going to tell me everything and you start off with a lie?"

"I swear! I didn't kill her."

"Look, we know about the Ebo knife you switched out from your collection to Andrea's. Your DNA is all over it." She opened the ever-present file in front of her and thumbed through a handful of pages. "We found the chicken blood you used to pour on her at the beach. And even the candles in your sanctum were the same brand as those found at the scene."

"Yes, I stabbed her. I moved her to the beach and simulated a ritualistic sacrifice," he said. "But she was already dead when I did it. You have to believe me."

"Why do criminals always say that?" She closed the folder. "Actually, Mr. Blakely, I *don't* have to believe you. That's part of my job description. What I do have to believe is the evidence and right now, it all points to you."

"Ask him about Elaine Shepherd," Silas shouted, knowing full well she couldn't hear him. He growled in frustration. Not being part of the interrogation that he'd worked so hard for was maddening. "Ask him about the working he put on Andrea!"

"I'm telling you, I didn't kill her," Blakely protested. "I had no reason to."

"What about Elaine Shepherd?"

"That's my girl," Silas chuckled.

Spenser Blakely's eyes widened at the mention of Andrea's co-worker friend. "What about her?"

"You don't know?" Becca was smiling. "We have her in custody right now. Conspiracy to commit murder."

"Conspiracy? Whose murder?"

"Andrea Alvarez. She went to Jacinto Garcia and asked him to kill her with a death curse. When he refused, she came to you. Isn't that right?"

"S-she told you?"

"No." Becca leaned back in her seat. She gave him a victorious look. "But it wasn't hard to figure out when we learned she'd secretly come by your work in the early morning hours. You might be a killer, but the one thing no one would mistake you for is a lady's man. You two weren't having an affair, so the only other thing it could be was that she asked you to perform the death curse on Andrea yourself." Shaking her head, she chuckled. "And you pretty much just confirmed my theory with your answer."

Blakely sat up straight. "Look, you've got it all wrong."

"You mean, she didn't ask you to perform a working on your girlfriend?"

"I, uh..."

"What's the matter, Blakely? I thought you wanted out of this town...even if you went to prison."

"I do!" he shouted, his eyes once more darting around the room. It was as if his outburst might have attracted the attention of some unseen thing. "I'm sorry," he said, more calmly. "I do, yes. But I also figured you wanted the truth and not just what you assume to be true."

"Okay. Then, start being straight with me. Did Elaine Shepherd reach out to you about putting a death curse on Andrea Alvarez?"

He hesitated a moment, then nodded. "Yes. She did. Andrea had apparently told her about me. Told her we'd met during our worship meetings. When Omo Sango had refused to do the curse, she came to the only person she knew who might be able to do it."

"Why would she come to you? I mean, you were dating Andrea. What would make her think you would do something like that?"

Blakely hung his head. "Because," he said with a sigh, "we had broken up."

# CHAPTER
# THIRTY-NINE

"Broken up?" Becca asked. She hadn't expected that answer at all. "Why?"

"It's complicated."

"Neither one of us are going anywhere anytime soon," she said. "So, try to *un*-complicate it for me."

He exhaled, looking down at his fingernails with feigned interest.

"Mr. Blakely?"

"I had done something foolish," he finally said. "Something I thought would help her. When she found out about it..."

The room suddenly erupted with banging from the two-way mirror. Someone—she assumed Silas—was pounding excitedly on it. She turned around and attempted to burn a laser-thin hole in the glass with her glare. The look had the desired effect. The banging stopped and she turned back to her suspect.

"And what exactly did you do, Mr. Blakely, that caused her to be that upset?"

The door to the interrogation burst open and Silas Mot dashed inside with Sergeant Tanner running after him.

"He placed a death curse on James Andrews!" Silas shouted.

"I'm sorry, ma'am," Jeremy said to Becca.

She nodded and waved him away. "It's okay. He can stay."

Tanner glared at Silas a moment, then backed out of the room, closing the door behind him.

"Now, what were you saying, Mot?"

"That's what his bilongo was doing in the print shop," Silas continued. "We assumed it was made recently. After Ms. Alvarez's death. We assumed that because he'd created bilongos for us, which would have only been done after we started snooping around." He leaned in closer to Blakely, giving him a threatening glare. "You know, that wasn't very nice, by the way." He patted the suspect on the head as he said it. "Anyway, truth is, he had performed the death curse on James Andrews, thinking that if he died, Jamie would automatically go into her custody."

Becca turned back to Blakely. "Is this true?"

He nodded. "Yes. She had tried so hard to get custody of Jamie back. She was devastated when that shyster of a car salesman refused. She tried to get legal help, but no one would give her the time of day and it was killing her a little inside every day she wasn't in that boy's life."

"So, she found out about it and didn't respond exactly how you thought she would?"

"No, not at all. She was furious with me. Broke things off right then and there."

Silas, who seemed brimming with enthusiastic energy after figuring out how James' bilongo fit into the case, sat down beside Becca with his chest puffed up. "And she went to work the next day and told her sister from another mister,

Elaine Shepherd, about the breakup and she thought maybe you might just be mad enough at Andrea to perform the curse," he said with a smug curl of his lips.

"Basically, yes," Blakely said. "She came to me and told me what she wanted. I didn't intend to go through with it, but considering Mrs. Shepherd wasn't a believer herself, she wouldn't know any better. So, we worked out a deal."

"What kind of deal?" Becca asked.

"She would convince her firm to send advertisers to my newspaper and I would create a bilongo doll to make Andrea think she'd been cursed." He looked up from his examination of his fingernails. "But there was no curse imbued with it. For all intents and purposes, it was nothing more than a rag doll. No power behind it at all."

"Why would you do that to her?" Becca asked. "Even if you didn't put your mojo into it, you knew how she would react to seeing it. You knew that she would believe in it and be terrified."

He gave a sad nod. "I did. But I wanted her back. I thought if she thought she was cursed and that Omo Sango was the one who put it on her, she would have to come back to me. Figured she would need my help to break the curse and we could start fresh."

"That is the stupidest thing I've ever heard!" Silas barked. "And most cruel."

Becca wanted to reprimand him for his outburst, but truth was, she was thinking the same thing. The man was the worst sort of parasite.

"And, of course, the curse and its implications couldn't hurt any in raising circulation for your newspaper, right?"

"Yes." His cheeks reddened as he said it. "It was a perfect opportunity. I could get Andrea back, sell papers, and, if I was lucky, get rid of Omo Sango in one fell swoop." Blakely tried to clear his throat. "Could I have some water or something? My throat's dry."

Becca glanced back at the two-way mirror and nodded. She knew Jeremy would still be back there and would have heard the request. When she was confident her officer was going to get the water, she returned to her next thought.

"So, what went wrong in this plan of yours?"

"Pardon?"

"Well, if everything went well, there was no need to kill her. Yet, someone switched her medications out without her knowledge and killed her. Since you and she were dating, that gives you plenty of opportunity to do it without her catching on."

"That's how she died? Her medications?"

"Actually, someone else's medications. They were switched, as I said."

"Why on earth would I kill her? I wanted her back!"

"You just admitted to stabbing her and dragging her to the beach," she said. "We're recording this interrogation now. Do you want me to let you hear what you said?"

"No, I know what I said. And I'm telling the truth." He fidgeted in his chair. "Look, I heard about her breakdown in Jacksonville. When I found out she was home from the hospital, I came over to check on her. When no one answered my knocks at the door, I let myself in using the key she'd given me." Sweat glistened across his forehead, illuminated by the harsh overhead lights. "I went up to her room and found her in bed. She was already dead."

"What time was this?"

"Around one in the morning."

"Why so late?"

Blakely shrugged. "You know my schedule, Chief Cole. I went there on my way to run the morning edition."

"And what did you see when you got to her place?"

"Exactly what I said. She was in bed."

"Under or on top of her covers?"

"Under. But she was wearing jeans and a t-shirt, which I thought was kind of weird."

Becca looked him up and down, weighing his words. He seemed pretty sincere, but a few things just weren't adding up.

"Okay, so how did it go from finding her body to you putting a knife in her back and dumping her body on the beach."

He coughed again, then cleared his throat. "Is that water coming?"

"Shouldn't be long now." She motioned for him to continue. "Go on."

"I thought about calling the police, I really did," he said. His voice was gravelly. Hoarse. "But then, I realized the opportunity I had."

"To pin her death on Omo Sango and the rumor of the death curse you spread with your paper."

"I wasn't trying to frame him, Chief. I was trying to point you in the right direction." He tried to throw up his hands in frustration but was hindered by his chains. "I still can't believe you've ruled him out as your suspect. There's no doubt in my mind that he's the one responsible for Andrea's death."

"What?" A lump began to swell in her throat. Had she miscalculated? She'd all but discarded Jacinto Garcia as the killer after meeting with him. "That doesn't make any sense. We know he didn't put the curse on her. Elaine Shepherd even admitted as much. The only motive he would have had to kill her was to ensure the public believed his curse actually worked. It was a matter of street cred. But if he publicly denied casting the spell, there was no reason for him to save face."

Blakely laughed, shaking his head. "You've got it wrong,

Chief Cole. He wouldn't have murdered her for that. In his world, it's up to the Orisha whether a curse works or not. If an Orisha chooses not to kill someone with one of his curses, that's on the Orisha, not the Babalowa. It wouldn't be a motive for..."

There was a knock on the door and Jeremy appeared with a bottle of water. He set it down at the table in front of Blakely and backed out of the room. The reporter unscrewed the bottle's cap and downed half the bottle before he continued.

"It wouldn't be a motive for murder."

"So, why would he kill her?" Silas asked, suddenly intrigued.

Blakely shook his head. His hand shook as he set the water bottle down in front of him. "Uh-uh. I've said too much already."

"But you've basically accused Garcia of murdering Andrea," Becca said. "If you don't give us a reason, we can't take it seriously and you're still our chief suspect."

"So be it."

There was a moment of uncomfortable silence in the room. This interview had taken a turn she hadn't expected. Sure, she hadn't thought Spenser Blakely would just roll over and admit to killing his girlfriend, but she'd never expected this twisted direction either.

"Esperanza," Silas suddenly said.

Blakely's eyes stretched wide at the mention of her name.

"Yeah, that's it, isn't it?" he continued. "You know Esperanza. She's got you spooked. That's why you're trying so hard to get out of town. Why you were hiding."

"Partially." Blakely nodded. "But if you knew what that woman...that creature...really was, you'd go into hiding too."

"Chuckles, I was *married* to that creature. Trust me. I feel your pain."

The man reeled back in his chair. If it hadn't been bolted down, Becca was certain it would have tipped over by his reaction. "Married to her? But...but..."

"Yeah, I know." Silas' grinned stretched wide. "You never can tell with some people, eh?"

Becca placed a hand on Silas' arm to shut him up and addressed Blakely. "So, this has to do with Esperanza?"

His head nodded emphatically, but his gaze remained glued on Silas. "I...she..." He drank more from the water bottle and sighed. "Andrea overheard the two of them one night over a month ago. Although she didn't quite know what they were talking about, she understood enough. Something about a powerful artifact that had the power...the power..."

"The power over life and death," Silas said. His grin had disappeared. "The Hand of Cain."

Blakely nodded.

"What did she overhear?" he asked, leaning forward in his seat.

"Like I said, she only overheard bits and pieces and even then, she didn't understand half of what she'd heard. But something about it being hidden where someone would never find it."

"Did they mention who this someone was?"

Blakely shook his head. "Problem is, she got caught eavesdropping. Omo Sango warned her not to tell anyone or he would unleash a bilongo on her like no one had ever seen before."

"Which is why it was so easy to convince her Garcia had cursed her," Becca chimed in.

"Yes. Of course, I had no idea about it, but when she discovered the doll, she'd told me everything she remembered about that night."

Silas sat in his chair, staring past Blakely's shoulder. Becca

269

could almost hear the gears inside his head grinding as he worked to process it all.

"If what you're saying is true and you thought Garcia or Esperanza—"

"Santa Muerte!" Blakely shouted, his terrified stare still fixed on Silas. "Let's call her what she is."

"Fine. If you thought Garcia and *that woman* had killed her..." Becca refused to call her Santa Muerte. "...why did you wait a few days after her death to start hiding out? I mean, you ran another story on her murder. You pointed a finger at Garcia in it. Heck, you even boldly proclaimed you were running for mayor to clean up the town of Santeria and its ilk."

"He thought he was protected," Silas said, still staring off into space. His voice had almost zero inflection in it, as if the statement was simply a matter of fact. "That's what all that stuff in his sanctum was. He was pulling resources from every magico-religious system he could think of to create a protective ward around himself. But something must have happened to let him know he wasn't nearly as safe as he thought."

Blakely drank the last of the water and nodded again. "That witch showed up in my house one night. As easy as you please. One minute, I was alone, surrounded by my protective charms. The next, she was standing right in front of me, kissing me on the lips."

Becca glanced over at Silas, but he didn't respond.

"She then warned me not to say anything about what Andrea had told me." The journalist pointed at Silas. "Especially to him. I didn't understand why at the time, but I swore I wouldn't say a word. As soon as she left, I went into hiding, hoping I could figure a way to get out of town without Omo Sango or that creature finding out."

Silas' eyes finally came into focus and he looked directly at suspect. "I've figured it out," he said. "I know who killed Ms.

Alvarez. Most importantly, I know why." He looked over at Becca. "But you need to call an ambulance right now."

"What? Why?"

He turned back to the man across the table from them. "Because Mr. Blakely is about to have a heart attack."

Then, as if his very words made it happen, the middle-aged journalist clutched at his chest. His face, stricken with pain and terror, contorted into a ghastly grimace. Becca leapt from her seat and rushed to the door. "Someone get EMS here now!"

# CHAPTER
# FORTY

"Dr. Stratton to the E.R., please," the woman's voice boomed over the hospital intercom. "Dr. Stratton to the E.R."

Becca paced back and forth in front of Spenser Blakely's room while a horde of medical staff worked to save his life.

"What are we doing here, Becca?" Silas asked, pacing in step with her while zipping his yo-yo around in vibrant patterns. "The guy's not going to survive this."

"Put that thing away." She crinkled her nose and shook her head. "And you don't know that!" Of course, he knew. He was Death. But she wasn't about to give him the satisfaction. As a matter of fact, her mind had been replaying the events that had occurred only minutes before their suspect had collapsed. They'd discussed Silas' ex-wife, Esperanza, placing her as a possible suspect. He'd gone quiet after that, lapsing into a fit of

272

concentration as the interview had continued. Concentration similar to what she'd seen when he'd used his finger gun to bring down three of Garcia's goons when they'd entered the storage facility that was the gang's headquarters.

Then, he'd proclaimed he'd solved the case—something he had yet to explain to her—and casually told her to call Fire-Rescue because Blakely was about to have a heart attack. It was entirely too coincidental for her liking.

"And just how do you know he's going to die?" She wheeled around on him. "Did you do something to him?"

"No, of course not!"

"Well, was it his 'Time', as you call it?"

"No, it wasn't. As a matter of fact, I believe he was sched-uled to have a few more years left, if I'm not mistaken."

"Then, how did you know?"

Silas put his hands down his pockets and squared off on her. "First, the profuse sweating. The dehydration. The fidgeting and nerves. And I also noticed, he kept stroking the left side of his cheek with his hand. He was having tooth pain, I believe. All signs of an eminent heart attack."

"Okay, but..."

"But, the most important thing is that I felt it, Becca. I felt the Hand of Cain being activated. I could sense someone directing its power at Blakely. I can't explain it, but I felt it nonetheless."

She eyed him. "And you had nothing to do with it?"

"For the last time, no. Why would I want him dead? He's obviously a link to whoever has the Hand."

"Someone like your ex, maybe?"

"If you think I'd kill a man to protect that woman—or her gangbanging henchmen—you don't know me at all. Besides, I know she doesn't have the Hand."

"How do you know that?"

"I've already told you...we can't touch the thing."

"That doesn't mean one of her followers can't do it for her. Seems to me, Jacinto Garcia would be a prime candidate for the artifact," she said. "As a matter of fact, sounds like that's what led to Andrea's death even. She found out about the Hand and they killed her for it."

Silas opened his mouth to protest, then obviously thought better of it. He sighed, relaxing visibly in front of her.

"I know how we can catch the killer...get them to confess even," he said. "But you're not going to like it."

"I'm sure I won't, but..."

A ruckus erupted from inside the partition leading into Blakely's room. The doctor shouted a series of orders. Others responded. A nurse ran from the room, moving toward a hallway door a few feet away, only to return a moment later with a vial of clear liquid. The commotion continued and Becca found herself biting her lower lip as she listened and waited.

Silas had moved over to one of the waiting room chairs and resumed his yo-yoing. She decided to ignore the impropriety. It wasn't important now. The only thing that mattered was that her suspect lived.

But a few moments later, the tumult in Blakely's room receded and one by one, nurses and orderlies filed out with downcast faces. Finally, the doctor—a Dr. Bernita Arruza—strolled out from the room and approached Becca.

Arruza, a middle-aged woman of what Becca guessed to be Mediterranean descent, looked at her with a somber expression. "I'm sorry, Chief Cole. We did everything we could, but we lost him."

"Any idea what killed him?"

The doctor shrugged. "At his age and physical condition, I'd say it's probably some type of cardiac event, but I can't be sure. Do you know if he has any medical history?"

"No, I don't," she replied. "And his wife died a few years ago. I'm not sure who his next of kin is or anyone else who might be able to tell us."

The doctor nodded. "Guess we'll call the M.E. then. Maybe they'll be able to get some answers for you."

With that, Dr. Arruza strolled toward the nurse's station to complete her paperwork. Becca turned to Silas, who had moved from the waiting room chair to her side without her even noticing. "Okay, Mot. What's this plan of yours I'm not going to like?"

He grinned.

# FORTY-ONE

SAND CASTLE CONDOMINIUMS
ANDREA ALVAREZ'S APARTMENT
SATURDAY, 8:30 AM

"I can't believe you actually talked me into this," Becca said, looking around the corner of Andrea Alvarez's kitchen into the living room.

The room was now filled with every living suspect in the case. James Andrews and Ceci Palmer sat uncomfortably on the loveseat facing the sliding glass doors. Elaine Shepherd, wearing the bright orange jumpsuit of the county jail, sat in the overstuffed reading chair. Sergeant Tanner, who was handcuffed to her, stood behind her with his usual stone-like expression. Finally, the massive figure of Jacinto Garcia hunkered down in the couch next to the loveseat, with the beautiful, but devious Esperanza by his side.

Two of her other officers and two sheriff's deputies stood at attention around the room, keeping their careful eye on all the suspects.

"Why not?" Silas whispered back. "This is going to be fun."

"Because we don't do dramatic killer reveals in real life. That's just something they do in the movies."

Ever since Silas had told her who he believed the killer was—and more importantly, why Andrea Alvarez was killed—her gut had been simply to arrest the person and sweat them out in the interrogation room. The problem was, the way in which Andrea had been killed had been brilliant. Short of having an eye-witness to someone seeing the pills switched, there was no way to tie the killer to the crime. That's how Silas had talked her into his crazy scheme. With it, he'd promised a confession by the end of the night.

"Yeah, but they're really good movies." He chuckled in her ear. "Besides, I can guarantee you no movie has ever done a killer reveal like the one we're about to do."

"Aren't you afraid of blowing your cover?" she asked, turning her attention back to the block of cheese on the counter top. She cut the block into twelve smaller wedges.

"Nah," he said, busying himself with pouring wine into five glasses. "Whoever's got the Hand already knows who I am. So, does Esperanza and Garcia. The others? Well, only you and the killer will actually see what I'm doing and they won't be saying much of anything when I'm done."

She spun around on him. "You're not going to..."

"Kill them? No way. Look, I know you think that because I'm the Grim Reaper, I'm all about..." He wiggled his fingers and spoke in a theatrical spooky voice. "...*harvesting souls*..." He chuckled again. "But truth is, if all this living in the mortal world has taught me anything, it's that life is just too sacred. Besides, I'm nothing if not committed to my Purpose. You know I don't abuse my power."

She did. It was one of the qualities she actually liked about the guy. He could be an immature child sometimes, but when it came to his job as Death, he was committed.

"So, you ready?" he asked her.

"As much as I'll ever be."

Silas nodded in the direction of the living room and she picked up the platter of cheese and started making her way toward their 'guests'. As she stepped down into the room, she laid the platter on the coffee table and waited until Silas had deposited the wine glasses before addressing their suspects.

"First of all, I'll like to thank you all for coming on such short notice," she said, standing in front of the bookcase. Silas, for his part, had skulked back toward the kitchen without a word. "We're here today as a sort of celebration."

"Celebration?" James Andrews said. "Does that mean you caught Andrea's killer?"

"Haven't you heard?" Elaine Shepherd asked him. "Spenser Blakely was arrested, though he died of a heart attack before they could formally charge him."

Jacinto Garcia's eyes narrowed as he stared suspiciously at Becca while Esperanza leaned back on the couch with a bored look on her face.

"It's true," Becca continued. "We did arrest Mr. Blakely and yes, he did die before we could make formal charges. This has been one of the most grueling investigations I've ever conducted and each of you have been exceptionally good sports about it."

"Um, hello?" Elaine said, holding up her hand to reveal the handcuffs. "I'm having some difficulty finding anything to celebrate at the moment. Now that Blakely's dead, are you going to drop the charges against me?"

"Charges?" Ceci Palmer asked. "Aren't you Andrea's work friend? Why have they arrested you?"

Elaine blushed at the question, then, embarrassed, lowered her handcuffed hand behind the chair's armrest.

"Mrs. Shepherd is being charged with conspiracy and solicitation to cause someone bodily harm," Becca explained. "She approached Mr. Garcia..."

There was a low growl that came from the large Cuban man.

"Sorry. She approached Omo Sango here, asking him to perform the death curse on Andrea."

"You're the one who cursed her?" Ceci asked Elaine, her voice rising in anger.

"Of course, not," she replied. "The charges are ridiculous. First of all, Omo Sango refused to perform it."

"It doesn't matter," Becca told her. "As the state attorney has informed me, the intent was there. To solicit someone to kill another person by use of a gun or ritualistic magic, it makes no difference. The gun might be unloaded, but it's still solicitation and conspiracy nonetheless. Same is true with trying to curse someone—especially someone predisposed to believe the curse will work." The chief smiled at the woman. "And you were determined, Ms. Shepherd. You weren't about to let Omo Sango's refusal stop you, were you? You just sought out someone else to do it. Like Spenser Blakely."

"Spenser was into Santeria?" James asked. "But that's crazy. He despised the whole lot of them."

"Only because he wished to abuse the Orisha," Jacinto Garcia spoke up. "He wanted to bend them to his will. To control them instead of serving them. I excommunicated him and he resented us for it from then on." The big man nodded to the food and wine on the coffee table. "Is that for us?"

Becca smiled, waving to the cheese. "Help yourself everyone," she said. "We have plenty."

James, Ceci, and Garcia took a few pieces of the cheese and

a glass of wine each, but Esperanza and Elaine didn't move from their seats.

"It's rather odd, isn't it? Putting out cheese and wine for people you've obviously viewed as suspects throughout your investigation," Elaine said.

Becca shrugged. "We know from the autopsy, that it was the last thing Andrea ate before she died. I just thought it was an appropriate way to honor her right now."

Esperanza let out a knowing little laugh with a disdainful curl of her lip, but she said nothing.

"And yes, Mrs. Shepherd," Becca continued. "Each and every one of you have been suspects at least once in this investigation. But fortunately, today, we can put all that behind us. Today, we can name the killer."

"Spenser Blakely?" Ceci asked.

"He was definitely the one who stabbed her in the back, yes. He also dumped her body on the beach in hopes of pinning her death on Mister...um, Omo Sango here." Becca turned her gaze on Elaine Shepherd. "And he also agreed to perform a death curse on her for a price, isn't that right?"

"That's his word against mine."

"Yes, but I already spoke with Mr. Neely on the phone. He told me you had spoken to him about getting prime customers of his firm to place ads in *The Summer Haven Chronicler*...the price you agreed to for him to perform the curse."

"Unbelievable," Ceci said, shaking her head. She put an arm around James and leaned into his shoulder for comfort. "Andrea really thought Spenser was a nice guy. I can't believe he'd kill her like that."

Becca turned to face her. "Oh, but he didn't actually kill her," she said. "When he found her, she was already dead. He just saw her death as another opportunity to drive a proverbial nail in Omo Sango's coffin while increasing newspaper sales.

The only thing he was really guilty of was desecrating a corpse, greed, and having really bad taste."

She suppressed an urge to smile as she spoke. Although she'd never in a million years admit it to Silas, the whole 'killer reveal' thing was much more fun than she ever imagined it would be. She knew it was horribly unprofessional, but there was something classic about gathering all the suspects in one room and sweating them out until the real killer revealed him or herself.

"If he didn't kill her, who did?" James asked.

Omo Sango placed the wine glass back on the table and leaned back on the couch with a sneer.

"The better question is 'how was she killed?'" Becca said. She was now pacing the floor, hands behind her back in classic movie detective fashion. "It puzzled us for quite a while actually and without knowing the precise mechanism of death, there was no way to identify the most likely suspect. That's why we looked at each of you very closely."

"And?" Ceci asked.

"And, what?"

"How was she killed?" The redhead was now sitting on the edge of her seat, her hand gripping James Andrews' tightly.

"Well, actually, we thought it'd be interesting to let the killer fill us in on that one." Becca looked at Ceci. "Care to tell us, Ms. Palmer?"

## CHAPTER
# FORTY-TWO

"Wait, me?" Ceci Palmer asked, rising to her feet. "You think I killed Andrea?"

"It's why I asked," Becca replied, stopping her pacing and leaning against the bookcase.

"Honey?" James said, looking up at the woman he loved. "What is she talking about?"

"Go ahead and tell him," Becca said. "Tell him how you started switching out Andrea's medications with Eldepryl." She looked at James. "We're still waiting on a court order to get your son's medical records, but we're guessing that's one of the medications he's taking?"

James nodded, his eyes still glued to Ceci.

"Go on, Ms. Palmer. Tell him," Becca pressed.

The redhead looked from the chief to James. As Silas had predicted, tears were already streaming down her face.

"She's lying!" Ceci shouted. "I loved Andrea. I would never hurt her. You know that, honey."

"So, you're denying exchanging her Ativan for Jamie's Eldepryl?" Becca asked.

"Yes! Yes!"

"Are you sure?"

"Absolutely. I didn't do it."

Becca put a hand to her mouth. "Oh my," she said. "Then we made a horrible mistake."

"Mistake? What mistake?" Ceci's voice squeaked.

The chief walked over to the cheese platter and made a show of counting the wedges. She looked back at Ceci and frowned.

"Well, we were certain you were the killer," she said. "Silas thought it would be fun to turn the tables around on you, so we put some Eldepryl in some of the cheese and used an old mentalist trick Silas knew to force the laced wedge to you."

"What?" Ceci's eyes widened. "Are you crazy? Taking that stuff with cheese and wine can kill me!"

"I know." Becca shook her head sadly. "That's why you are so careful over the foods you give Jamie, right? Elaine told us as much. She said Andrea called you little more than a cook. You spent your days scheduling Jamie's meals. You were so thorough. So careful about what he could have to eat. Just because of those MAOIs he was taking."

"Exactly! That stuff is deadly when consumed with anything fermented. Alcohol. Cheese. And even some chocolate." Ceci looked around the room, shaking her hands as she began to panic. "Oh, my God. Oh, my God. Oh, my God."

Becca looked over at Sergeant Tanner. "We've made a horrible miscalculation, Jeremy." Her voice was calm. Unhurried. "Maybe you should call for EMS. Ms. Palmer is about to have a dangerous episode."

James Andrews stared at his girlfriend, confusion and anger alternating across his face. "Honey? Tell me what she's saying isn't true."

"What does it matter?" she screamed. "I'm dying! Help me!"

"Ms. Palmer, you're the only medical professional here right now," Becca said. "Help us help you. What symptoms can we expect?"

She wiped a stream of sweat from her brow. "It's...it's already happening," she said, taking deep breaths. Now she was pacing the floor. Her eyes darted around the room. "My blood pressure is rising. I feel my heart fluttering. I'm going into a hypertensive crisis."

Becca rushed over to her, taking her by the arm and leading her back to couch. "Maybe you should sit down," she said, helping her ease down onto the cushion.

Then, Becca heard it. From the saucer-like size of Ceci's eyes, she knew the redheaded tart had heard it too.

"*Ceci Palmer!*" A deep booming voice echoed around the room.

The woman's head swiveled, trying to track where the voice had come from. Becca looked around, but no one other than Esperanza showed any sign of hearing it. Esperanza, however, grinned from ear to ear.

"*Ceci Palmer, your Time has come!*" The voice boomed again.

"Who's there?" She rose from the couch, spinning three-hundred and sixty degrees. "Who is it?"

James looked at Becca. "What's happening to her?" he asked.

"From what I understand, the Eldepryl causes hallucinations," she told him. "I think she's hearing things."

"Oh, my God!" Ceci shouted, trying to back away and tripping over the couch. She sprawled onto the floor, pointing toward the entrance of the living room. All eyes turned in the direction she was pointing, but no one—other than Becca and Esperanza—had any clue what she was seeing.

Of course, Becca herself struggled not to react to the ghastly image now searing into her own brain. Hovering about a foot off the floor was an amorphous cloud of smoke and shadow, weaving in and out of itself like the raging waves of a tumultuous sea. The most brilliant display of blinding pure light swirled around from deep within the thing. It glided into the room, silent as the night, and then began to churn and swell as it took shape.

"Help me!" Ceci said, now crabwalking backwards, away from the thing.

*"There is no help for you, Ceci Palmer,"* the voice from the cloud said. *"Death comes for you today!"*

She screamed, scrambling to her feet and running straight for the sliding glass door where Officer Robinson grabbed her, holding her struggling form.

"What's happening, Chief?" he asked Becca. His voice was wobbling a little, a sure sign he was freaking out a little bit.

But she couldn't blame him. He wasn't even seeing what she and Ceci were seeing at that moment. The miasma of shadow and blazing light stretched and contorted until soon, it was the relative shape of a man, robed in a cloak and hood. A long instrument of some kind, with a three-foot black blade, was clutched in the thing's hand.

She had to admit, it was truly terrifying to behold.

"Don't let him get me!" Ceci pleaded with Officer Robinson. "Please! Don't let Death get me!"

"Death?" James Andrews said. "Isn't that what Andrea was screaming in that restaurant two nights before she died?"

"Must be guilt," Becca said.

*"Ceci Palmer!"* The shrouded figure of smoke drifted toward her, its scythe lowering to point its curve blade at her head. Ceci whimpered, sliding down on the floor with her back

against Officer Robinson's legs. *"Confess! And if you do, you may still live!"*

Becca rolled her eyes. *Geez, Silas. Ease up on the melodrama, will you?*

"Please don't let him get me," she cried, looking up into Robinson's face. "Please don't let him get me."

Becca stepped forward, crouching down to get eye to eye with her. "Ceci, honey...maybe if you tell us what happened, he'll go away."

She shook her head, her eyes clinched tight. "No, no, no!"

"Get it off your chest," Becca pressed. "Look, we know it wasn't your intention to kill Andrea. At least, at first. You switched her Ativan with the Eldepryl at first, just to elevate her serotonin, right? You were just trying to elicit the paranoia and hallucinations, hoping she'd think her schizophrenia was getting worse. You hoped it would get her to back off from fighting for custody of Jamie. Isn't that right?"

She was rocking back and forth, keening in terror. If Becca wasn't dealing with a cold-blooded murderer, she would have felt bad for the woman. But what she was experiencing now was nothing compared to the terrors that Andrea Alvarez had faced the weeks before her death.

"Isn't that right, Ms. Palmer?" she emphasized.

"Yes!" Ceci shouted. "I didn't want to kill her!"

"Dear Lord, Ceci what did you do?" James asked.

Silas, in the spectral form of the Grim Reaper, continued to drift nearer. His size had grown to the point where he almost filled the entire room. Esperanza chuckled, obviously amused by the audacity of the drama playing out before her.

"I just wanted her to give up trying to get Jamie back," Ceci cried. "Just wanted to make her think her treatments weren't working anymore. I knew mixing Jamie's medications with Andrea's would trigger hallucinations." Her eyes were glued to the growing miasma of smoke in front of her. Tears streaked her mascara into dark gashes down her cheeks. "Then, she went nuts and was forced to go to the hospital. They'd asked her what medications she was taking. That's when she put two and two together."

"She figured out what you were doing," Becca said.

Ceci nodded. "That's why she asked me to drive her home when they released her. She wanted to confront me about it. We argued on the car ride home. She threatened to go to the police. She was going to tell James what I had done."

"And what happened then?"

"I asked her for a chance to talk about it. To explain my side of the story. We agreed to meet at her house and do what we've always done when we were at odds...drink our troubles away. I brought the wine and the cheese."

"Knowing full well that it would be deadly to anyone taking MAOIs."

She nodded. "I'd done something so terrible to her, I couldn't imagine her ever forgiving me. And that meant she would tell James and my life would be over. He'd break up with me. I'd be taken away from Jamie too. I just couldn't let that happen."

Becca noticed the room was getting a little less crowded. Silas' specter was starting to diminish...to dissolve.

"And so, you let her eat the cheese. You let her drink the wine. And all the time, you knew it would send her into a hypertensive crisis that would kill her without medical treatment."

Ceci sniffed. "She passed out on the couch," she said. "She was such a little thing. It was no big deal to carry her upstairs and put her to bed before I left."

"Which is why you freaked out so much when you came

here the next day and discovered her body wasn't where you left it."

She nodded again. "I couldn't understand it. The plan had been to come by that morning and discover the body." She made air quotes with her finger at the word "discover". "I was then going to call the police and figured it would either be blamed on the curse everyone in town was talking about or natural causes."

Ceci looked around the room and blinked.

"Wait, where did he go?"

Everyone in the room, except Esperanza, looked around as well, wondering who she was talking about.

"Where did who go?" Becca asked.

"Death. He's not here anymore."

Silas had indeed removed himself from the gathering. Becca knew that even now he was busy reconstructing a new body in which to inhabit, though she wasn't entirely sure what that meant. He'd told her it would take a while—between twenty to forty-five minutes or so—before he could appear as human again.

"Maybe that's because I lied to you, Ceci," Becca said. "I'm sorry. But you were never given Eldepryl. I made that up to get you to talk."

"What? You mean...you mean, I'm not..."

Becca shook her head. "You're not dying. Whatever you were experiencing must have been psychosomatic. Or a product of guilt. Who knows?" She reached out a hand to help Ceci to her feet. "But whatever happened, I'm sorry to say, I'm placing you under arrest Cecilia Suzanne Palmer, for the murder of Andrea Alvarez."

# EPILOGUE

Silas sat at the bar, enjoying the shade of the palm frond-roofed pagoda and the exquisite fruity alcoholic beverage with the colorful umbrella. It wasn't as good as the concoction Courtney Abeling had made for him a few nights earlier, but the new bartender, Scott, had tried hard to recreate it—not knowing what it was called—and had done a pretty good job nonetheless.

He took a sip from his straw and looked up at the cloudless blue sky. He breathed in deep, enjoying the salt air. The mournful cries of seagulls and the explosive crash of waves against the beach were the symphony he'd engrossed himself in while Becca Cole busied herself with the mundane task of booking and charging Ceci Palmer with the murder of Andrea Alvarez.

Although Ms. Alvarez was still dead—taken long before her Time—there was, he had to admit, a certain amount of satisfaction he felt in finally solving the murder. He was still no closer to discovering the whereabouts of the Hand of Cain, but he now had a few ideas of where to look, and the inkling of a plan forming in his mind.

He glanced over at the row of beach chairs a few yards away. Each chair was now shaded by large, round umbrellas. Elliot Newman was the only one occupying any of them. His pasty white legs were already turning all kinds of red in the beach sun as he too enjoyed the fruity concoction Silas had grown to love.

*I think I'll call it 'Death on a Beach',* he thought, taking another sip. *Seems appropriate somehow.*

"Is this seat taken?" A velvety Hispanic voice asked from behind him.

He swiveled his head to see Esperanza, decked out in a thin cotton pullover—her skimpy string-bikini evident under the garment—standing behind him with one hand on the adjacent chair.

"Suit yourself," he said.

The two sat together in silence for a few uncomfortable minutes, enjoying the scenery.

"That was quite a show you put on this morning," she finally said after she'd ordered her own drink. Silas noticed that the bartender had practically undressed her with his eyes, which had tickled her to no end.

"We needed a confession," he said quietly. He kept his sight fixed on the rolling waves beyond the tiki bar. "She wasn't about to admit she'd killed her best friend...especially knowing it would ruin her relationship with James Andrews. The drama just gave her the push she needed, that's all."

"Oh, I'm not judging you," she laughed. "You know me. I love a good show of theatrics."

Silas nodded while taking a deep pull on his straw.

"Like you appearing to Spenser Blakely and laying that threatening kiss on him so soon before he dropped dead of a heart attack?" He finally said.

Esperanza tilted her head back and laughed louder this time. "He told you that, did he?"

"He did."

"What can I say? I didn't want you to know."

"That your boy Omo Sango has the Hand?"

"Oh, he doesn't have it," she said. She was scowling now. "Not anymore anyway. He did. His crew were some of the first scavengers of that wreck. They retrieved it, but then, it was stolen."

"Stolen? Was this before or after Andrea Alvarez overheard you talking about it?"

"After. It was stolen about a week before she died, as a matter of fact."

Silas pondered this a bit.

"Any idea who took it?"

She tsked at the question. "You know me better than that. If I had a theory about who stole it from me, do you really think they'd still be alive to use it?"

"It never hurts to ask."

She nodded at this, pushed her empty glass forward, and stood up. "Well, *mi esposa*, I suppose it's time to catch some rays."

"Enjoy." The sooner she was gone, the sooner Silas could get back to enjoying this glorious afternoon.

She leaned in and kissed him on the cheek. "*Buenos dias*, Love." She turned to walk toward the beach when she came to an abrupt halt and gasped. "Ankou, what have you done?"

Silas smiled, not bothering to look. He knew she'd just spotted Elliot Newman, alive and well, and taking a nice relaxing beach day instead of being dead and worm food in a big claustrophobic box.

"Whatever do you mean, Essie?" he asked, grinning and taking another sip from his drink.

He could feel her burning glare at the back of his head.

"Don't think for a minute I'm going to let this stand," she said. "It's bad enough when you take one of mine. Now, you've moved on to restoring souls I've taken as well. It's an abuse of your station."

He chuckled and handed her a customer satisfaction card he'd taken from the motel lobby. "Feel free to fill this form out and send it to our boss, Chica."

With a grunt, she wheeled around and stormed down the steps to the beach without another word.

Amused, Silas stood up and moved over to Elliot, taking the beach chair next to him.

"Enjoying your day, buddy?" he asked.

Elliot nodded. "Ya know, I never really ever took time off to go to the beach when I was alive. It's much more relaxing than I ever imagined."

"Stick with me, kid, and you'll be a relaxation king in no time."

Elliot smiled and took a drink from his coconut tiki mug.

"So, tell me, Elliot. You've never mentioned it," Silas said. "But with all this talk about that pirate ship wreck, I've never thought to ask. Do we have any idea what the ship was called when it sailed the seven seas?"

"Oh, that's actually quite fascinating," the archaeologist said. "It's why I've been so excited to excavate the ship, really. See, it doesn't officially exist. I mean, not really. It was supposed to be as legendary as its captain within the scholarly world."

"Really?"

"Yes, yes. For centuries, scholars believed it was merely a superstitious myth. Something to scare pirates and sea dogs while they drank their profits in pubs in Caribbean harbors."

"Tell me more."

"The ship is known as *The Lord's Vengeance*."

Silas' gut instantly twisted into tightly wound coils at the name.

"It was captained by a creature of myth and legend. A being revered by the practitioners of vodou in the Islands. A man named..."

Silas' throat was suddenly parched. He was going to need something a lot stronger than a *Death on the Beach* to quench his thirst this afternoon. "A man named Baron Tombstone," Silas said, his voice a mere whisper.

"Exactly!" Elliot said, smiling. "Have you heard of him?"

"Oh," he replied. "You can definitely say that."

He'd finally discovered the being behind the approaching enclave. The one who'd raised the motion to vote on Silas' ability to handle the station of Lord of Death. The one vying for his throne. His dilemma was worse than he ever imagined.

"And I can assure you," he said to his new friend. "This makes things a lot more complicated."

9 798987 684719